BLACK CAIRN POINT

BLACK CAIRN POINT

CLAIRE McFALL

HOT
KEY
BOOKS

First published in Great Britain in 2015 by Hot Key Books
Northburgh House, 10 Northburgh Street, London EC1V 0AT

A CIP catalogue record for this book is available from the British Library.

ISBN: 978-1-4714-0487-0

1

This book is typeset in 10.5 Berling LT Std using Atomik ePublisher

Printed and bound by Clays Ltd, St Ives Plc

www.hotkeybooks.com

Hot Key Books is part of the Bonnier Publishing Group
www.bonnierpublishing.com

ALSO BY CLAIRE MCFALL

Bombmaker
Ferryman

For Harry.
You saved me from the monsters.

CHAPTER ONE

Now

Waiting. My fingers drum out an uneven rhythm on the hard plastic armrest of my chair. The noise jars against the light, methodical patter of the receptionist on her ergonomic keyboard. I see her wince and know I'm rubbing her up the wrong way, like nails down a chalkboard.

Good.

My non-verbal protest is the only complaint I can make because waiting, it's a privilege. It means I've moved up one rung on Dr Petersen's 'ladder of trust'. One rung on a ladder that stretches all the way up to the cloud-covered sky. I'm at the bottom. And I have no intention of climbing to the top. Still, my small ascent has its advantages. I'm wearing my own clothes, for a start. My hands are free and I can continue my discreet torture of the snooty-faced secretary. Smiling serenely at her, I increase the volume of my tapping.

The door opens. Both the receptionist and I look towards the rectangle of space, but no one appears. Through the doorway I can just make out the cream wall, covered with certificates, and the plush shag of the crimson red carpet. At no sign that I can see, the receptionist takes her cue.

'Dr Petersen will see you now.'

She's perfected that sickly-sweet voice. Professional, polite and dripping with disdain. I avoid looking at her as I rise out of my seat. The rubber soles of my plimsolls – real shoes are at least another six rungs – make no sound on the cheap laminate. Instead, slightly out of step with me, the heavy tread of my escort announces my presence; loud enough for Dr Petersen to know I'm coming. Loud enough for him to look up and greet me.

He doesn't.

'How are you today, Heather?' he asks the piece of paper in front of him.

It doesn't answer. There are at least eight seconds of silence before he deigns to lift his eyes to me.

'Hmmm?' He raises his eyebrows, his expression open, pleasant. As if we're friends. Confidants.

We're not.

I hold his gaze as I ease myself into the plush leather chair facing his desk. No ugly moulded plastic in this room. He drops his eyes first and I allow myself a small smirk of victory as I watch him go through the rigmarole of shuffling the papers on his desk, clicking his engraved silver pen several times and adjusting his tie, his shirt. Then he clears his throat and fixes me with a piercing look.

Now we're really playing.

2

'Are you ready to talk today, Heather?'

To you? No.

He reads it in my face and sighs. Leaning forward over the desk, he drops the pen and presses the fingers of both hands together into a steeple. The soft yellow spotlights inlaid into the ceiling make the signet ring on his right little finger sparkle. I can't see what's imprinted on the circular face, just the hint of etchings rubbed worn with age. Like the lines around his eyes, the repugnant folds of his jowls surrounding a mouth puckered by dislike – the expression he wears every time he looks at me. The feeling is mutual.

'I have a report to make to the court, you know.'

I lift one eyebrow disdainfully. Have you?

'The judge wants an update on your progress, your state of mind. Heather, I can't do that if you won't engage with me.'

Written down, these words seem considerate, the rhetoric of a doctor who cares about his patient, about her welfare. When this is transcribed by the receptionist outside – and I know I'm being recorded, even if I can't see the equipment – I'm sure that is how it will read. Only I can hear the razor edge of threat.

I have the power to send you somewhere where there will be bars on your window instead of straps on your bed. That's what he's really saying. Play nice, open up to me, let me inside your mind and you can climb up the ladder until one day blue sky and blazing sun will be the only things hanging over your head.

What Dr Petersen doesn't understand is that I'm not safe. Whether I'm here, in prison, not even if I'm free. It doesn't matter where I am. I'm not safe. A darkness infinitely more potent than his bureaucratic intimidation hovers. Makes this puppetry a ludicrous sideshow.

And he just wouldn't understand. So why the hell should I play his game?

He sees the thought shining clear as day from my eyes and grimaces. Momentarily defeated, he flicks through the sheaves of paper about me – reports, medical notes, facts and figures – and scans for something, anything, to fill the minutes. He's not quite as comfortable with silence as I am. Suddenly his eyes light up. In response, mine narrow to slits. What has he found?

'I have a release form here,' he says, waving a single piece of blue paper in the air for a brief moment. Before I can focus on it, he returns it to the pile. Release form? He has my interest now. There's no hiding it. Victory number two goes to him and he is not above preening. 'I have to sign to say that you are stable enough to be allowed out of this establishment temporarily for the surgery on your right hand to be performed . . .'

My hand. I look down at where it's folded into my lap, unconsciously shielded from view by my unblemished left. I can't see it, but I can still feel it: the puckered rivets, the rough unevenness of the scars. Slowly I shift position and lightly place a hand on each knee. Stare at the difference.

Left: pale white skin, fingers long and thin, nails bare and unvarnished but as long as they'll let me keep them. They could be a weapon, after all. They have been, when I had the chance.

Right: ravaged red, misshapen, nails missing or twisted. More a claw than a hand. Ugly. Monstrous.

I feel my eyes tear up and I'm helpless to stop it. My hand. Petersen's still talking, but I can't hear him.

'Heather? Heather, are you listening?'

No.

'For me to sign this, you need to show that you can communicate. That you're rational enough to be allowed out of this establishment for the procedure. You have to talk to me today. It's important.' He lifts another document; this one is thick, its multiple pages straining the staple that holds it together. 'We're going to go over your statement to the police. What you told them.' He pauses, as if he's waiting for me to say something, give him permission to go right ahead. 'Your own words, Heather. Exactly as you said them. Let's start at the beginning.'

The beginning?

I think about it as I cradle my hand. Close my eyes and imagine I'm not here, but that I'm flying down the motorway, surrounded by my friends. I can almost hear the song blaring from the radio.

CHAPTER TWO

Then

The music erupted out of the speakers, but the smashing drums and high-pitched screech of the lead singer were lost under the cacophony of our five voices, all trying to out-compete each other. The band took over once again as the melody twisted and turned its way across the bridge, then there was a collective intake of breath followed by laughter: none of us knew the words to the verse.

'I love that song!' Emma, flip-flopped feet propped up on the dash, turned round and grinned at Martin, Dougie and me, squashed into the back seat.

'Yeah? Who's it by?' Her boyfriend – Darren – took his eyes off the road to raise an amused eyebrow at her, lips twitching into a smirk.

There was a moment's pause, punctuated by a quiet snort of laughter from the boys on either side of me. I kept quiet: I'd no idea either.

'I don't know,' Emma huffed, put out. 'It's ancient!'

'It's by The Small Faces,' Martin said quietly. 'They were Rod Stewart's band before he became famous.'

Ah. I'd heard of him.

'Whatever,' Emma replied airily. She tossed her long, blonde hair. I wasn't fooled – the gesture was something she did when she wanted attention rather than when she was genuinely upset – but it was enough to get Darren to take his left hand off the steering wheel to rub her thigh in apology.

'I'm just joking,' he assured her.

His hand continued to run up and down the length of tanned skin from her knee to the hem of her skirt. Stuck in the tiny middle seat, his fondling fingers were directly in my field of vision. I counted to ten in my head while I waited for him to cut it out, but he didn't, so I twisted to my left and contented myself with staring past Dougie's profile, becoming hypnotised by the dazzling sunlight and green of the Ayrshire countryside. Feeling me shift in his direction, Dougie turned to look at me. The corners of his lips quirked up, putting a matching pair of dimples in his cheeks. I loved those dimples, just like I loved his eyes, blue and warm – and looking right at me. I lasted three seconds under his scrutiny before I had to turn my head and fix my stare out of the other window to hide my burning cheeks. This time Martin eyed me quizzically, registering the heat in my face, but him I could ignore.

The view wasn't as good from this side: the rolling hills and farm fields were interrupted by two lanes of traffic charging in the other direction. Safer, though. It'd do until my pulse stopped pounding.

'Pit stop,' Darren announced from the driver's seat and I felt the car swerve as he peeled off into the slip road at the last second. Emma squealed dramatically and gripped the seat as he floored it up the hill. I did likewise, although much more quietly, my nails digging into Martin's leg to stop myself being pushed over into Dougie's lap.

'Sorry,' I muttered, as he massaged the bruised skin.

He smiled briefly at me, telling me I was forgiven, then shot Darren a look. I smothered my own grin. Since we'd set out that morning, I didn't think Martin had exchanged more than ten words with Darren. He'd referred to him (outside of Emma's presence) as a meathead – 'that muscle-bound moron'. But it was Dougie's birthday, and that meant making nice.

Initially it had been just the three of us going camping, but my parents had gotten all funny about me going off with two boys. Dougie had been the one to suggest we invite Emma and Darren along (because Emma would never have come without him). I'd been disappointed at first, worried their presence would ruin things, but Dougie convinced me we'd still have fun, we could still do everything we had planned. And Darren had a car, so we were able to head further afield, out to the middle of nowhere rather than just the outskirts of the city.

'What are we stopping for?' Dougie asked over my shoulder.

'Supplies.' Darren swivelled round to wink in the direction of the back seat.

I raised my eyebrows. The car was already chock-full of stuff for the trip. We had enough to stock a bunker and survive a nuclear winter, never mind four nights in a tent.

'Right –' Darren cruised into a supermarket car park far too fast, causing a woman in a Micra to steer herself hurriedly into the kerb – 'you lot stay here. Dougie and I will get stuff for everyone.'

'What?' Emma complained. She stared beseechingly at her boyfriend. 'Why can't we come?'

Darren squealed into a space then yanked up the handbrake as he shot her a grin that revealed two rows of dazzling white teeth. No dimples, though.

'Because I'm the only one with ID and if I go loading up a trolley with you lot trotting along behind me, they won't serve me. Then we'll have to drink seawater all weekend.'

Or cola, or orange juice, or any one of the eight types of soft drink squashed into the boot. But Darren had something a little harder in mind. Beside me, Martin shifted on the seat, clearly disapproving but not wanting to say anything. I kept my mouth shut, too. I wasn't a big drinker – mostly because I wasn't allowed – but I was curious and not so pure that I'd turn the opportunity down.

Fresh air tickled my side as Darren and Dougie threw their doors open in tandem.

'How much do you want us to spend?' Dougie asked as he slid across the vinyl.

'Twenty each?' Darren suggested. Twenty quid? My eyebrows slithered up my forehead. 'It's for four nights, mind,' he continued, reading my expression, which I knew would be echoed and then some on Martin's face.

'Twenty's fine,' Emma replied, shooting me a warning look. I made a face at her, unimpressed. My best friend Emma didn't drink, said it turned people into mindless idiots. Darren's girlfriend Emma, however, apparently thought differently. Resignedly I reached for my purse.

There was a definite air of disgruntlement in the backseat as Dougie and Darren shut their doors on the three of us. Emma didn't seem to notice; she was too busy staring at Darren's broad shoulders as they disappeared into the warehouse-style supermarket.

'Isn't Darren gorgeous?' she sighed.

Martin huffed a laugh that he managed to turn into a half-convincing cough. Emma slanted her eyes at him before turning her attention to me.

'Isn't he?' she prompted.

'Um . . .' I shrugged.

He was good-looking, I supposed, in a thuggish kind of way. He was a big guy, one of those compulsive gym-goers, and his clothes came from the sorts of shops that blared out dance tunes and sold shirts with brand names emblazoned in huge letters across the front. Two years older than us, he had a job as a labourer in the building company Emma's dad managed – that was how she'd met him. He was confident, too, walking with a pronounced swagger. But it was all very deliberate, very affected. A paper-thin facade. To be honest, I thought he looked a bit like an idiot. Dougie, on the other hand . . .

Dougie was as laid back as Darren was pumped up. He was just as tall as Darren but nowhere near as bulky. Nicely normal-sized. He had similar blue eyes, but they were usually smiling rather than eyeing the world with barely veiled aggression, and his thick brown hair stuck up everywhere, nothing like Darren's gelled masterpiece.

'Heather?' Emma waved a hand in front of my face, pulling my attention back to her and her question.

'Sure.' I smiled at her, putting just the right amount of enthusiasm in my voice.

I'd had quite a lot of practice at that recently. For the last six months, Emma and Darren had been inseparable. If I wanted to spend time with her, I had to put up with him too. Which didn't make me happy because the Emma I knew, the one I'd been friends with since we were shy five-year-olds together on the playground, turned into someone completely different as soon as she was within swooning distance of Darren.

'He is!' she asserted, smiling dreamily. 'And he's such a good kisser.'

Given that I knew for a fact Emma hadn't kissed a single boy before she'd caught Darren's eye, I wasn't sure how she was in a position to judge, but I kept my mouth shut.

Martin gave a cough – a real one this time – and squirmed uncomfortably on his seat. Emma didn't notice.

'And he knows what he's doing, if you know what I mean.' She gave me a saucy look. 'I mean –'

'Emma!' I cut across before she could expand. 'Enough details.'

'What?' She looked at us, wide-eyed, the picture of innocence. I was saved from answering by the reappearance of Dougie and Darren.

'Here they come,' I said, relieved. Then my eyes widened. 'Did they buy the whole shop? Where the hell are we supposed to fit all of that?'

The answer: at our feet, on our knees, in the millimetres of space between the seats. Basically anywhere Darren could find a gap. If I was uncomfortable before, now I'd less space than a sardine in a can. To make matters worse, Darren forced a case of beer between Martin and me so I was pushed up tight against Dougie's side, so much so he had to chuck his arm along the back of the seat and press against me just so Darren could shut the door. I was burning up under the heat of it resting lightly across my shoulders. How many times had I daydreamed about sitting close beside him, his arm casually flung round me? In none of those dreams were we quite so closely surrounded by boxes of booze – or people.

'How long do we have to go?' I asked. The sun streaming in was turning the car into a greenhouse and sweat was already gathering at the base of my back.

'An hour, maybe a bit more,' Darren replied, twisting the key in the ignition. The car spluttered and heaved before dying completely. There was a long, drawn-out moment of silence.

Darren tried again, pumping the accelerator with his foot. The car vibrated, clanking noisily, but refused to catch.

'Darren, what's wrong?' Emma simpered.

The look he gave her was priceless.

'The car won't start,' he hissed between gritted teeth.

Aggravated, he tried again, turning the key and holding, letting the choking, grating noises go on and on and on. People in nearby cars began to turn and look. I tried to avoid their stares, wishing there was room for me to slink down and hide.

'Are you in the AA or the RAC?' Martin asked, leaning forward.

'No.' Darren turned the key back, waited several seconds, then twisted hard. After just a moment of protest, the engine roared into life. 'Yes!'

Throwing the car into gear, Darren backed out of the space and navigated his way out of the car park. With the extra weight we were carrying, the car was riding low on its axles and I felt every bump and rut in the tarmac.

'Darren, is this thing likely to die on us when we're in the middle of nowhere with no mobile phone reception?' Martin asked quietly as we accelerated back onto the M77 motorway.

'Have a little faith,' Darren replied. 'She's never let me down before.' He patted the Volvo symbol nestled in the heart of the steering wheel.

'Yes, it has,' Emma piped up. 'Didn't you have to call your dad last month to give you a tow back from the gym?'

'Apart from that one tiny incident, she's never let me down before,' Darren corrected. 'Shut up!' he snapped good-naturedly at the titter of amusement that rumbled across the back seat. He gave us a one-fingered salute before fiddling with the settings on his top-of-the-range stereo, its shiny buttons and flashing digital display incongruous in the ugly plastic dash of the ancient car.

'Right, Martin,' Darren called suddenly. I felt Martin stiffen beside me before fumbling to react to the small missile being hurled towards him over Darren's shoulder. He caught it – just – and I realised it was an iPod. 'Your turn to choose the music,' Darren told him.

Martin shot him a surprised look before offering half a smile.

'Cheers,' he said, and a minute later the strains of John Mayer filled the car.

'Good choice,' Darren muttered before spinning the volume up high.

We drove along without talking, listening to the music and watching the scenery race by. Under the noise from the stereo, the car engine screamed as Darren pushed it faster and faster, showing off to Emma who was giggling and shrieking in the passenger seat. I was relieved that I couldn't see the dials on the dash, didn't know exactly how fast we were going; Darren was passing other cars as if they were standing still. I wasn't about to complain, though. I was desperate to get there and stretch my legs, rub at the bruises from where the sharp edges of the boxes of booze were digging into me.

I shut my eyes and leaned my head back. Both boys had opened their windows, allowing a cooling breeze to whip across the tight space, pulling strands of my hair free of the plait I'd constructed and making them dance around my face. It was nice, relaxing. I smiled to myself, letting my shoulders slump down, forgetting, momentarily, that I was leaning back on Dougie's arm. My life over the past few months had been madness. If my eyes were open, they'd been stuck in a book, going over notes, watching my hand scrawl out answer after answer. But now the exams were done and it was the first week of July: six weeks of holidays stretched out before me. In theory I still had another year to do at school but I had a tenuous agreement with my mum that, if I got the results I needed, I could skip sixth year and go to university at the end of summer. I wasn't seventeen until September so she told me I'd have to stay at home, for the first year at least, but I'd be a university student.

14

Better yet, Dougie had a conditional offer from the same place, the same course in Archaeology. That hadn't been why I'd chosen it – digging into the past, seeing the way people lived, the things they believed in, had fascinated me since I was a child – but it was a definite plus. Dougie. Unconsciously, my smile edged a little wider. I'd had a thing for him for a while now. We'd always known each other, had been in the same class ever since primary school. But Dougie and I had never really been friends. Not until the last few months, since Emma had taken a fancy to Darren and disappeared, leaving a gaping hole in my life that Dougie had stepped in to fill. I owed her for that. Now we saw each other almost every day. More, even, than Dougie saw Martin. We had so much in common. Kindred souls, he said.

But friends, only friends. Unfortunately.

'Heather.' His voice whispered in my ear, taking me by surprise. I jumped a little, but I didn't open my eyes.

'Mmm?'

'You're kind of making my arm go to sleep.'

Oh God.

Embarrassed, I yanked my head forward so fast I almost gave myself whiplash.

'I'm so sorry,' I muttered as he tried to rub life back into his limb.

'Don't worry about it.' He grinned at me, but the blush refused to fade from my cheeks.

'You should have said . . .'

He shrugged.

'You looked comfortable. Well –' He glanced down at the collection of stuff packed around me – 'as comfortable as you're going to get.'

'Right.' I gave him a timid smile. He was still grinning at me. My face flushed flame red once again as I tried to think of something to say. Something intelligent. Nothing came. 'So . . . where are we going again?'

He wriggled his eyebrows. 'Black Cairn Point.' He hissed the words at me, low and menacing. Despite the humour in his eyes I felt a little thrill roll down my spine.

'Sounds creepy!' Emma purred from the front. 'Like the sort of place serial killers go to dispose of the bodies!'

Dougie ripped his gaze from mine, releasing me.

'Well, it's named after a graveyard, sort of,' he told her.

'What?' Emma blinked at him, looking horrified.

'A cairn's a burial monument,' Martin explained from over my other shoulder.

'Darren, you're not taking us all out there to do away with us, are you?' I asked, addressing the eyes that were watching our exchange via the rear-view mirror. Dougie snorted quietly beside me and I grinned. 'Because –'

But at that moment the music cut off, silencing me.

'Hey!' Emma complained, reaching for the buttons. She pressed several randomly, but nothing came out of the speakers, not even crackle.

'The light's gone out,' said Dougie. 'Has the fuse blown?'

'Better not have,' Darren replied, knocking Emma's hand away and taking over the fiddling, but with no more success. 'The damned thing's new.'

'Darren, watch the road!' Martin yelped. Darren turned his attention back to the motorway just in time to swerve out from behind the lorry he'd been about to climb over the back of.

'Christ, sorry!' he huffed.

He pressed down on the accelerator to take him past the truck and I watched as we cruised along beside the advert, a child's face covered in yoghurt laughing happily in at me. It drifted out of sight as Darren sped on, but then started to coast back into view until the lorry was undertaking us.

'What the hell?' Darren hissed.

'What is it, what's wrong?' Dougie leaned forward, peering around me.

'I don't know . . . the dials have all died. I've got no power.' Darren was still kicking at the accelerator, but nothing was happening.

'Darren, we're in the fast lane,' Martin reminded him, urgency in his voice.

'I know!' Darren snapped.

'Get into the slow lane,' Dougie ordered. 'Look, there's a slip road coming up. See if you can coast down it. That'll get us off the motorway at any rate.'

Darren did as he suggested and the Volvo rolled slowly down the exit until we reached a junction for a much quieter road where the gradient started to tilt up. Eventually gravity called a halt to our progress. Darren did his best to force the car onto the dirt hard shoulder, out of the way of any passing traffic. We sat for a minute, no one speaking, before Darren elbowed open the door and stomped around to the front. A moment later he'd thrown up the bonnet, hiding his glowering face from us.

'Shit,' Dougie sighed and got out. I watched him jog round to join Darren.

'You're not in the RAC, are you, Martin?' I asked quietly.
He laughed.

'Not much point when I don't have a car, is there? Come on, no sense baking in here.'

He stepped out onto the hard, compacted mud on the roadside, offering me his hand so that I could slide along, navigating the obstacle course that was the back seat. Though it wasn't any cooler outside, standing in the direct path of the sun, the air felt fresher, kept moving by a gentle breeze, and I was able to stretch out the kinks in my muscles.

'How's it going?' We moseyed round to join Darren and Dougie, who were standing motionless, staring into the inner workings of the machine. Neither of them answered me, which I took to be a bad sign.

Gathered around the engine, I followed the boys' gaze, not quite sure what I was looking at. Under the bonnet was a mass of pipes and oddly shaped boxes. The whole thing was covered in grime, metallic surfaces glittering with coppery rust.

'Try starting it,' Dougie offered.

Darren gave him a sidelong look, as if it was clearly pointless, but he got behind the wheel again and obligingly turned the key.

Nothing happened. No coughing, no spluttering, no clicking. The engine stayed inert.

'Battery,' said Martin. He stuffed his hands in his pockets and scuffed at the loose stones around his feet.

'What?' Darren asked, curling his body back out of the car.

'The battery's flat,' Martin repeated.

'How can it be? If the battery was flat, the car would never have started in Kilmarnock.'

18

'It still had charge then. Your alternator's knackered. It hasn't been charging. Happens all the time with this type of car.' He kicked at the ancient Volvo's dented bumper. 'The brushes get clogged and they don't spin right.'

We all gaped at him. Martin, with his wiry frame and specs, was more pocket protector and calculator than spanner and automobiles.

'What?' he said defensively, seeing the way we were all looking at him. 'I can't know about cars?'

'So what do we do, then?' Darren asked, staring at Martin with newfound respect. Martin smiled wryly at the change.

'Give the alternator –' Catching our confused expressions, he pointed at a silvery cylinder near the front of the machinery – 'give *that* a bang to clear the brushes, then we just need a jump start. After that we should be good.'

'And have you got a hammer?' Darren asked dryly.

Martin nodded.

'Got a rubber one in the boot for putting in tent pegs. Give me the keys and I'll grab it.'

I followed Martin to the rear of the car.

'How the hell did you know all that?' I whispered.

He winked at me conspiratorially.

'My cousin's a mechanic. He used to babysit me. Spent most of my time in his garage handing him screwdrivers. Don't ask me to actually do anything, though . . .'

I laughed.

A minute later Martin had unearthed his rubber mallet and Darren had given the alternator a couple of good whacks, after fixing Martin with a searching look to make sure he was serious.

'Now we just need someone to give us a jump,' Dougie said, rubbing his hands together.

The four of us looked both ways up the road. Nothing was coming. We waited in silence as a minute trickled past. Then another.

'Come on!' exploded Darren. 'This road's five foot from the motorway! How can there be no traffic?'

'Guess no one lives out this way,' I offered. Looking around, there were only a few houses dotted in the rugged landscape.

'What's that?' Dougie asked, pointing to a faded green building down the road in the distance.

'Workshop or something,' Martin replied.

'Well, there're cars parked there. Maybe someone will help us?'

We all looked at each other.

'Who's asking?' Darren said finally.

Martin chipped in at once. 'It's your car.'

I thought he had a good point but Darren's eyes narrowed.

'Yeah, and if it wasn't for me we wouldn't be going further than the back garden,' he shot back. 'And we wouldn't have anything to drink, either.'

'What do you think they do in there?' Dougie asked, shading his eyes so he could peer at the building. I followed his gaze. I couldn't see a sign or anything written on the side to give it away.

'Probably welding or something,' Martin offered. 'Something industrial.'

'So it'll be almost all men . . .' Darren said slowly.

'Yeah.'

His face brightened.

'Well, that settles it, then,' he said, slamming down the bonnet. 'We send the girls. They can charm them for us.' He winked at me, ignoring the curdled expression on my face.

The worst thing was that the other two boys seemed to be in complete agreement with him, although Martin was somewhat sheepish about it, refusing to look me in the eye. Outnumbered and outvoted, I huffed and puffed as I dragged Emma out of the passenger seat and we traipsed off towards the small warehouse.

'Remember – be alluring!' Darren called to our departing backs.

CHAPTER THREE

We walked along the narrow hard shoulder of the road without talking, only the quiet slapping of Emma's flip-flops breaking the silence. I could feel the gazes of the three boys burning into my back along with the sun and I folded my arms across my chest, cross.

'I can't believe we're doing this,' I complained. 'Your boyfriend's an arse!'

Emma didn't respond, which I took to mean she agreed with me.

We didn't spot a sign until we were almost on top of the place. I was relieved to see it looked fairly professional, announcing the place to be a metalworking shop run by J. P. Robertson and Sons. The driveway hadn't been tarmacked, though. It was just a dirt road running a hundred metres to a large circular parking area where several vehicles – mostly small vans – had been abandoned haphazardly.

We had a quick look around the outside, hoping there would be a lone friendly soul lurking about so we wouldn't have to go in, but there was no sign of life. Gritting my teeth, I headed for the small door to the right of the huge warehouse roll-top shutter, which was firmly closed.

'You talk,' I said to Emma as we hesitated on the threshold. 'You're the pretty one. And he's your boyfriend,' I added as she opened her mouth to argue.

I had her with that one. She pursed her lips but stalked through the door when I held it open for her. She didn't go very far, though, grinding to a halt just inside. I almost walked into the back of her, barely stopping myself in time before squeezing past so I stood alongside her. We glanced around, feeling a little stupid. The room was big, partitioned by giant machinery. Here and there I caught movement, the backs of shoulders as men bent to their work. The noise was incredible, like I'd stuck my head inside a vibrating drum. I couldn't hear myself think.

No one seemed to notice us. I looked to Emma, who stared back at me uncertainly. Should we just wander about? It didn't seem safe. Everywhere the walls were dotted with hazard and warning signs.

'Can I help you?' The words were hollered from our right. I turned my head and saw a girl, maybe eighteen or so, dressed in oil-smeared overalls, short dark hair slicked back, looking at us questioningly. She waved us into a small glass cubicle, which I guessed served as an office, and shut the door. The noise of the machinery was immediately halved. I sighed in relief.

'Can I help you?' she repeated.

There was a short pause whilst I waited for Emma to take the lead. She didn't.

'We're looking for a jump,' I explained. 'Our car's just died up on the road. Something to do with the alternator?' I gave a brief smile and spread my arms helplessly, thinking she'd empathise with my distinct lack of mechanical know-how. Instead she frowned, thinking.

'Clogged brushes?'

'Eh, yeah. Think so.'

'You'll need a hammer.' She moved across to the opposite wall and started to rake through a drawer.

'We've done that,' I said hurriedly. 'We just need the jump.'

'Okay.' She smiled at us. 'I've got a charged jump battery in my boot.'

'You just keep this in here?' I asked moments later as we watched her dig a plastic box about the size of a shoebox out of the back of a battered Ford Fiesta.

'Yeah, my dad didn't want me driving around out here without one. Mobile signal's not very good if you get stuck.' She stood up. 'Where's your car?'

I pointed with my fingers to where the Volvo was just visible, glinting in the distance. I couldn't see the three boys but guessed they'd taken refuge inside the car.

'Hop in then.'

I grinned to myself as we drove back in her car, imagining Darren's face when I arrived with my heroine. She wasn't exactly what I'd been sent for.

'Where are you heading off to?' she asked, her low voice almost masked by the rumble and rattle of the Fiesta.

'Camping,' I offered. 'There's a beach down near Stranraer, nice and quiet. Black Cairn Point?'

'Oh right.' She smiled at me. 'Hope your alternator doesn't die again down there!'

I smiled back, but my stomach dropped. What *would* we do if the damned car died again? The girl caught the thought on my face.

'Don't worry,' she said, pulling over just in front of Darren's car and flinging her door open. 'You're never too far away from someone around here. You'll just be in for a bit of a hike. Hi!' She waved a cheery welcome to Darren, who was sidling out of the driver's side, watching our approach. I saw his face crumple a bit – he'd obviously expected us to come back with a man – but his eyes zeroed in on the bulky thing in the girl's hand. 'I hear you need a jump.'

'Yeah.' He recovered himself, plastering an ingratiating smile across his jaw. 'Yeah, we do.'

He popped the bonnet then stepped back and folded his arms across his chest, watching as she went to work, deftly attaching two cables somewhere in the maze of car parts. I saw him raise two eyebrows and noticed with a smug sense of satisfaction that he was impressed.

'Do you want to try starting it?' the girl asked.

He did, and seconds later the car roared to life.

We left the leads attached for ten minutes, letting the battery charge itself back up, during which time Darren managed to find the decency to thank the girl. No gratitude for Emma or me though, I noticed.

When the leads came off, the car kept running and we were back on our way.

The beach we were heading for was somewhere none of us had ever been. It was a place Dougie's dad used to go fishing and camping with his friends when he was a teenager. He'd given us a scrap of paper with directions scrawled across it, something Darren resolutely ignored until we hit the seaside town of Stranraer.

'Right.' He pulled over, idling illegally alongside double yellow lines. 'Emma, get out. You're swapping with Dougie.'

Emma looked outraged.

'What? Darren!'

'Sorry, angel, but I have no confidence in your ability to direct me. In the back you go.'

'Because I'm a girl? That's totally sexist!'

'Not because you're a girl. Because you're you. I might have let Heather have a go –' I focused incredibly hard on not letting a fleeting wave of smugness show on my face – 'but you'd get us lost in about five seconds.' He paused, stared at her. 'Come on, shift before I get a ticket.'

She glared back at him and for a moment I thought she wasn't going to move. I watched, proud of her defiance and eagerly anticipating fireworks, but Dougie had already climbed out and when he opened the passenger door she vacated the seat without complaint. Muttering venomously under her breath, she plonked herself down next to me. There was more room with Emma next to me instead of Dougie, but her disgruntled aura filled the space and I soon found myself wishing for my old seating partner back.

Looking to escape her bad mood, I leaned forward between the front seats, watching Dougie and Darren navigate, drinking in the scenery.

'Are we close?' I asked. I didn't recognise any of the names on the signs we passed and hadn't seen any for Black Cairn Point, the place we were heading.

'Yes.' Dougie twisted his
there now. Turn here, Darren.

Darren steered the Volvo round
road. High hedges closed in on us on b
from view. Then the road dipped down ɑ

'The sea!' I said, instantly sitting up stra.

It glimmered deep blue in front of us, almost ⟨ ⟩ ıst
the paler sky. I stared at it eagerly. Living in the hear ⟨ ⟩ ɔtland
it was a sight I rarely saw, especially in such glorious weather.

'Is that it, is that where we're going?' I asked excitedly,
sounding a decade younger than my sixteen – almost seventeen
– years.

'Sort of. The road hugs the coast for a bit before we drop
down,' Dougie replied, studying the hastily drawn map.

It was an impatient wait for me as Darren guided the car
along the road, which twisted and turned, narrowing further
until it was a squeeze for us to force our way through. Windows
were wound up as nettles, brambles and long grasses from the
hedgerow scraped against the sides of the car. For once, Darren
drove at a sensible speed, trying to dodge potholes and the
worst of the crumbling tarmac.

'Where is this place?' he asked tersely, finally provoked as
the bottom of the car grated noisily, wheels dipping into a
particularly deep crevice.

'I think we're nearly there,' Dougie replied, frowning intently
at his paper. 'My dad says there's a dirt track off to the left
that'll take us right down to the beach.'

'How long since he's been here?' Martin asked. 'Is the track
definitely still there?'

mumbled. 'Yeah, apparently his friend was
ng last summer. He said it was still the same, still
serted. Just . . . just keep your eyes peeled. It might be pretty
overgrown.'

We continued forward in near total silence, the music turned off, only the growl of the engine and the whir of the fan – working overtime now we were closed in by the attacking plants – breaking through the quiet. Each of us stared to the left intently, convinced we'd miss the turning if we so much as blinked.

It proved remarkably easy to find.

'There!' Dougie shouted, pointing.

A wide gap in the hedge, tousled by a breeze that none of us could feel, seemed to wave at us. Darren smiled, easing the car round the tight bend. From there it was a steep drop, the road scything its way across a hill that was so devoid of plant-life it was really more of a cliff. At the bottom was a narrow parking bay of compacted dirt, a low stone wall separating it from the grass-covered dunes. Beyond them I could make out smooth sand and the vast rippling blue of the ocean.

Darren parked haphazardly in the centre of the makeshift car park. He barely even had the handbrake yanked up before all four doors were open and we tumbled out.

Like children, we clambered excitedly down the narrow sandy path between the dunes, eyes set on the wide expanse of shimmering sparkles thrown up as the sun tickled the sea. It was a totally deserted landscape. Not even a bird swooping in the broad blue sky to interrupt the peace and quiet. The beach, several hundred metres long, curved in a thin crescent like a new moon. Tumbles of rocks hemmed us in at both ends and behind us hills covered in heather and long grasses provided a backdrop. With the road hidden from view, the spot seemed completely inaccessible, completely protected. Completely isolated.

'All ours,' Darren smiled. 'I bet there's not a soul for miles.'

'Awesome,' Dougie grinned back.

Awesome, right. I spun in a slow circle, taking in the glorious beach, the rugged hills, the absolute emptiness. I tried to keep the sudden nervousness I felt off my face. So we were alone, big deal. That was what we wanted, right? I looked to Dougie to reassure myself.

'Shall we get our things, then?' I forced my voice not to tremble.

It took several trips back and forth to the car to unload our provisions. Parental permission had been based on the fact that we separate into two tents – girls and boys – and our stuff was split pretty much fifty-fifty. I had to lug most of Emma's and my gear alone. On the first return trip to the car Emma spotted a fish that some fisherman had hooked and discarded, leaving it baking on the top of the low stone wall. It was dried out and rotting, maggots writhing in its belly. It stank and was repulsive to look at. Emma absolutely refused to go near the thing, and it was cart our load myself or go without our tent, clothes, toiletries . . .

I was sorely tempted just to take my own things, but I didn't want to look petty. My irritation was plain on my face, though, and I made sure to scatter sand over Emma's prone body – sunbathing as she 'watched our stuff' – every time I dumped something new on the pile. It was mid-afternoon and the heat was suffocating. I was sweating as I stormed back up the short hill, trying not to breathe so I wouldn't inhale the putrid stench of decomposing fish. Hissing out a string of profanities at her newfound selfishness, I rounded the back of the car, arms already reaching for the heavy bag containing Emma's assortment of beauty products (another new development) and the two sheathed sleeping bags. My fingers closed on air; the boot was empty.

'Hey, has anyone seen –' I looked around just in time to see Martin and Dougie heading back towards the beach, the rest of our stuff slung awkwardly across their shoulders.

I watched them go, bemused. I wasn't used to anyone doing things for me. Well, boys doing things for me. Something about me didn't scream damsel in distress.

After a second I shrugged, grabbed the last couple of things from the back seat – an air mattress and a can of insect repellent – and ran after them.

'Thanks,' I said, a little breathlessly, as they plonked everything down by the rest of our gear.

'No problem.' Martin smiled.

Dougie gave me a half grin and a wink.

A wink?

I blushed scarlet. Luckily both boys had already turned their attention to their own pile. Darren was busy picking through the boxes and bags, so only Emma was left to see my burning cheeks, but she had her eyes closed, sunglasses staring up into the fiery heat of the sun.

'Right, Emma!' I barked, exasperated by my motionless teammate. 'Help me.'

She flipped her shades up and eyed me speculatively. 'What?'

'Help me,' I repeated. 'We need to get the tent set up.' 'Now?'

'Unless you'd rather do it in the dark,' I replied acidly.

Five minutes later I wished I'd left her lounging in the sand. Emma was worse than useless. She just stood around, hovering ineffectually, fiddling with the straps on her top or the hang of her skirt, glancing over to see if Darren was looking back at her. Without her help, I managed to get the canvas unravelled and oriented on the lumpy beach. Then I dug out the poles and snapped them into a long, bendy line.

'Just hold this here. Like this,' I ordered her.

She ambled over and stood obediently where I'd asked, keeping one end of the pole jammed into the ground whilst I ran round attaching clips and forcing the tent to assume its erect shape. After several seconds of watching me, Emma looked over to where the boys – or rather, Martin and Dougie – were having much more success. They were already hammering in the tent pegs to hold the fly-sheet. Darren appeared to be 'supervising', standing with his legs planted in the sand, finger pointing imperiously.

'Their tent is bigger than ours,' she pouted.

'There are three of them,' I reminded her.

'And theirs is taller.'

'Well, this is what we've got,' I huffed, struggling to heave the fly-sheet up and over the apex of the tent. 'You can let go of that now.'

She released the pole and I waited anxiously for a few seconds, but the tent remained standing. I grinned at it, pleased with my handiwork.

'Are we done?' she asked, eyes once again on Darren, now lounging in a camping chair and arranging bottles and cans in the cooler.

I exhaled heavily, but it didn't register with Emma.

'*You're* done,' I said.

Emma pretended not to hear the emphasis in my words.

'Okay.' She smiled brightly and trotted over to her boyfriend, leaving me with a jumble of ropes and twisted pegs.

I got finished fairly quickly on my own, quicker when Martin and Dougie came over to help me get proper tension on the lines and blow up the air mattress with Martin's little electric pump. Even so, it was close to dinner-time once we flopped down onto the folding chairs that Darren had deigned to dig out and arrange for us – pretty much the only contribution he'd made to the whole pitching-camp operation.

'Drink?' Darren asked, holding out a beer in the general direction of Martin, Dougie and me.

I stared at it. It was glistening, chilled from its bed of ice in the cooler, perspiration dripping down the shining silver can. But I didn't really want it. My mouth was dry from exertion, sweat beading on my forehead. My head was aching from the heat and the hassle of trying to get the damned tent up mostly by myself. What I really wanted was one of the bottles of water or cans of fizzy juice hidden beneath what seemed a mountain of alcohol. I could imagine Darren's expression if I said that, though. More importantly, what would Dougie think? I grimaced at the dilemma.

Not wanting to look immature, I started to reach out, but stopped at the look on Dougie's face. He was wrinkling his nose, half shaking his head at Darren.

'Later,' he said. 'I'm starving. Barbecue?'

CHAPTER FOUR

Now

'Shall we talk about your issues with self-esteem, Heather?'

Dr Petersen's voice cuts through my reverie. I'm not sure how long he's continued to talk; I haven't been listening. This question rankles, though.

'I don't have issues with self-esteem,' I shoot back, then scowl. I'm annoyed at myself for letting him goad me into speaking.

Two–one to him. Another reason to scowl. He smiles, gloating.

'Do you deny that you have difficulties talking about your emotions? Or believing your self-worth? Let's talk about your feelings for your friend, Douglas.'

I open my mouth to correct him – Dougie hates to be called Douglas – but then close it again. Take a deep breath. Rearrange my cool, nonchalant expression. I won't talk about Dougie. Not with him.

I can all but feel the tables turning as the hour passes, handing the advantage to Petersen. The smugness I had when I walked in now lies in tatters around my feet. With a tremendous effort, I force myself to smile at him. It's not warm but something more akin to manic. I watch as he squirms uncomfortably under my stare, and my smile becomes real. Almost uncontained. He clears his throat.

What will be his next avenue of attack? The self-esteem thing sideswiped me, but I wasn't concentrating. I am now. Focusing like a boxer in the ring, waiting for my opponent to make his move. A sharp jab, a hook, an uppercut. What does he think will land that knockout blow?

While Petersen deliberates, I decide to defend with feigned indifference. I sigh, look away as if I'm bored.

I am bored; bored of the circles that we spin around and around in. Bored of trying to pretend I'm sane now, when I was never insane in the first place. Bored of dreaming about getting out of here.

At least, I tell myself I'm bored, and I almost believe it.

What I really am is afraid. Fear, my constant companion, churns in my gut, but I've lived with it for so long now I can almost ignore it. Here, in the light, the shadows in my mind are pushed back, almost vanquished. The only monster sits opposite me.

'I spoke to your mother, Heather.' He pauses, watching keenly for my reaction. I blink, nothing more. 'She tells me you've been refusing to take her calls . . .'

He tails off, hoping I'll fill the silence with a response. Any response.

I have one: I have nothing to say to her.

But I don't say that. And it's not just because I don't want to give him the satisfaction of thinking I'm opening up to him. It's because I don't want to admit it, even to myself. But it's true. I have nothing to say. To her or to any of my family. Because they didn't believe me . . . and there's just no way past that.

Neither did Petersen. But I don't give a shit about him.

While he lets the silence drag on – hoping I'll break – I let my gaze wander across his desk. Half my mouth lifts up in a smirk. The silver letter opener is gone. It was there, in pride of place, the first day I came here. It's been there every time since. Silly thing for a shrink to have in his office, really, something like that. Sharp. Deadly. I don't believe for a second that I'm the only person to have tried to stab him in the neck with it. I *do* wonder if I got the closest . . .

'Heather?'

At the sound of my name like that, like a question, I look up. It's involuntary. Still, it annoys me. I glare at him, eyes sparkling in defiance. He sits up straighter, thinking he sees tears.

'She'd like to see you.' He's dropped his voice and made it patient, kind, indulgent. Almost loving.

It's like the squeak of wool between teeth. But I don't react. Well, my lip curls a little, but I can't help that.

'Your mother's offering you a second chance,' he scolds gently.

Is she? I laugh bitterly to myself. It's *me* who should be offering *her* the second chance. If I ever decide to.

I compose myself once more and go back to smiling at him. I'm sure I know what's coming next. Another barbed threat.

Something about how healing the division with my family will show I'm making progress. Maybe a reference to moving up his stupid ladder.

He surprises me.

'Tell me about the cairn, Heather. Tell me what you found there.'

CHAPTER FIVE

Then

By the time we'd managed to cook burgers on the tiny portable barbecue Dougie had brought with him, the sun was sinking low in the sky. It hovered an inch above the horizon, the first hues of a beautiful sunset ebbing out over the cloudless blue. I leaned back in my chair, stuffed full of food, and let the last of the day's heat play across my face.

'Time to get the fire going, d'you reckon?' Martin asked quietly.

At the word 'fire', both Dougie and Darren jumped up, their expressions eager and enthusiastic, Darren losing the cool, superior look he usually wore. It made him look a lot younger suddenly. Nicer. I almost smiled at him as he rubbed his hands together, practically gleeful.

'Definitely,' he said.

Neither Emma nor I moved. It was obvious that this was a boy thing. I wondered, as I watched them dig a hole and then rearrange a hastily gathered bundle of firewood, whether any of them were ever boy scouts. Martin, maybe. He seemed to be moving the most purposefully, taking charge of constructing the twigs into a tepee shape, cradling a crumpled wad of paper in the centre and setting a match to it.

'This'll get it going,' Darren announced, holding up a bottle of something. Vodka, I realised.

'No!' Martin yelped, jumping up with an arm aloft to halt Darren, who was already halfway towards pouring the alcohol onto the smoking wisps of fire.

In an instant the friendly camaraderie was gone. Darren bristled, narrowing his eyes in annoyance. Martin took in Darren's posture – the way his fingers curled themselves into a fist, the broadness of his shoulders and curve of his bicep revealed under a ludicrously tight t-shirt – and his expression went from alarmed and irritated to supplicating.

'Don't want to waste it,' he said, attempting a smile. 'The fire will catch, just give it a second.'

'But since you've got the vodka out . . .' Dougie appeared behind Darren, a stack of plastic cups in his hand.

There was an awkward moment where Darren continued to stare at Martin, aggression barely veiled, before he turned and started to fill the cups as Dougie held them out to him. I watched as the liquid inside rose at least halfway up the side of the transparent plastic before Dougie topped it up with Coke. This time, when he handed me one, I didn't hesitate. After all, it wasn't like I'd never had a drink before . . .

I took a sip and, aware that Dougie at least was watching me, did my utmost to keep the grimace of distaste off my face. The Coke did nothing to disguise the sharp tang of the alcohol. It was nasty. Like drinking hairspray. Still, no one else was complaining so I took another mouthful. It didn't improve. Making my way back to my seat, I made a mental note to sneakily add some more fizzy cola as soon as possible.

'So what shall we do?' Darren asked from across the circle. As Martin promised, the fire had caught and Darren's face was illuminated by flickers of orange light. Dusk had fallen quickly and behind him the landscape melded into layers of darkening shadows.

'How about Truth or Dare?' Emma suggested with a giggle.

'Truth or Dare?' Martin repeated. His tone was scathing but it was apprehension that I read in his eyes.

I was with him. My stomach dropped at the very thought, imagining what I might have to say or do in front of Dougie, but he was grinning enthusiastically.

'Sounds good,' Dougie said. He turned and raised a questioning eyebrow at me. 'Heather?'

What else could I say?

'I'm in,' I muttered.

Martin sighed unenthusiastically. 'Fine, then.'

'All right, Truth or Dare.' Darren emptied his cup and quickly poured himself a refill, pausing to top up Emma's drink before stashing the already half-empty bottle protectively between his feet. 'Who's going first, then?'

'Why don't you?' Martin suggested, sure, as I was, that Darren would refuse.

'All right,' Darren said, rising to the challenge.

'Truth or dare?' Emma asked eagerly.

'Dare.'

She pouted and I knew she'd had some awful question planned for him – probably whether or not he loved her! I doubted Darren had drunk enough for something like that. Neither had I. I took another swig, knowing it would soon be my turn.

'I've got one.' Dougie leaned forward, rubbing his hands together. 'I dare you to go into the sea. Right up to your chest, then duck your whole head in.'

Darren gaped at him.

'That's the friggin' Irish Sea. It's freezing!'

'Chicken!'

The word seemed to animate Darren. He jumped up from his chair in one sudden movement.

'All right then.' He began stripping off his clothes carelessly, almost tossing his jeans into the fire before Emma snatched them free of the flames. 'I'll keep my kecks on, seeing as there are ladies present.'

He winked at Martin, wickedly amused, then took off, jogging across the sand.

It was a good fifty metres to the shore, but we still heard his gasp as his feet touched the water. He ploughed on, though, his outline silhouetted against the last of the light. When he was out almost far enough for his shoulders to disappear beneath the waves, he dropped, leaving the horizon flat once more. Just a second later he emerged, half-swimming, half-running back to the beach. As soon as he broke free of the water he burst into a flat-out sprint for the warmth of the fire.

'Christ, it was Baltic!' He juddered, dancing on the spot, holding his hands out to the heat. His body was covered in goose bumps, impressive muscles twitching beneath the skin. His boxers were soaked, clinging indecently to his body. I tried not to look, especially as he yanked them off before diving back into his jeans.

'Aren't you going to put your shirt back on?' Martin asked sourly as Darren settled himself back into his chair, still topless.

'Think I'll dry off a bit first.' Darren grinned at him. He held Martin's eyes and twitched both pecs, one after the other, in an obscene little dance.

'Show-off,' Martin muttered, so quietly the words only reached me because our chairs were close enough for the arms to touch. Darren smirked a little wider, though, and I wondered if he could guess what Martin was thinking.

'Who's next?' Darren asked.

'You get to choose,' Emma told him, prodding his splayed thigh with her toe.

'Then I choose you. Truth or dare, gorgeous?'

Emma giggled, revelling in his attention. I turned my head to the side and rolled my eyes, catching Martin's gaze. He discreetly mimed shooting himself in the head and I laughed silently.

'Ooh, I don't know.' More giggling.

'Pick one, Emma,' I said, perhaps a little too sharply. She stuck her tongue out at me.

'Dare,' she said eventually.

'Okay . . .' Dougie began, but Darren held up his hand.

'I've got one.'

'What?' Emma eyed Darren apprehensively. As did I. I didn't want him to set a precedent of humiliating dares, because I knew exactly what Emma would ask if I opted for truth.

'Lose your top.'

'What?'

'Come on, babe. I'm feeling exposed, half-naked here all by myself.'

'You could just put your shirt back on,' Martin offered, but Darren ignored him, gazing at Emma, wiggling his eyebrows suggestively.

She bit her lip indecisively for a moment, then whipped her sleeveless t-shirt up and over her head. Underneath she wore a string bikini top. I would have died. Emma, my Emma, *should* have been mortified, but instead she seemed to enjoy the attention. I saw her glancing around, checking that all three boys were looking at her. Of course they were, though Martin tore his eyes away after a moment. Dougie continued to stare, his eyebrows lifting in appreciation, a half-smile on his lips.

My stomach squirmed uneasily. Firstly that he was looking at her like that. Secondly . . . there was no way I was taking *my* clothes off. Was that the way this evening was going? I gulped down the rest of my cup to douse the apprehension writhing in my belly. Darren saw the gesture and offered me the bottle. After just a moment's hesitation, I held out my cup and let him pour me another healthy measure. Dougie passed me the Coke and I filled it up to the brim.

'Okay,' Emma purred, pleased with her moment in the spotlight. 'I pick Dougie.'

'Truth,' he said, not even pausing to think.

Emma looked pointedly at me and I felt ice slither through my veins. Don't, Emma. Please don't, I thought.

'Do you fancy someone?' she asked.

I tried to swallow another mouthful of vodka, but it wouldn't go down. The world in front of me seemed to be receding a little, as if I was viewing it through a tunnel. I wondered if it was the alcohol or just my intense embarrassment.

Dougie didn't seem bothered by the question.

'Yes.'

'Who?'

My heart stopped in my chest as I waited for his answer, but he leaned back in his chair, his grin still in place.

'That's two.'

'What?' Emma blinked, confused.

'That's two questions. You only get one.'

I breathed again as Emma's face crumpled.

'But that's not fair!' she squealed.

'Yes, it is,' Dougie disagreed.

'Darren!' Emma turned to him for support, but he was laughing.

'Sorry, angel. You need to work on your questions.'

'That's rubbish,' Emma grumbled.

Dougie shrugged his shoulders, hands spread, the picture of innocence. I kept quiet, hoping no one else could hear the way my heart was pounding with the after-effects of adrenaline. He fancied someone, then. I felt the weight of crushing disappointment as I wondered who it was. Please not Emma, I thought. Anyone but her.

'Right, Heather or Martin, Dougie?' Darren asked.

I didn't let myself look at Dougie as I waited for his answer. I wanted him to pick me, in exactly the same way as I wanted him not to. The silence dragged on, until eventually I had to glance at him. He was staring at me thoughtfully. I stared back, but after just a second he turned his face away.

44

'Martin,' he said.

An evil grin spread across Darren's face.

'Truth or dare, Martin?'

Martin adjusted himself in his chair, looking uncomfortable. No doubt he was trying to work out what sort of torture Darren might have lined up for him. 'Truth,' he said slowly.

Darren's grin widened.

'Who do *you* fancy?'

There was a pause. Everyone looked at Martin, but he shook his head and folded his arms across his chest.

'I'm not answering that,' he said flatly.

'Oh, come on,' Emma chided. 'Everyone else has.'

'I don't care. I'm not.'

'Then you have to take a dare,' Darren told him. I could hear the malicious delight in his voice, but there was no way out of it for Martin.

'Fine. What is it?'

Darren answered so quickly I knew he'd been brewing this one up for a while.

'I dare you to kiss Heather. A real one, not a peck on the cheek.'

As soon as I heard my name, my insides squeezed. My gaze flew to Darren for a millisecond before I turned to Martin. I knew my own eyes were wide with shock and shared embarrassment; Martin's expression, on the other hand, was completely blank. He stared at me for a heartbeat before drawing his eyes slightly to the left, focusing over my shoulder. Where Dougie sat. I absolutely could not spin to see the expression on his face; I'd have doused myself with the rest of my drink and jumped in the fire first.

After a horrible few seconds that felt like a year, Martin turned to Darren.

'No,' he said firmly. 'I'm not doing that either.'

'Why?' Darren challenged.

'Because it's stupid. I'm not going to embarrass myself, and I'm not going to embarrass Heather. And –' another flicker in Dougie's direction – 'you know you're just trying to be an arse. Well, forget it.'

'You have to do one or the other, that's the game. Choose.' Darren's voice was hard. Aggressive. The fight I'd predicted earlier seemed to be very close to the surface.

'No, I don't,' Martin disagreed, shifting forward in his seat like he was preparing to stand up. Darren moved in tandem as the testosterone rose up another level.

'Martin, that's the point of Truth or Dare,' Emma chimed in, siding with Darren.

'Well, then I'm not playing.'

'Are you chicken?' Darren asked quietly. I could see that Darren had rankled Martin. He stood up, towering over the rest of us.

'No,' he said slowly, emphasising the word. 'It's not that and you know it.'

'Yes, you are. Chicken!' Darren moved to stand too, but Dougie was quicker than him, jumping to his feet and putting a restraining arm on Darren's shoulder.

'Right, enough Truth or Dare. I'm hungry. Who's up for toasting marshmallows?'

CHAPTER SIX

Though they took a while to get organised, the marshmallows worked out just like Dougie had hoped, providing a distraction that allowed the tension to slowly dispel. We used sticks that were too spindly to be any good as firewood, piercing a mallow on the end and thrusting the pink and white blobs into the heat until they melted into strange shapes and their edges blackened. I threw the first one straight into my mouth, my senses dulled by Darren's vodka, forgetting the centre would be molten hot. I scalded my tongue and the roof of my mouth, squawking like an agitated parrot until someone handed me a can of icy cold liquid to quell the stinging. I chugged down half the contents before I realised it was beer. It tasted foul. I tried to spit it out but only succeeded in spilling much of it down my top.

It took a long minute after I'd wiped myself off before I could join in with the laughter.

'You know,' Darren told me, a saucy leer in his eyes, 'you're all wet. You might as well join the topless ranks.'

'Darren!' Emma smacked him hard on the arm. That made me smile, though I was mostly just embarrassed.

'I think I'll just put a jumper on,' I muttered. 'It's getting cold anyway.'

It was dark in the tent. I unzipped the doorway in one smooth motion and stepped inside. It was supposed to be a four-berth tent, but there was really only room for the double air mattress, our sleeping bags waiting side by side on top. Where the other two people were meant to go I'd no idea. I edged around the mattress to the top corner where I'd stashed my rucksack of clothes and pulled out a thick black hooded jumper. It caught in my hair, ripping out my ponytail. Impatiently, I yanked the bobble free of the last few tangles. My hair probably looked like a haystack, but hopefully it would be too dark for anyone to notice. I was too woozy to attempt to put it back up.

Back by the fire, the marshmallows were well on their way to being finished and a quiet calm was settling on our circle. I wondered what time it was – not late, I didn't think – but when I tried to read my watch the dials jumped in and out of focus.

'Here.' Dougie handed something to me as I sat down; I took it before I realised what it was. 'You didn't finish your beer.'

'Thanks,' I said, my fingers curling round the can.

'Your hair looks nice down,' he commented. 'I didn't realise it was so long.'

I flushed bright red at the compliment and didn't know what to say, so I settled for an awkward smile and took a large mouthful of beer. It tasted slightly better, I noticed. Maybe that was just because the marshmallow had burned off all my taste buds.

'What time is it?' Martin asked, giving me an excuse to look away.

'Midnight,' Darren replied, lowering his voice to give it a spooky tone. 'The perfect time for some scary stories.'

'And I suppose you've got one for us, have you?' Martin asked, but his tone lacked the scathing quality it had before and he was smiling slightly. This seemed to be one activity he was happy to join in with.

'I have,' Darren beckoned with his finger. 'But you'll have to come closer, children. This tale can only be told in a whisper. Nothing more.'

It was melodramatic and over the top, but we obediently slid off our camping chairs and gathered closer around the flames. I was glad. Middle of summer or not, it was still Scotland and the temperature was dropping, icy air whipping in off the sea. I shivered as a gentle breeze sought out the gaps in my clothes.

'Cold?' Dougie asked, folding himself down onto the sand right next to me.

'A bit,' I admitted as Martin settled down on my other side. Darren had hunkered down across the campfire from us, Emma practically draped across his lap, both of them still shirtless. That just made me shiver all the more.

'Here.' Dougie chucked an arm around me and started rubbing at my upper arm. 'I'll warm you up.'

It was meant as nothing more than a friendly gesture, I knew, but I still tensed, shy and awkward. I managed to look in his direction long enough to offer him a tentative smile before I fixed my gaze on the flames, letting the blinding dance of white, yellow and orange dazzle me into a trance. Opposite, Darren unearthed a bottle of something else to pass around – this time a dark amber colour – before he began to speak.

'This is a story told to me by my father, told to him when he was our age by a local who lived in these very hills. It's the story of the Wicker Man.'

He drew out the final two words and whether it was the chill of the night, the eeriness of the inky landscape or the quick gulp from the bottle I took as he spoke – whisky, I think – I trembled involuntarily, a goose walking over my grave.

'You all right?' Dougie whispered to me. His breath in my ear tickled, but his concern made me feel like an idiot. I resisted the urge to move so much as an inch.

'Just cold,' I mumbled back.

He responded by squeezing me tighter to him, tucking my head against the warmth of his shoulder. I tried to keep my breathing even, concentrating on Darren, who was grinning wickedly, delighting in being the centre of attention.

'Hundreds of years ago, in the Dark Ages, Pagans roamed over the land . . .'

'No, they didn't,' Martin interjected quietly.

'What?' Darren snapped, dropping out of his eerie voice and breaking the spell, clearly annoyed at the interruption.

'They were Christian in the Dark Ages,' Martin said, straightening his glasses on his nose. 'Pagans were more the Iron Age.'

'Does it matter?' Darren barked back, glaring.

'Just saying,' Martin muttered.

'Anyway.' Darren took a deep breath, swept his eyes around the circle to recapture his audience. 'Hundreds of years ago, in the Iron Age –' he shot Martin a glowering look; Martin nodded back with twisted satisfaction – 'Pagans roamed over the land. Cloaked in black, they gathered in the night to worship their evil, savage gods. Minions of the devil, these spirits demanded more than just adoration. They wanted *sacrifice*!'

There was a smattering of laughter around the campfire. Darren's voice reminded me of a children's TV presenter, being deliciously – but incredibly melodramatically – ghoulish for the Halloween special. Darren's lips twitched, acknowledging the ham acting, but then he frowned us all into silence before beginning again.

'The worst of these, my friends, was a powerful wraith. It was nameless and formless, and the Pagans feared this phantom monster more than any other. Not satisfied with the quick death of a martyred virgin, her throat cut upon the stones, the wraith craved pain and torture and suffering. It craved fire.'

Beside me I heard Dougie chuckle again and out of the corner of my eye I could see Martin rolling his eyes – even Emma was gazing at Darren's muscles rather than paying attention to the story. Darren didn't seem to care. His gaze fixed on me and I tried to look suitably enthralled and wide-eyed with terror.

'In order to satiate the wraith, every year the Pagans would erect a gigantic statue in its honour, made of wood and hazel strips, fashioned into the shape of a man. In the middle of this wicker man, right at the heart, would be an empty space, just big enough for a person. Now, it just so happened that a traveller was passing by the Pagans' lands at that time. He stopped, looking for supplies and passing news. The Pagans were delighted: here was a ready-made sacrifice!'

He paused, stared round at each of us in turn, as if ramping up the tension. I swallowed my giggle.

'One night they got the traveller drunk on the local wine. Then, once he'd passed out – for it was strong stuff – they tied his hands and feet, and imprisoned him in the wicker man. And then . . . then they set it on fire!'

There was a moment's silence. No one spoke. We just waited. It was clear Darren wasn't finished.

'That's not the end of the story,' he said. 'The traveller awoke as the flames started to take hold, as the smoke started to fill the air. He realised where he was, saw the Pagans standing round the fire chanting, robed in black with hoods pulled forward to hide their faces.'

'How'd he know it was the same Pagans then?' Martin muttered, but Darren carried on as if he hadn't heard.

'At first he tried to free himself, pushing against the confines of his wicker cage, hunting for a weakness, but the Pagans knew their business. The sacrificial statue was strong. Finally he had to face the truth: he was going to die.' A pause; a quick flash of Darren's teeth as he grinned devilishly. 'And this is where it gets interesting. See, the Pagans weren't the only ones to dabble in the dark arts. The traveller . . . was a Voodoo priest!' Darren announced this with a flourish and Dougie coughed derisively beside me. I knew he wanted to correct Darren's appalling mangling of history – even I knew Pagans were *way* before Voodoo, not to mention the fact that they originated on opposite sides of the globe – but he held his tongue. 'He cursed the Pagans. Around his neck he kept a talisman of his faith, and as his flesh melted from his body he called to his

Voodoo gods, demanding that anyone who ever set a fire in the same spot would be cursed to die a horrible death. When the fire smouldered down to ashes that melted into the sand, the curse was set in place. The next year, the Pagans once again made their sacrifice, stealing a girl from a nearby town, and each and every one of them died that night on the beach. Their bodies were swept into the sea. This sea, boys and girls, this beach. It's cursed.'

Darren sat back, obviously pleased with himself.

'Of course,' Dougie chipped in, breaking the silence, 'in the sequel the hero comes along and saves the day, freeing the villagers from the curse before snogging the virgin sacrifice senseless.'

'Ah, you've seen it!' Darren laughed before chucking a handful of seaweed across the circle at Dougie.

'Of course we've seen it! Mr Crooks makes everyone in fourth year watch it in RMPS, remember? You took some serious liberties with the storyline, though!'

'Oh yeah.' Darren looked slightly crestfallen, to the hilarity of everyone around the circle. Except me. I hadn't seen the film – I'd had glandular fever in fourth year and missed months of school.

'I didn't know there was a sequel,' Martin said, head tipped to the side. 'Any good?'

'No!' Dougie said emphatically, setting off another chorus of laughter like baying hyenas. 'Don't watch it, it's bloody awful! Anyway –' Dougie pulled his arm away from me and shifted to his knees until he towered over us – 'you want a scary story, guys? I've got one that will make sure you never sleep soundly again. Because every single word is true.'

'Oh yeah?' Darren smirked across the circle.

'Yeah,' Dougie replied softly. 'Because I hate to tell you, Darren, but there weren't any Voodoo priests mincing about the hills of Dumfries and Galloway . . . but there were witches.'

'Flying about on their broomsticks, were they?' Darren asked derisively and Emma giggled.

Dougie just smiled. And let the silence go on. And on.

'Witches,' he repeated at last, his voice so quiet I had to strain to hear it over the soft sound of the water behind me and the low pops and hisses of the fire. 'Do you know how witches get their power?'

It was a question, but none of us answered.

'Sacrifice.' The same word that Darren had used, but out of Dougie's mouth it made me shudder. As if on cue, a sinister wind whipped around the campfire, making the flames snap and jump. For a moment the fire was almost extinguished entirely and we were engulfed in a shocking blanket of black. I gasped, but just as suddenly the light flared into life again, illuminating Dougie's cheeks and jaw, leaving his eyes ghostly dark pits. The effect was frightening.

'They practised sacrifice. If a creature could bleed, if it could feel pain, then it had the ability to provide the witches with power. They used animals sometimes, if the spell was small. But when the enemy was great, when the witches needed to delve deep into the darkness of their souls – the sacrifice would have to be human.' Dougie smiled at us softly, but there was no warmth in it. Despite that, I found myself leaning closer towards him, drawn by the cadence of his voice, the hypnotic gleam in his eyes. 'Witchcraft began with the Pagans. More

54

specifically, the druids. They believed in the power of sacrifice, that through it they could commune with the gods, drink of their might. Just across that water –' he pointed to the sea with one ghostly pale arm – 'that's where it happened. Because one year men from the south came, armed with weapons and soldiers, intent on taking over the Pagans' lands. Romans. Outnumbered, outmatched, the druids fled to one of their holiest places, Ynys Dywyll. An island, rocky and bleak. It means, 'the Dark Isle'. There they set up their altar, chose their victim. Her name was Ygraine, and she was the daughter of the lord. With the Romans gathering round, with time running out, the druids slaughtered her as a gift to their gods.

'First, they strangled her, taking her right to the brink of death. Then, calling upon their gods, asking them to strike down the cursed army that had invaded their lands like a plague, they slit her throat and watched her blood spill out upon the stone. As the life drained out of her, the leader cut open her chest and drank directly from her heart. It's said her spirit screamed as she watched him do it.'

Another pause. This time there were no interruptions. Dougie let the silence linger for almost a minute.

'What happened?' Emma finally managed to whisper.

'The Romans stormed the island and killed them. Every single one. A mass sacrifice, the blood flowing so freely it stained the rocky ground red. And at last, at last the gods were appeased. The druids had lost their lives, but the gods let them return, as spirits, to guard the land. To haunt it.'

Dougie finished exactly as he'd started: quietly, softly. Eerily. Seconds passed but the silence drew on.

Eventually there was a tittering, then a confused bark of gasping and laughter as the tension that had gripped our little circle for the duration of Dougie's story was dispelled. Martin's face broke into a grin; Darren shook his head ruefully as he swigged from the bottle of booze. Emma was rubbing her arms, getting rid of imaginary goosebumps in such a way as to shove her cleavage higher up her chest, her side pressed against Darren's.

But not me. I was eyeing the inky landscape, sudden fear twisting my stomach. Not a single house light anywhere; not a single soul. Just empty blackness where, I now imagined, evil spirits lingered.

Suddenly our campfire seemed far too small, far too insubstantial. Its glow barely illuminated our faces, close as we were to the flames. How near could evil get without us noticing?

Beside me, Dougie rose and brushed the sand from his jeans, then yawned and stretched.

'Right, I'm knackered. I say we sleep.' His voice was back to normal and as he looked down at me, hand outstretched to help me up, all at once he was my friend again, his mouth tugging into a smile, dimples winking in his cheeks.

There was a murmur of agreement. Only Darren looked put out, though I wasn't sure whether that was because his story hadn't had the same spellbinding effect as Dougie's, or because of the sudden end to the night. He was holding mulishly to the remains of the whisky. No doubt he wanted to stay up till dawn, drinking. This probably wasn't his idea of a party. Still, Dougie's actual birthday wasn't for another two days.

I made my way wearily to our tent, chilled now that I was away from the flames. Teeth chattering, I pulled off my clothes and yanked on my warmest pyjamas before I turned on the torch, aware that my outline would be silhouetted against the faded red of the tent. Shoving my feet back into my trainers, I tripped back outside, toothbrush in hand. The boys were dumping spadefuls of sand onto the fire, trying to douse the final flames. At least, Dougie and Martin were. Darren stood to the side, his arms around Emma, lips locked against hers.

They were still like that, glued together, when I returned from the bushes where I'd created a makeshift bathroom. I forgot, momentarily, about evil figures in the dark. I looked at them, half amused, half uneasy. I'd made it quite clear to Emma that the tents were single-sex. I hoped she hadn't thought I was saying it just for the benefit of our parents. If she wanted to shack up with Darren, she'd have to sleep in his car.

'Night,' I called to Dougie and Martin as I slithered for the final time into the tent.

As I'd hoped, my farewell acted as a spur to Emma. She disengaged herself from Darren's octopus grip and, after planting one final kiss on his cheek, ambled in my direction. She didn't bother getting changed or brushing her teeth, but buried straight down into her sleeping bag, watching as I shoved clothes and toiletries back into my rucksack, tidying up the space.

'That story was really spooky,' she commented as I unzipped my own bag and crawled inside. 'You looked totally freaked out.'

'It was creepy,' I replied honestly. 'Dougie really knows how to tell a scary story.'

'Mmm,' Emma agreed. 'Think it was really all true?'

'Most of it,' I replied. At least, I hoped it was only most of it. The idea of druid spirits haunting the land freaked me out too much to contemplate.

'You reckon? How does Dougie know all that, then?'

'Well, he's really interested in that stuff.'

'What, ritual sacrifice?' Emma stared at me, her expression wide-eyed with put-on horror.

'No,' I scowled. 'History and archaeology and things. He's got loads of books on it. It's what he wants to do at university.'

'Oh, that's right,' Emma purred. My ears pricked up at the change and I turned to look at her. She was grinning slyly. 'You've both applied, haven't you?'

'Yeah.' I knew where she was going with this and I didn't want to talk about it. I held my hand over the torch, ready to douse the light. 'You all sorted?'

Emma nodded and I hit the switch, plunging us into darkness.

Everything was immediately different. Blind, my ears automatically tuned in to every noise, inside the tent and out. I could hear Emma's quiet breathing, the rustling of her covers as she shifted, trying to get comfortable on the air mattress. Further away, I caught the quiet murmur of the boys, huddling down. Comforting noises, reminding me that I wasn't alone. Below that, though, there were more eerie sounds: the rhythmic whoosh of the water, hissing like a whisper; the higher pitch of the wind through the reeds high up on the sand dunes like a scream. The distant bark of a dog, snapping and jarring at my nerves.

Stop it, I told myself. You're surrounded by people.

Still, the haunting tones of Dougie's voice murmuring his tale of druids and bloody sacrifice seemed to have followed me into the tent. I couldn't shake the feeling that I was being watched. That there was something out there in the dark, something other than Emma lying beside me or Dougie, Darren and Martin in the other tent . . .

My scalp started to tingle and the alcohol I'd consumed churned uneasily in my stomach.

'It's a pity Martin's here,' Emma said, carrying on what I'd hoped was our finished conversation in a voice loud enough to carry to the adjacent tent.

'Emma!' I hissed. 'Keep your voice down.'

'Well, it is,' she repeated, only a little more quietly.

'What? Why?'

I stared in her direction, though it was impossible to see her in the pitch black.

'Think about it,' she said, as if it was glaringly obvious. 'If it was just the four of us . . .'

If it was just the four of us, Emma would disappear with Darren, and Dougie and I would be left to look awkwardly at each other, trying to think of things to say. No, I was very glad Martin was here.

'Wonder who it is Dougie fancies,' Emma mused. 'It's rubbish that he wouldn't answer that.'

'Mmm,' I replied half-heartedly. I wondered, too. But given that I wasn't going to get the answer that I wanted, I was pretty sure I didn't want to know.

'Maybe it's you,' she suggested.

'Doubt it,' I shot back, not even wanting to discuss the possibility. No point getting my hopes up. 'Maybe it's you.'

I tried to infuse my voice with indifference, like it was just a throwaway comment, but the words were bitter on my tongue.

'Might be,' Emma mused, not seeming remotely disconcerted or embarrassed by the idea. 'I don't think so, though. I've never seen him looking at me like that or anything.'

'He was looking at you tonight,' I pointed out, scowling at the memory.

Emma's laugh tinkled across the space.

'Of course he was, I was half-naked! You should be more worried if he wasn't looking.'

'Shhh!' I growled. If we could hear the boys, they could hear us.

'Stop worrying,' Emma replied, refusing to lower her voice. 'Besides, don't you want him to know?'

'No.'

'How's anything supposed to happen then?'

'It's not going to,' I snapped. 'He likes someone else, remember?'

'It might be you, Heather,' Emma reminded me.

It might be. But I doubted it.

'I'm tired,' I said, shutting down the conversation. 'Let's go to sleep.'

I turned my back on her sigh of frustration. Shutting my eyes, I tried to lull myself to sleep with thoughts that Emma was right, that I was the one Dougie had his eye on, but instead my dreams were filled with formless black shadows, swooping down with glowing eyes and gaping mouths.

CHAPTER SEVEN

I woke much earlier than I wanted to. The sun was rising on what would be yet another glorious day and its penetrating rays turned the tiny interior of the tent into a sauna in a matter of minutes. One moment I was snuggled tightly in my sleeping bag, covers up over my face to warm my nose, the next I was sweltering, fighting my way free of the thick cocoon, pyjamas sticking to my body. I didn't hesitate but scrambled across the space and yanked the zipper to open the door.

At once frigid air poured in through the gap. I gulped it gratefully, oblivious to Emma's mewls of protest.

'What time is it?' she muttered groggily.

I reached for my wristwatch, abandoned in a corner, and peered at the dial. Whoops.

'Just before six,' I admitted.

'Heather! What the hell is wrong with you?' Emma flopped over in disgust, bashing her pillow into a more comfortable shape before burrowing back down. 'Shut the door or get out,' she griped, her voice muffled by the thick padding of her covers.

It was stupidly early but I knew I wasn't going to sleep. Snatching up my jumper and shoes, I stole outside. Stretching the stiffness out of my back – and trying not to grin about the fact that my disappearance had shifted the air in the half-deflated air mattress, dumping Emma on the floor – I saw that I wasn't the only one up early. Martin sat perched on one of the folding chairs, watching the lightening sky and sipping at a bottle of water.

'Couldn't sleep?' he asked as I wandered over.

I shook my head.

'Me either, too hot. Plus, Darren snores worse than my dad.' He grinned. 'How's your head?'

'It's –' I stopped short of saying fine. 'Bangy,' I realised.

'Here.' He handed the bottle of water to me. 'Booze makes you dehydrated. This your first hangover?'

'Yeah.' I took a gulp, sat down on another of the chairs. 'It's not as bad as I thought it would be.'

'I think it varies in strength relative to your alcohol consumption,' Martin said sagely.

'I see.' Another grin to smother. Such a Martin answer.

Taking another large mouthful of water, I leaned back in the chair and sighed. Yanking my jumper on over my head, I contented myself staring in the same direction as Martin. We sat in companionable silence. It wasn't awkward the way it would have been with Dougie. Or uncomfortable like it would have been with Darren – and it would be damned impossible with Emma! It was relaxing, listening to the rhythm of the waves – a nice sound now that daylight showed it was nothing more sinister than the gentle stroking of water on sand. I shut my eyes and leaned my head back. I might even have fallen asleep again if it hadn't been for the taut fabric of the chair, digging into my neck.

No one else emerged until almost eight. By that time Martin and I had succumbed to hunger and dug out the little gas-fired burner. He was slathering slices of bread with butter and ketchup while I prodded half-cooked rashers of bacon around the frying pan with a spatula.

'I thought I smelled something,' Darren commented, scratching his head. 'I'll take two.'

He gave me a wink to solidify his order, then disappeared into the privacy of the long grass behind the tents.

'Would it be wrong of me to spit in his sandwich?' Martin asked me in an undertone.

I laughed. 'Only if he catches you.'

'Need any help?' Dougie emerged from the boys' tent fully dressed, only his feet bare, a toothbrush hanging from his mouth.

'We're just about done.' I smiled brightly at him. 'You could dig out the orange juice?'

'We need that to mix with the vodka!' Darren hollered from behind the dunes, somehow hearing me across the distance.

Dougie rolled his eyes.

'I think Darren's an alkie,' he joked. 'I'll go hunt it out of the car.'

Emma climbed lithely out of our tent just as the bacon sandwiches slid onto paper plates, her expression expectant. Despite the fact that she'd gone to sleep in last night's clothes, she was now wearing pyjamas. It wasn't hard to work out why. The little camisole and shorts set was clingy and revealing, showing off her long legs and tiny waist. As she sauntered over every pair of eyes was fixed on her, mine the only two that were disdainful.

'Oh, I'm sorry. Am I too late to help?' she asked, eyes wide and innocent.

I suppressed my sigh. When had my best friend turned into this complete and utter airhead?

'Don't worry, we made you one.' Dougie held the plate out to her, smiling, and I wondered yet again if she was the mysterious girl he fancied. At least I had the comfort of knowing he'd never act on it, not when she was going out with someone else.

For a short while everyone was quiet as they munched on breakfast, washed down, despite Darren's complaints, with the orange juice.

'So what are we going to do today?' Martin asked, licking the grease and tomato sauce from his fingers.

'Do?' Darren asked, looking at him with feigned confusion.

'Yes, do,' Martin repeated. 'You're not planning to just sit here all day, are you?'

'Sunbathing,' Emma asserted, lifting one leg to run her fingers along her silky-smooth calf. 'That's what I'm doing. I'm pale.'

Martin pulled a face that made it clear sunbathing was about as appealing as stabbing himself in the eye.

'I'm up for a bit of exploring,' Dougie offered. 'My dad said there are some ruins of an old castle or something up over the hill.'

'Exploring sounds good.' Martin grinned.

Dougie turned to me. 'Heather?'

'Heather's going to sunbathe with me,' Emma announced.

I raised one eyebrow at her, then turned to Dougie.

'I'm up for some exploring,' I said quietly.

Darren opted to stay behind to 'watch Emma sunbathing', he said, eyes trailing her provocative outfit, so it was the three of us who made our way slowly up towards the car park. We passed by the Volvo, finding a trail that wound its way in a zigzag from the beach, in the opposite direction to the road. It was a steep climb and I soon found myself lagging behind the two boys, panting for breath. Luckily the sun still hung low in the sky and the air was cool. Even so, I had to yank off my jumper, knotting it around my waist.

'Check out the view,' Dougie said to me as I crested the top.

He pointed back the way we'd come and I spun on the spot, using it as an excuse to hide my flushed cheeks and heaving lungs. He was right, though. It was beautiful. The sea spread out like an undulating blanket of blue, bordered by a thin strip of cream-coloured beach. Beyond the sand was a carpet of greenery, emerald in the sunlight. It was breathtaking, maybe more so than the hike to get up there.

'I think I can see the ruins your dad was talking about, Dougie,' Martin called from behind me. I turned to see him pointing to the peak of another hill. The ground dipped away from us, so although the blurred jumble of stones didn't look to be any higher than we were, it would involve trudging up another steep incline. I groaned inwardly.

There was no trail up on top of the hill so we clambered three abreast across the rugged heathland. Despite the sun, the grass was damp with dew that quickly soaked the bottoms of my jeans and slithered into my trainers.

'So how do you think the exams went?' Dougie asked me as we walked.

I shrugged, made a face. 'Not sure. English was okay, I think. Maths . . . who knows? I probably failed physics.'

'Reckon you did enough to get your uni place?'

Another shrug. 'Hope so. You?'

'I think they went all right,' said Dougie, smiling impishly.

I snorted a laugh. Dougie had been named the Dux – the top pupil in the school. He was practically guaranteed to get five As.

'Martin,' I turned to my other side. 'What about you?'

He sniffed, shoved his glasses back up on his nose.

'Sciences went well. English will probably be my downfall.'

'Think you'll leave school?' I asked.

I knew he hadn't applied to any courses yet, but there was always Clearing. Universities offered last-minute places on any courses that weren't full. Martin was shaking his head, though.

'Not allowed. My parents say I'm too young. Plus I'd quite like to do a couple of Advanced Highers. Maths and Chemistry. Maybe Biology if I get a good enough grade.'

'Will you miss us?' I asked teasingly.

He gave me a strange look, not matching my jokey tone.

'Yes,' he said soberly.

My grin vanished.

'Well, don't worry,' I said. 'I'll probably be back in August, doing re-sits.'

He still didn't laugh.

'No, you won't,' he said quietly.

I looked away, feeling awkward although I wasn't sure why.

The rapidly inclining hillside cut off the conversation, although it had been dead already. For several minutes there was just the uneven melody of three sets of lungs, panting. The sun, climbing steadily higher in the sky, began to reach out with its heat until I could feel it starting to burn my bare shoulders. I hadn't thought about sunscreen.

Finally we made it to the top and there, taking centre stage at the very peak, were the ruins Dougie had told us about. He'd said it might be a castle but looking at what was left it was hard to discern any sort of building. There were no walls remaining, just one large mound of stone that spilled over at the edges, sending irregular lumps tumbling into the grass.

'I don't think it was a castle,' Dougie commented, hands on his hips, a thoughtful look on his face. 'My dad probably just looked at it from the beach; he's not much of one for exercise. I don't think this was even a building.'

He moved over to get a closer look.

'Look at this,' he called, waving Martin and me over. 'There's a sort of entrance here.'

I looked to where he was pointing, trying to see what he saw. This was exactly the sort of thing I wanted to study at university, but I had to admit that all I saw was a jumble of stones. I squinted, trying to create any sort of identifiable shape. It reminded me of when my cousin had shown me her baby scan and she'd pointed to blobs and circles, telling me they were limbs, a head. I hadn't seen anything then, and now was no different.

'Do you see it?' Dougie asked. 'Right there.'

Martin circled the spot, eyeing it critically.

'Okay, Indiana,' he joked, his face sceptical.

At least I wasn't the only one.

Dougie wasn't giving up, though. He stood there for ten minutes, gesturing with his arms and trying to talk us through lumps and bumps that he said were an entrance, a roof, a protective wall. At first I was just as lost as before, but the more Dougie talked, the more some sort of hazy structure started to appear. Little by little I began to see what he was talking about.

'So what do you think it was?' I asked, when I was sure I had the outline straight in my head. 'A house?'

Dougie shook his head.

'A tomb,' he said. 'A cairn,' he expanded, seeing my puzzled look. 'This is probably what the place is named after. When important people died they used to bury them at the top of the hill then pile all these stones on top. If you could get into it, there'd be a sort of chamber in there. That's if it hasn't collapsed.'

I nodded along as he spoke, trying to look as if this wasn't all new to me. Martin's sceptical look folded into an incredulous frown.

'They hiked all these stones up here? Seems it would have been easier to just do it at the bottom. Prestige, I suppose.'

Dougie nodded.

'You know,' he said, turning to me, a wicked gleam in his eye, 'this is exactly the sort of place a druid spirit, hungry for vengeance, might choose to lurk.'

My stomach lurched, a burst of adrenaline making my skin crawl like hundreds of spiders were slithering over me as I stared at the cairn with a sudden horror – and fascination – before I gave myself a shake.

'Shut up, Dougie,' I said. 'You made that bit up!'

'Did I?' He grinned, then he turned his back on me to bend over and start hauling at some of the large stones covering what he'd identified as the entrance.

'What are you doing?' I asked.

'We might be able to get in,' he said.

In. To a tomb.

'You don't think there's a body in there?' I said, revolted yet somehow drawn forward. I didn't want to see the cracked, yellow curve of some skull come tumbling out and land at my feet.

'Doubt it,' Dougie puffed, still trying to yank a particularly large stone out of the way. 'This will be thousands of years old. There won't be anything left. People used them as sacred sites, though. They didn't know what they were. So you never know what you'll find if you rake about.'

'My money's on an empty bottle of cider and a crisp packet,' Martin quipped.

'Wrong!' Dougie announced, at last getting the stone out of the way and delving deep inside with his hand. 'It's a can of juice!'

He held it up triumphantly as Martin and I let out matching cackles of laughter. The can had obviously laid there for a long time; the colours had seeped from the metal so you could no longer tell the brand. Rust surrounded the rim and a gash in the centre.

'Better call the National Museum,' Martin chortled.

Dougie ignored him. He was down on his knees, poking his head deep inside the hole he'd made.

'Anybody have a torch handy?' His voice was muffled, coming out distorted.

'Oh yes, I always carry a torch. That and a defibrillator, a pocket guide to Wales and a pair of bicycle clips.'

'Ha ha.' Dougie leaned back and threw Martin a scathing look. 'How about a phone, then?'

'I've got a flashlight app on mine,' I offered, holding my mobile out.

'Cheers.' His face already back in the depth of the cairn, he reached for it clumsily. His fumbling fingers grabbed mine instead of the phone, sending a wave of heat up through my hand. 'There's something else in here,' he called. 'Maybe I can reach it.'

'What is it this time, a Durex wrapper?' Martin snorted.

Dougie made a face at him, his body turned to the side so that he could wedge his shoulder into the gap and reach an extra few inches.

'I've nearly got it,' he said, straining. 'Ah-ha!'

This time when he held it up we were all silent. Wordlessly, Martin and I edged closer for a better look.

'What is it?' I asked.

It was small, flat and circular. The centre had been cut out, with a thin line connecting across the diameter. The surface was textured, bobbled and pitted like rusted metal, and it was coated in dirt. Beneath that, though, I could just about make out the faded etchings of curves and shapes carved into the facade.

'I don't know.' Dougie spat on his finger and rubbed at the surface, removing the top layer of dirt. 'It's metal, anyway. And old. It's pretty cool. Here.' He chucked it at me. 'Take a look.'

I snagged it with my fingertips, almost snapping the fragile, corroded circlet. Turning it over in my grasp, I traced the hinted-at carvings.

'It needs cleaning up,' I murmured. 'You can't really see it right.'

'We'll dunk it in the sea,' Dougie agreed.

I looked up at him, a little shocked.

'You're going to take it?'

'Sure, why not?' He smiled at me, puzzled by my tone.

'But, that's . . .' I stopped short of saying stealing, not sure if it was. 'But this is someone's grave.'

Grave-robbing was definitely illegal, I was sure of that.

'This isn't a grave-good,' Dougie disagreed. 'Probably someone left it as an offering or something. Cairns are a bit like stone circles; people forgot their original purpose, just remembered that they were important.'

I pursed my lips. That didn't feel any better. But I made no move to stop him as Dougie reached out and plucked the object out of my hand. I watched as he ran his fingers over it one final time and then slid it into his pocket.

'Want to head back down?' he suggested. 'It must be just about lunchtime. I'm starving.'

With Martin's help he replaced the stones he'd disturbed and then led the way back down towards the beach, pointing out more archaeological features in the hillside as we went. I tried to pay attention to what he said, hoping I might learn something to prepare me if I did manage to get on my course – but it was hard to focus. My mind was still up at the cairn, at the deep, black hollow surrounded by ancient stones. The druids' haunt, as Dougie had joked.

I couldn't help thinking we'd done something wrong, somehow. Time and time again my eyes were drawn to Dougie's pocket, where the thing he'd taken was safely nestled.

I felt like a thief.

CHAPTER EIGHT

Now

The phone rings. Its shrill, agitated tone cuts through the thick tension in the room like a chainsaw through butter. Dr Petersen glares at it. The offending machine is sleek, black and looks old-fashioned. Not antique, though. Just made to appear that way.

I raise one eyebrow at him. Isn't he going to answer it?

He sighs, shoots an annoyed look at the door. Or through it, really, to the secretary who has dared to interrupt our session.

I'm not annoyed. I'm grateful. It's a reprieve, a chance for me to take a breath. Refocus.

With an exaggerated tut, Petersen picks up the stylish handle and presses the brass-edged mouthpiece to his lips.

'What?'

I can't hear the response, but Petersen's eyes widen, then narrow.

'I'm in the middle of a session, Helen.'

Helen knows this. She let me in here, after all. Guess it must be important. Maybe important enough to cancel the rest of this 'therapy' session. I cross the fingers on my good hand hopefully.

Just the phone call is a plus, though. It's eating away at the minutes before I can leave. Because no matter how long we're interrupted for, Petersen will despatch me precisely on the hour. Nothing messes with his meticulous schedule.

He gives another sigh. I look away from the bookcase I've been examining – full of books with spines that are yet to be broken – and go back to gazing at Petersen. He's looking right at me, frowning.

'No, I can't talk just now. I'll have to call him back.' Pause. I imagine I can hear the tinny whine of Helen wittering on the other end of the phone line. 'Yes, I know that!'

Ooh, snappy. Petersen immediately takes a deep breath, reining in his irritation. Not before I smile at him, though.

It's a fake smile. What I really am is disgruntled. How has insipid Helen managed to get under his skin when everything I've done – and I've done a lot to try to antagonise this man – has been met with nothing but measured calm? I tried to stab him, for God's sake!

'Tell him . . . tell him I will call him after my next patient . . . Yes, one o'clock.' He hangs up, grimaces at me. 'I am sorry about that, Heather.'

Don't be. I'm not. I'm back on the defensive. Walls up, mind alert, ears pricked. But that's just on the inside. Outwardly, I'm slumped in the chair, eyes heavily lidded like I'm so bored I could fall asleep; feet scuffing against the carpet. I blow out a breath, making sure he knows I think that sitting here is dull and mind-numbing and beneath me.

'You were going to tell me about the cairn,' he prompts, when it's clear I'm not going to acknowledge his apology.

No, I wasn't.

I set my lips, stare at him. I don't blink. I'm good at this, the silent treatment; I've been doing it to my mother since I was six years old. I can keep it up for a long time, easily long enough to see out the hour.

'Do you want to talk about it today?'

I can hear the oh-so-slight emphasis he puts on the word *today* and I know we're about to take a trip through my previous transcripts. Back to the days when I actually tried to talk to him, tried to explain. Back when I thought he was here to help me, when I believed his bullshit.

'Do you remember telling me about the burial site, Heather? Do you remember what you said, about the thing you took from the cairn? The artefact?'

Not my exact words, no, but I'm sure you're going to tell me.

He rifles in a drawer in his desk and comes up with a huge folder, papers spilling out. It's my old file. Crazy Heather's back catalogue. Spreading it out on the desk, he begins to flip through sheaf after sheaf. I can't read what's written there, but I can see row upon row of spiked calligraphy. Dr Petersen's notes. All about me. I don't want to read it, but at the same time I'd love to know what ludicrous theories the man has come up with about my 'deluded' state of mind.

'Ah, here it is. You told me it housed the spirit of a druid, an ancient being. Sent back to wreak havoc and vengeance. Do you remember saying these things?'

I stare at him steadily. It's subtle, just the merest hint, but I know he's mocking me. He may as well say, *'Do you remember when you were off your head, Heather? Does that ring any bells?'*

No, Dr Petersen, I can't say I do remember talking to you about that. But I remember having my arms hauled back so hard I thought my shoulders would dislocate. I remember the needle that was jammed into my arm. And I remember waking up with a pounding headache and a horrible sense of hopelessness. Tied down, trapped. Terrified. Not of the room but of something I could never outrun.

He waits. Just in case I'll suddenly and miraculously open up to him. Sorry, Dr Petersen. No miracles today. He sees that in my eyes.

Searches for another angle.

'Druids, Heather.' A pause. 'The occult. It's something that interests you, isn't it? Fascinates you, even?'

I shake my head in disdain and Petersen mistakes it for denial.

'No?' He raises his eyebrows in apparent surprise. 'You aren't? I've been to your house, Heather. Some of the books you've collected are quite . . . unusual for a young lady of your age.' He rifles through more notes. 'Ah, here we are: *Sickles and Mistletoe: The Druid Way.* Not exactly light reading. And *Blood and Dust: The Dark Rites of Human Sacrifice.* Why would you have these books, Heather? If you aren't drawn to the arcane, to dark magic?'

Staring at him stonily, I clench my teeth. I do not like that he's been in my home, my room. He probably had a cup of tea and slice of cake with my mum, holding her hand sympathetically while he reassured her about how insane I was.

The books I'm not bothered about. They aren't mine, they're Dougie's. He loaned them to me when I put in my application for the archaeology course at university, along with a whole host of other titles. Preliminary reading, so that I could get a step ahead. But I don't see Petersen mentioning *Introduction to Archaeology* and *The History of the British Isles* that are also taking up space on my bookshelf. That wouldn't fit with the little scenario he's creating in his head.

And he thinks I'm crazy.

'Okay.' He gives in after several long moments, shoves the file back down onto his desk. 'Okay, let's try something else.'

Like what? Electric shock treatment?

No, it's worse.

'Let's talk about your friends. Let's talk about Martin. Now in your initial statement to the judge you said he disappeared –'

'He *did* disappear,' I hiss through clenched teeth.

This is one topic I will not be silent on. I don't even care that Petersen is all but beside himself with self-congratulation that he's finally got me saying *something*. I will not let them accuse of me of . . . I can't even bring myself to think it.

Because I didn't.

I. Did. Not.

CHAPTER NINE

Then

The beach was empty when we returned. Emma and Darren had disappeared, leaving all our gear unprotected. We increased our speed, practically jogging down the narrow dirt path to the beach – which was fine by me as the rotting fish was still there, still stinking – but a quick inventory showed everything was accounted for.

'Where do you think they've gone?' Martin asked, glancing round at the empty landscape. 'Think they went for a walk as well?'

'No.' I shook my head, my expression amused at the thought of Emma and exercise. Now that I was thinking properly, it was supremely obvious where they were. 'I think they're taking a *nap*.'

I used my fingers to add air-quotes to the final word.

'Oh!' Dougie huffed an uncomfortable laugh. Then he raised his voice. 'Darren?'

'What?' The response was muffled and accompanied by a high-pitched giggle.

'Nothing. Just making sure you're not dead.'

'Not dead.' More laughter, this time abruptly cut off.

I grimaced as Dougie shook his head indulgently. 'Lunch?' he suggested to Martin and me.

'Lunch?' Darren's super-sensitive hearing was not just limited to conversations involving alcohol, it seemed. He emerged from the tent – fully dressed, much to my relief – with Emma trailing behind him looking both sheepish and smug. 'Did I hear someone mention lunch?'

We ate a meal of cheese, cold meat and crackers, knowing that our supply of ice and ice-packs was thawing rapidly and the cheese at least would go off if left out in the heat. The hike had reinvigorated our appetites and I was stuffing food into my mouth like I hadn't seen a decent meal in days.

'So how was your walk?' Darren asked, his mouth full of food. 'Exciting?'

Emma snorted into her can of juice and I knew they must have been having a laugh at our expense. Not that I cared. In fact, I was having a chuckle of my own at the scarlet red patches on Emma's knees, arms and nose. She'd given herself wicked sunburn lying out and if it wasn't already stinging like crazy, it soon would be.

'It was pretty cool, actually,' Dougie replied, not rising to Darren's dig. 'We went up to my dad's ruins, it's really a cairn. Found something funky.'

He dug the disc out of his pocket and chucked it over. Darren caught it deftly then turned it in his fingers.

'So what am I supposed to be looking at, saddo? I haven't seen as many episodes of *Time Team* as you.'

Dougie lifted one shoulder in a half-shrug.

'Don't know. An offering, maybe? I was going to try cleaning it up in the sea.'

'Go on then.' Darren tossed the object back. 'I'm curious.'

Dougie reached out to catch it, but his fingers clipped the edge and sent it spinning away from him. It landed neatly in my lap. I stared down at it and my fingers moved of their own accord to trace the strange etchings scratched into the surface, still impossible to see clearly under the dirt and rust. Despite having being in Dougie's pocket, and the midday sun beating down on us, the metal was still cold to the touch. The pads of my fingertips started to tingle and I snatched them away. Did some metals emit nasty chemicals as they corroded? I wasn't sure.

'Pass it over,' Dougie said, reaching his hand out.

But for some odd reason I didn't want to. Like Darren, I was curious to see what lay hidden underneath the filth.

'It's okay.' I smiled at him. 'I'll do it.'

The soft sound of footsteps dogged mine as I paced towards the water. I looked round to see Emma just behind me. Still a little bit annoyed at the way she and Darren had laughed earlier, I didn't say anything but turned my back and continued to the seashore. Just a few feet away, where the sand became compacted and wet, I kicked off my trainers and socks and padded the final distance into the surf.

'It's freezing!' I exclaimed involuntarily.

Freezing wasn't really a strong enough word. The cold instantly penetrated down to my bones, making the nerves in my feet throb and ache. Goosebumps erupted and a shiver ran the length of my body.

'Freezing,' Emma agreed, suddenly beside me. 'I can't believe Darren went all the way in last night!'

She sighed as she said it, her admiration clear. I rolled my eyes as I bent over, ready to dunk the disc into the water.

Emma splashed deeper, looking like she was going to try to repeat Darren's daring exploits.

'I wouldn't,' I warned.

'Why?' she asked, though she stopped when the water reached halfway up her shins.

'The salt water on your sunburn will sting like crazy,' I replied, pointing to her blotchy pink knees.

'Oh, wow,' Emma gazed down at her scalded skin, shocked. 'Whoops! Who'd have thought you'd need sunscreen in Scotland!'

'Yeah,' I agreed half-heartedly. I was concentrating on the thing in my hands, half worried I'd lose it in the tiny waves lapping around me. The dirt came off easily enough, but as I rubbed I was also flaking off layers of bubbled and rusted metal. I hoped it wouldn't fall to pieces on me.

'So what is it?' Emma asked, gazing across the water. She looked down when I didn't answer. 'Hey, it's shiny!'

It was. Underneath the outer coats, the metal gleamed. As more and more of the tarnished stuff came off, it was regaining shape. The edges smoothed out and the surface was satiny. Almost like new. I frowned down at it, confused. I was no alchemist but I was pretty sure it wasn't supposed to do that.

'It must be modern,' I told Emma, standing up. Now sparkling in my hands, the object looked perfect, like it had just come out of the shop. I could see what it was after the clean-up, too – a brooch. The line across the centre was the pin, designed to hold it in place against whatever fabric it was attached to.

I'd never seen anything like it before. It wasn't gold, but something a little pinker. Copper, maybe. And it wasn't a perfect circle. It looked more like a horseshoe, although the ends had been connected to make the rounded shape. I could now see the engravings clearly, but I had no idea what they were. They seemed to be a mixture of symbols and creatures, but exaggerated. Arty-farty. I didn't recognise anything. Maybe Dougie would, he'd studied art.

'Let's go show the boys,' I suggested.

But back at the beach the enigma of the brooch was driven from my mind. It was obvious before we got close enough to hear the words that something had kicked off. Darren and Martin were standing several metres apart, with Dougie in between them – once more piggy-in-the-middle. Instead of a ball, it was a barrage of insults that was being tossed to and fro. Darren's voice reached us first.

' . . . Mister Goody Two-shoes. Can't do a thing unless Mummy and Daddy say it's all right. Why don't you grow up? You're a big boy now.'

'Grow up? Like you, you mean? Be the big hard man, all fists and no brain? Did the steroids melt the little sense you had?' Martin's response was steel. He wasn't standing the way Darren was – fighter's pose, arms up and fists clenched – but his mouth was set in a thin line and his eyes were flashing angrily.

'Guys –' Dougie tried to interject, but neither Darren nor Martin even glanced at him.

'You don't know how to have fun, that's your problem!' Darren spat.

'Fun?' Martin laughed, but it was a black sound. 'Getting steamin' and making an arse of yourself? I'd hardly call that fun.'

We stopped a distance away and lingered just within earshot. I didn't really want to go any closer, but Dougie turned and caught sight of the pair of us out of the corner of his eye. The relief on his face was clear. Immediately I felt obliged to help him, though it was with reluctance that I licked my suddenly dry lips.

'What's going on?' I asked, stepping forward.

'Nothing. It's fine,' Dougie said.

'Aye, fine,' Darren added bitterly. 'Just misery-guts over here trying to ruin the party.'

'Darren –' Dougie flashed him a warning look.

'What? He's only here because he's hoping to –'

'Shut up!' Martin barked, making me jump.

Darren grinned slyly, pleased that he'd ruffled his feathers. 'What's the matter, scared to say it?'

'Darren, leave it.' Dougie was angry now, turning his back on us to glower at him.

'You're not much better, kiddo. The pair of you are pathetic.' Darren dismissed both of them, shouldering past Dougie and throwing Martin a filthy look. He paused halfway to the boys' tent, glanced over his shoulder. 'Emma, you coming?'

There was an awkward moment's pause then Emma scampered after Darren self-consciously. When she reached his side she looked back at us guiltily, but as Darren continued towards the beer cooler, she followed him, drawn like metal to a magnet.

As soon as they were far enough away to be out of earshot, Dougie blew out a breath. His shoulders slumped back down and he grimaced.

'Sorry,' he muttered.

'It's not your fault,' Martin conceded, though he still looked furious.

'What was that about?' I asked hesitantly.

'What do you think?'

Martin glowered over to where Darren was releasing the tab on yet another beer and I had my answer.

Dougie swung his arms back and forth, looking around uncomfortably. I bit my lip as I stared at him. The tension between Martin and Darren was putting a dampener on the trip. If things continued as they were, it wouldn't be much of a birthday for Dougie to look back on. 'How about a swim?' he suggested, gazing at the water. 'Help us cool off?'

I gave a nervous laugh and he smiled at me tightly.

Martin seemed to consider it for a moment, but then he shook his head.

'I think I'm going to go for another walk, get away from here for a little bit. Heather, what are you doing?'

Both boys looked at me. Martin's expression was hopeful and I realised he wanted me to go with him, probably to bitch about Darren. I could probably calm him down, too, I thought. Persuade him just to ignore Darren's snide remarks and superiority complex, and his constant drinking.

On the other hand, it was Dougie's birthday trip. It didn't seem right to abandon him. And, if I had to choose, he was the one I would rather hang out with.

'I'm going to swim with Dougie,' I mumbled, guilt stealing the volume from my voice.

'Right, fine.' Martin's expression didn't alter, but I sensed his disappointment. I almost changed my mind, but then Dougie grinned at me gratefully and I decided just to keep my mouth shut.

Martin headed off in the opposite direction to the trail we'd taken that morning, walking the length of the beach to avoid going past Darren and Emma who were now sprawled on two of the folding chairs. Dougie and I watched him shrink as he walked away until finally he clambered over the rocks and out of sight. The suddenly empty beach made me feel guilty, but it was too late to change my mind.

'Are you serious about swimming?' I asked Dougie as he led me back to our tents. 'It's *really* cold.'

'You chicken?' he challenged.

'Yes.'

He laughed, just like I'd hoped he would.

'Come on, you can't bring your swim stuff and not use it. It's unlucky!'

Swimwear. My blood ran cold at the same time as my cheeks flooded with heat. That was more naked than I'd intended to be this weekend and more naked than I *ever* wanted to be in front of Dougie. Well, in public. In private there were the fragile fantasies that I was trying very hard to keep a lid on because they were never going to happen.

'It's not unlucky – you made that up,' I accused, stalling whilst I looked for a way, any way, to get out of removing my clothes. The prospect was made even worse by the fact that he'd been eyeing up Emma's scantily clad form last night. I was blisteringly aware that I did not compare well.

Dougie wiggled his eyebrows at me.

'Are you willing to take that chance?' he asked. 'To spend the rest of your life haunted by the Speedo Spectre?'

I gave in, smiling though my teeth were clenched together. 'I guess not.'

I disappeared into my tent to change. At least I could be grateful that my costume covered a lot more than the string bikini Emma had brought with her. It was utilitarian, made for purpose, high-cut at the legs and with a neckline than only dipped two inches from the hollow of my throat, completely black apart from two vivid blue stripes up my sides. I was in my local club and the coach warned us to pick swimwear that would make us faster, not win us any fashion awards.

At least I knew I wouldn't make a fool of myself in the water.

'You ready?' Dougie's voice right outside the tent made me jump.

'Eh, just about,' I called back.

Giving myself a shake, I grabbed up a bobble and pulled my hair into a ponytail. I ignored my goggles and my swimming cap, sure that we were just headed in for a splash around rather than to do any serious swimming. Then I took one deep, steadying breath and stepped back out into the heat of the sun.

Dougie had his back to me as I emerged, blinking against the brightness. I was glad I hadn't tried to hide by wrapping myself in the huge beach towel I'd brought, because he was clad in nothing more than a pair of shorts-style trunks. I had three seconds of sweeping my eyes across the broadness of his shoulders before he turned and I had to rake my gaze up to his face.

'I tried to convince Emma and Darren to join us,' he said, 'but Darren said he'd rather be shot, stabbed and run over by a bus than get back in there.'

'And you still want to do it because . . . ?' I raised one incredulous, amused eyebrow at him.

'I'm insane?' He turned it up at the end, made it a question.

'I'm not going to argue with that,' I said, but I found myself following him anyway.

I baulked as soon as my toes touched the coolness of the damp sand, anticipating the much colder water to come. But Dougie kept on going, not hesitating when he broke the surface of the water. He didn't pause until the waves were lapping around his knees, and then it was only a cursory glance behind to check I was still there. I hurriedly closed the final few feet to the water before he could realise what a wimp I was.

It was just as cold as before. The iciness took my breath away, made my hair stand up on end. And I was only in up to my ankles. How cold would it be when it was waist height? Chest height? I shuddered as I imagined sticking my head beneath the murky surface.

'Maybe Darren's right,' Dougie commented as I drew level with him. 'You definitely need a drink in you to brave this.'

I huffed a laugh, though it came out oddly through the shivers that were wracking my body.

'I wish he'd stop being such a git,' he continued bitterly.

I nodded mutely but I didn't hold out much hope. Every time I'd met him, Darren had been exactly the same.

Dougie sighed. 'Martin's ready to smash him one. Hope he doesn't, Darren'll break his nose.'

'Martin will cool off,' I reassured him. 'And I'll tell Emma to make sure she keeps Darren occupied. She can get him to take an inventory of her make-up bag, that'll take him at least two days.'

Dougie snorted and winked at me. I would have blushed, but all of my blood was busy keeping my internal organs going. I'd already lost the feeling in my feet.

'Right, we doing this?' Dougie looked at me questioningly.

'Only because it's your birthday,' I told him.

'Come on.' He grinned. 'Race you to chest height!'

He was off before I could object, sending a wave of icy spray cascading over me as he bashed forward through the water. I shrieked in protest but that just meant I got a mouthful of nasty, salty water. Spitting and retching, I closed my mouth and followed him.

Actually, once you were all the way in it wasn't so bad. Even better once I got up the courage to dunk my head beneath the surface. The saltwater was foul, though, and I found myself wishing for the sterile environment of a chlorine-saturated, heated swimming pool. We didn't really swim, but stayed far enough out for the water to flutter round my throat if I stood on my tiptoes. Dougie was tall enough for his shoulders just to clear the waves. He stood motionless but I lifted my feet and trod water, trying to stay warm.

'You're not swimming,' I commented, bobbing up and down as my arms and legs beat rhythmically, keeping me afloat.

'I think my limbs might have frozen solid,' he admitted,

grinning at me sheepishly. 'Maybe this wasn't such a good idea.'

'Oh no,' I said. 'We're in now. Imagine it's the Aqua Centre.'

'Minus the kids peeing in the pool!' he replied, laughing. 'And the angry lifeguard who hates his life.'

'And the grannies who don't want you to splash and mess up their perfect hair,' I agreed. 'So it's better really.'

'Yeah, it's –' Then a comical look of shock came over his face and he tumbled back into the water, disappearing below the surface.

'Dougie?' I stared at the water, waiting for him to reappear. He didn't. 'Dougie?'

I swam forwards, searching the water with my hands. Nothing. I was right over the spot where he'd dropped, my fingers reaching, eyes scanning the murky depths for his silhouette beneath the waves.

'Dougie?' I was starting to panic, aware of each second as it ticked by. Was that a minute now? More? I half-turned, about to scream to the shore, to Emma and Darren, when the water exploded right in front of my face.

Dougie sprang up, dousing me with another sheet of icy spray and scaring ten years off my life.

'You . . . you idiot!' I yelped. He was laughing between gasps, a wide grin on his face. 'I thought you were drowning!'

'Sorry.' He didn't sound it. He wiped at his eyes and gave me an impish look. 'My dad and I used to do that, challenge each other to see how long we could stay underwater. I always won.'

'Well, you could have warned me!' I snapped, feeling foolish now. 'That wasn't funny.'

'Yes, it was.'

I opened my mouth, planning on lecturing him on all the ways that it *wasn't* amusing . . . but something slithered past my leg.

'What was that?' My breath froze in my lungs and my limbs tensed. I immediately forgot about Dougie's antics, focusing on the water around me. Another soft brush ticked the base of my spine.

'Something touched me!' I squealed.

'Jellyfish?' Dougie suggested, trying not to laugh at what I'm sure was a look of absolute panic on my face.

'There are jellyfish in here?' My voice was just a squeak, inaudible to all but dogs.

'Probably.'

Another 'thing' grazed my forearm, seemed to curl around my elbow. The gentle contact threw me into action. I dived forward towards Dougie, thrashing my arms hysterically. Convinced I could feel tendrils creeping across my lower back, I grabbed for him, clutching at his shoulders with my hands, wrapping my legs around his middle. I didn't even realise I was screeching in his ear until he twisted his head away, trying to escape the noise.

'I'm sorry, I'm sorry,' I babbled, but I still didn't let go. 'Get me away from them,' I begged.

Dougie was wickedly amused – I could feel his chest shaking with laughter – but he started wading back towards the shore, practically carrying me as I refused to let go. Somehow the terror of creatures of the deep had made me forget to be self-conscious. Luckily Dougie didn't seem bothered by my feebleness. In fact, he seemed to be enjoying it, grinning hugely at my wide-eyed hysteria.

'If only I'd known that all it'd take to get you to throw yourself into my arms was a couple of jellyfish,' he joked, dropping me down onto the shore but keeping his arms wrapped round my waist. 'What will you do if I have to come to your rescue when there's a spider in the tent?'

'Marry you!' I blurted out. He threw back his head and laughed.

CHAPTER TEN

It took a *long* time to heat back up after our dip in the sea. I huddled in a towel in my chair, my arms wrapped around my knees, teeth chattering, thinking. Thinking about Dougie's throwaway comment about the jellyfish. Was it just a jokey thing to say between friends, or was it something else? Something . . . flirty?

I was embarrassed, too. My face burned – it was the only part of me that was warm – as Dougie recounted the tale for Emma and Darren, both of whom had heard my hysterics but been too far away to see what was happening. They laughed at me, but it was good-natured and, better yet, Dougie chucked me another wink as he got to the part where I'd practically thrown myself at him.

'I'm sorry,' I mumbled back, not quite brave enough to say something playful, something suggestive, like Emma would have.

'Don't be, I enjoyed it.' Dougie lifted one eyebrow at me. Then he laughed at the expression on my face.

I looked down shyly – and a little annoyed at myself for not being able to come up with a witty comeback – and the conversation moved on.

To fishing. That was what Dougie's dad had always come here for. Dougie wasn't sure if he'd ever actually caught anything – except, one time, the flu – but Darren was itching to have a go, to prove his manly skills. Only he didn't have a fishing rod. Or even a line and hook. The only thing he could come up with was a long length of twine from the junk-filled boot of the Volvo and a cold cooked sausage that he planned to tie on the end. He was adamant that it would work and was deaf to Dougie's criticism. I offered no opinion – I knew as much about fishing as I did about alternator brushes – although it seemed a bit optimistic. He'd have more chance of catching a passing Irishman. Emma was ignoring us, lying in the sun, trying to tan away her sunburn. I was dubious as to whether that plan would work either.

The fishing argument continued but after a while I tuned it out. I contented myself staring at the sparkles dancing in the sea. Then suddenly they disappeared.

'Hey!' Emma complained, lifting her sunglasses and glaring at the sky.

I hadn't noticed their approach but thick clouds now covered the sun, cutting off the light. They were innocuous enough, fluffy white cotton hovering in the sky, but behind us, crawling over the hill, they darkened to steel grey. Rain.

'We need to get our stuff inside,' I warned, watching with alarm as the rainclouds made steady progress across the sky.

'It's not going to rain,' Darren disagreed, shaking his head disparagingly.

Just then a stiff breeze blew up out of nowhere, bringing with it a spattering of droplets.

'It is,' Dougie replied, standing up and staring at the approaching weather. 'Pretty heavily, too.' He looked at me. 'Is your tent waterproof?'

I made a face. 'Theoretically.'

The tent was old. It belonged to my cousin. Hoping for sun, I hadn't thought to ask him how it would fare in a deluge.

'Sit it out in our tent,' he offered. 'Our fly-sheet's good for a pretty heavy downpour.'

'Thanks.' I jumped up, wrapping my towel tightly round me, and dashed for our tent. Once inside, I yanked on my clothes as quickly as I could, shoved everything else in my bag, hoping that would offer some protection, and bolted back out. The two boys were ferrying food and other provisions in through the empty opening of their much bigger tent, chucking everything on top of the three multicoloured sleeping bags. Three. I frowned at that.

'Hey, has anybody seen –'

The heavens opened.

There was no warning. No pitter-patter or sprinkle before the storm. A sheet of water dropped from above. I was soaked in an instant, rainwater dripping down my nose, saturating my hair, barely dry from swimming. The t-shirt I'd thrown on now clung to me like a cold, uncomfortable second skin. There was no trace of the summer we'd been enjoying just moments ago.

I dived into the boys' tent.

'Shall I zip up the door?' I asked, trying not to step on any of their possessions with my wet, sandy shoes.

'Just the screen,' Dougie told me. 'The porch'll keep the water out.'

We sat in a line, staring out of the half moon-shaped screen and watched the rain continue to fall. It was a torrent: big fat globules pitted the sandy beach and battered the waves. Time lost meaning as we sat there; it was mesmerising to watch. The clouds were so heavy an early twilight seemed to descend. Like looking at the world through a filter, the colours leached out.

'Who's got the torch?' Darren asked.

There was some scrabbling around on either side of me, but the light in the tent remained muted.

'Where was it last?' Dougie wondered aloud.

'I stuck it just by the opening, in case we needed it to pee in the middle of the night,' Darren said, his voice right at my ear as he felt around the groundsheet surrounding me. 'Heather, I think you're sitting on it.'

'Am I?' I couldn't feel anything, but I shifted obediently so he could check the space under me. Nothing was there.

'What are you looking for?' Emma asked, a dreamy quality to her voice as if she was in a daze. 'Here, this'll help.'

I heard a click and the tent was flooded with light.

'That,' Dougie laughed.

'Emma, sometimes I don't think you're on this planet,' Darren grumbled, but the look on his face was indulgent as he reached to take the torch from her.

'What?' She blinked and looked around at us, bemused.

'Never mind, angel. At least you're pretty.'

I rolled my eyes and shifted back to my original position. Every time I thought Darren wasn't quite so bad he'd say something patronising like that, voice showing no hint of humour, and I'd revert back to my original assessment: he was an arse.

'Ow!' Something dug into my hip painfully as I let my weight settle back down. Were there two torches?

No. Whatever was hurting me was in my pocket. I ferreted around in my jeans until I could draw the thing out.

'Oh.' I stared at it, surprised.

The brooch. I'd almost forgotten it. The argument between Darren and Martin had totally driven it from my mind. In the torchlight it glittered, the curved edge throwing off sparkles. The light wasn't quite good enough to show the carvings, not like I'd seen them earlier in the sunshine, but running my finger over the surface I could feel the grooves.

'You cleaned it!' Dougie said, surprised.

I turned to see him peering eagerly over my shoulder.

'Yeah,' I replied. 'Yeah, it came up really well.'

'Can I have a look?' I surrendered it into his waiting palm. He held it up close to his face, angling the torch so that he could get a good look. 'Wow,' he said. 'That's crazy. Guess it's not that old then.'

He seemed fascinated by the markings on the surface too.

'What do you think the engravings are?' I asked, pointing at one swirl that was just about visible.

'Don't know.' Dougie shrugged. 'Wonder what it was doing there?'

We lapsed into silence again. Dougie was still studying the brooch, picking at the pin on the back. I watched him, trying to imagine how the piece of jewellery had ended up buried deep in the middle of a collapsed cairn. The hill was in the middle of nowhere. I supposed there were probably walkers going past, but it seemed unlikely that whoever had left it there had discovered the place by chance. My stomach turned uneasily as another theory presented itself. What if it was a love token? What if it had been left there by a distraught widow, a gift to a husband or wife, one no longer here, left in a spot they loved? Once again I had the feeling that we shouldn't have taken it. Maybe I would suggest to Dougie that we return it.

I glanced around the tent as I thought about it and my gaze drifted towards Darren, staring broodingly out towards the beer cooler, half buried in the sand outside. Yes, that's what I'd do. But I'd wait until Dougie and I were alone first. Darren wouldn't get it, he'd laugh at me. I hoped Dougie wouldn't.

It felt like a weight off my mind to have decided. I went back to watching the rain.

'We might find our stuff swimming in water after this, Emma,' I told her ruefully. The bag I'd stuffed everything into wasn't waterproof either and I hadn't thought to bring our sleeping bags with me earlier. That was stupid.

'I'm not sleeping in a wet bag!' Emma complained.

'There's always the Volvo,' I replied, looking at Darren hopefully.

He grinned. 'Don't worry, ladies, we'll make room for you in here.'

'Where?' Emma looked round. Every inch of the tent was covered with the boys' gear.

'Believe it or not, this is meant to be a six-man tent,' Dougie explained.

'Ha!' Emma snorted derisively. 'Heather says ours is a four. Four what, midgets?'

The talk of numbers pushed a thought back into my head.

'Hey!' I exclaimed. 'Where's Martin? He still isn't back.'

Darren laughed. 'Specky's going to be drenched!'

I scowled at him, irritated. 'Don't call him that!'

'Ooh, touchy!' He grinned at me. 'Something you want to tell us about you two?'

'Darren, shut up.' Dougie glared across the narrow space, and for once Darren did what he asked. Dougie looked at me, his eyes uncertain. 'Do you think we should ring him?'

I looked out at the rain, the darkening sky.

'Yeah,' I said. 'Yeah, we should. Hang on, I've got my phone.'

I dragged it out of my pocket and flipped through the contacts. Finding Martin's name, I smacked my finger down on his entry and the screen jumped to *calling*. It last two seconds before it cut off.

'What?' I stared at the phone, confused. Then I remembered what the girl from the metalworkers' had told me – the one who gave us a jump. 'Oh. No signal. There goes that idea.'

Dougie pulled out his own mobile and stared at it. He sighed. 'Me either. How long do we give him before we go out looking?'

I looked at my watch. Martin had been gone for hours. Dougie caught my expression.

'Now?'

I hesitated, then nodded.

'Emma and I will stay here,' Darren said loudly. 'You know, in case he comes back.'

Emma's noise of agreement was lost under the rustling sound of Dougie rising to his feet.

'We're all going. Darren, get your jacket on.'

Though Emma accepted Dougie's edict with resigned silence, Darren muttered and moaned for ten minutes while we got geared up for heading out into the downpour. Typically, the moment we were ready to go – suitably clothed in waterproofs and boots, both Emma and me clutching umbrellas – the rain stopped. We ditched the brollies and replaced the jackets with thick jumpers – the wind hadn't died and there was a definite bite to the air – before heading across the beach in the direction I'd seen Martin go.

'Hasn't it occurred to anyone else that he might be going in a circle?' Darren asked. 'Just because he left in this direction doesn't mean he'll come back this way. He'll probably turn up back at the camp while we're traipsing about in the dark.'

'Then he'll wait there and we'll find him when we get back,' Dougie said firmly. 'You're not getting out of going, Darren.'

Darren didn't complain after that, although I did catch him casting dark looks at Dougie and mumbling under his breath. Things between him and Martin weren't going to be any better after this.

There was only one path at this end of the beach. It wound along the rocky coastline before veering steeply up the hillside. At the top it spat us back out onto the same road we'd driven in on. There seemed only one sensible direction for Martin to have taken: we followed the road back towards the dirt car park. It felt even longer on foot than it had squashed in the sweltering heat of the car. By the time we tripped down the sheer section running back down towards the beach, night had fallen.

We'd been gone for two hours, maybe more. At the car park next to our campsite, Darren's rusting Volvo waited for us, along with the smell of rotting fish that the rain had done nothing to dampen. I barely noticed it, however. I was staring intently at the beach, hunting for a torchlight beam or flicker of flames from the campfire to tell us Martin was back. There was nothing, just distant milky-white moonlight reflecting on the water now that the clouds had finally moved on.

'Martin?' I called as I stumbled my way down the narrow path. There was no answer. 'Martin, you there?'

Silence. My trainers sank into the soft sand, grains spilling into my shoes to irritate my feet. I didn't notice. Light played out in front of me as Dougie shone the torch left and right, scanning the area. There was no one there.

I shouted again anyway.

'Martin?' I could hear the panic in my voice now, tinged with guilt. I should have gone with him. He'd wanted me to. What had happened to him? My stomach twisted uneasily and I hurried on ahead.

I stopped in the middle of the campsite, practically empty now that most of the gear was in the boys' tent. The swirling breeze distorted the sound of three people murmuring quietly behind me. I turned to stare at them.

'He's not here,' I said pointlessly.

Their faces all reflected the worry I felt eating away at my gut. Even Darren looked bothered.

'Where else could he be?' Dougie wondered, frowning thoughtfully.

'Maybe he's fallen somewhere,' I suggested. 'Broken his ankle or something and can't walk?'

A horrible image of Martin huddled in a ditch, drenched and cold, flashed before my eyes. In front of me Darren shook his head, shattering the picture.

'No, we walked the entire loop. We'd have seen him, or he'd have heard us, called out.'

'Maybe he's unconscious –' I started.

Darren cut me off.

'You're jumping to conclusions.'

'Well, where is he then?' My voice was sharp, biting. I saw Darren's expression curdle in response.

'I don't know,' he said, folding his arms across his chest. His muscles bulged menacingly. 'Maybe . . . maybe he left, hitched a ride up on the road.'

'Without telling any of us?' Dougie looked sceptical. I was too. Martin wouldn't do that.

'He was upset,' Darren continued, warming to his idea. 'He was raging at me –' (Not without cause, I thought.) '– and then neither of you would go walking with him. Maybe he just decided to disappear. Five's a crowd and all that.'

'It wasn't like that,' I argued feebly.

But maybe it was like that, at least for Martin. Darren's words stabbed at the heart of the unease I already felt. What if that was exactly how he'd seen it? He'd been having a miserable time, clashing with Darren every five seconds. And then Dougie and I – who were supposed to be his friends – had let him storm off alone so we could go swimming together. Maybe he'd felt isolated, left out; maybe he'd decided to get out of the way.

Looking at it that way, Darren's suggestion didn't seem quite so unfeasible. I bit my lip, not wanting to admit it, ashamed of myself.

Dougie rescued me.

'Even if he did think that, I still don't think he'd just leave. He wouldn't have got into a car with total strangers. Plus, we walked all the way along that road, not a single motor went past.'

'*We* didn't see anyone,' Darren said. 'But that doesn't mean Martin didn't.'

'And that one car just happened to be willing to stop and pick up a stranger?' Dougie argued back.

Darren shrugged. 'It's possible. Or maybe he went the other way, up to the turn. There was more traffic there.'

'Maybe.' Dougie's voice was hard, disbelieving. 'You really think he'd just abandon all his things, though?'

'Who says he did?' Darren asked.

We all looked to the boys' tent. Then back to each other.

'I'll check.' Darren disappeared from the circle of the torch beam.

I heard the ripping sound of the tent flap being opened and then a rustling. A smaller light flared inside the canvas, whiter than the torch, like the glare from a mobile. It danced and flickered as Darren searched the tent. We could have gone over too, but for some reason none of us moved. We just stood there, clustered round the fire pit from the night before, waiting.

The light in the tent went out and I shivered, though it wasn't really cold. Agitated, I stuck my hand in my pocket and began to fiddle with the brooch. Finally Darren reappeared, pausing to zip the door and straighten the porch before he spoke.

'Well?' Dougie prompted, pinning him in the torch beam, tired of waiting.

Darren shrugged.

'He must have gone,' he said. 'His bag's missing, and all his clothes. The only things of his left are his sleeping bag and the air mattress pump.'

Dougie scowled, unconvinced. 'And just when did he have time to come and get them?'

'That would be when we were out searching the countryside for him,' Darren shot back. 'I told you Emma and I should stay. We could have stopped him, talked some sense into him.'

Dougie snorted and I knew what he was thinking. Darren would have been more likely to help Martin pack, offer him a lift up to the road. Frustrated, he ran his hand through his hair, making it stand up on end in disarray.

'Dammit,' he muttered. 'I can't believe this.'

Neither could I. We'd driven Martin away. Darren with his drinking and his temper, but it was Dougie and I who had pushed him out. I swallowed painfully, feeling sick at myself.

'What do we do?' I asked.

'We should go get him,' Dougie replied at once.

I blinked, then nodded. Of course that was what we should do. Only . . .

'How?' Darren's voice was acerbic.

'What?' Dougie looked more annoyed than confused.

'How are we meant to go and get him? We've no idea where he is; in fact he's probably halfway home. We haven't got any signal on our phones. Are you suggesting we hike all over bloody Dumfriesshire?'

'We'll take the Volvo,' Dougie spat back, as if it was obvious.

'You driving then? I'm over the limit.'

Dougie frowned at that, and so did I. Darren hadn't had a chance to have a drink in hours. Just how much had he consumed earlier on? Or was this just a convenient excuse?

It was a good one, though. If Darren couldn't drive then looking for Martin was out, at least for tonight.

'Look.' Darren's tone changed, became more ingratiating. 'We can't do anything tonight. Let's just stay here and then, in the morning, we'll drive up to where we can get a signal and you can call him and sort this out. He'll be home safe with his mammy. Guaranteed. I promise to drive you up tomorrow.'

Dougie considered that. 'First thing?' he asked.

'First thing.'

I didn't like the idea of waiting all night. Despite Darren's plan, the lead in my stomach refused to shift. Maybe it was the darkness. It was pitch black on the beach apart from the dimming light of the torch, in need of new batteries, and the watery glow of the moon. I agreed readily when Darren suggested trying to get a fire going. Didn't even complain when he dragged out the whisky. I needed something to warm my insides.

I tried to shut out the thought in the back of my mind that whispered that Martin wasn't halfway back to Glasgow, chatting merrily in the back seat of someone's car, but was somewhere much darker, much colder. Somewhere alone.

CHAPTER ELEVEN

The fire took a while to catch. Most of the wood we collected was damp and the breeze kept snuffing out any flames we managed to coax to life. Eventually, though, with the help of a little bottle of lighter fluid that Darren produced from the car, we got it going. It had an immediate effect on the atmosphere. Radiating warmth, it banished the shadows outside the circle.

We were still quiet, though, still subdued. For a while the silence was kept at bay only by the crackling of burning wood and the hiss and spit of the burgers Dougie was cooking on his tiny grill. We were all starving, having missed dinner in the search for Martin.

Every time she got up to go into the darkness to pee, or dart into the tent for a jumper, or a brush, or to fetch a drink, Emma shifted her chair a little further away from me, a little closer to Darren. I didn't see him move so much as an inch, but somehow his chair also migrated away from Dougie's, until I looked up and saw there was a clear divide: Darren and Emma on one side of the fire, Dougie and me on the other.

To be honest, I wasn't particularly bothered, but I did worry, as I watched them intertwine fingers, Emma giggling and Darren winking at her, a lascivious leer about his grin, that they would use Martin's disappearance as an excuse to pair up, to push me and Dougie into being a 'couple'.

Had Dougie noticed? I looked at him slyly out of the corner of my eye, saw he was staring in my direction. I waited for him to say something, but he didn't. He just kept looking at me.

'What?' I eventually asked.

He shrugged.

'Nothing.'

There was a pause, then I asked, 'Do you really think Martin hitched out of here?'

Another pause, before Dougie finally nodded.

'Yes,' he said.

And it was probably true. It wasn't hard to believe that Martin had wanted to escape, possibly badly enough that he'd ask strangers for a ride. I felt bad about it, knowing part of that was my fault, but I was also pretty annoyed with him by now. He must have known we would worry. Would it have been so hard to leave a note? Maybe it was part of our punishment. I could imagine his self-righteous, aggrieved expression as he marched away up the hill without looking back. Muttering that we deserved it.

I let the resentment build up, because it made it easier to convince myself there was no need to worry. But . . .

'I just . . . what if we call tomorrow and he doesn't answer?' I said. 'Or he does answer and he's in a ditch somewhere, been there all night, and –'

'He won't be, Heather.' Dougie cut me off. I let him, because talking about it was bringing that horrible uneasy feeling back again. I took a deep breath, looked around for a safe topic of conversation. There was only one real option.

'Emma and Darren look pretty cosy.'

'Yeah.' Dougie gazed across the flames at them, faces just a foot apart, grinning at each other. 'Yeah, think he really likes her.'

'Wonder why,' I murmured, finishing the thought I could see lingering on his lips.

Dougie laughed. 'Well, Darren's no picnic,' he said quietly. 'He can be a tosser.'

I grimaced my agreement, not really wanting to say it aloud.

'Guess they're perfect for each other, then,' I offered, smiling wryly.

'Guess so.' Dougie smiled back.

We didn't speak for a while after that and, for the first time, I felt perfectly comfortable just sitting there beside Dougie quietly, doing nothing more than watching the flames.

'Right, kiddos, bedtime.' Darren's voice startled me. I raised my eyebrows at him, confused. That was very sensible for Darren. It couldn't be much past midnight and he'd hardly had anything to drink. Maybe the Martin thing had actually unsettled him. Maybe he had feelings after all.

As he stood up, though, I saw a bulge up his sleeve that was suspiciously cylindrical and my eyes narrowed. What was he up to?

But I was tired so I readily agreed, dragging myself up and heading in the direction of my tent. I yanked on my pyjamas then stood, undecided. I needed to pee, but it was dark and my sleeping bag was calling to me, a little damp on the cover but mercifully dry inside. I knew if I crawled in it, however, that I'd just have to get up and go in the middle of the night. Grumbling audibly, I stamped my way outside.

Uncomfortable lingering in the dark, I was back in record time. Emma was already inside, because a light was glowing and the door was closed. I bent to unzip it, then paused, shocked, in the entrance.

Darren waved at me from inside the tent, sprawled nonchalantly across the double air mattress.

'Hi, gorgeous.' He winked cheekily.

'What are you doing in here?' I demanded, too surprised to be polite.

Emma appeared from out of nowhere to stand at my side.

'Darren's sleeping in here,' she said breezily. I gaped at her, aghast. I thought I saw a slight sheepishness in her eyes, but then she stepped past me and turned to block my way.

'Where the hell am I meant to sleep?' I ground out.

'Oh, I don't know.' She winked coyly at me. 'Somewhere else.'

'Emma, don't do this to me,' I hissed, but it was already done. Ignoring me, Emma reached out to zip the tent closed.

'You'll thank me for this later,' Darren called as I was shut out.

My mouth dropped as I registered what he meant. Not only was she shutting me out of our tent, but she'd told Darren about my feelings for Dougie. Darren, who couldn't keep his mouth shut about *anything*. I gritted my teeth against the swear words rising up in my throat.

Then my shoulders slumped. There was no way I was up for a confrontation with Darren tonight so I turned to contemplate my only other option. Like a condemned man to the gallows, I walked hesitantly towards the other blob of glowing light. The boys' tent. Dougie's tent.

I stopped just short and hesitated, squirming from foot to foot, too mortified to announce myself. I would have liked to knock, but canvas made that impossible. Instead I cleared my throat and, after sending a final frustrating and pleading glance towards Emma and Darren, inside *my* tent, I took a deep breath.

'Dougie?' I croaked as quietly as I could manage. I didn't want Darren or Emma to hear.

He didn't answer, but I heard shuffling from inside and a moment later his head appeared.

'Hey,' he greeted me. 'What's up?'

He wasn't aware of Darren and my 'friend's' treachery, then.

The words wouldn't come out and I watched as his face grew more confused, then amused.

'Can I sleep in here?' I mumbled eventually, dying on the spot.

The confusion was back.

'What's wrong with your tent?'

'There's a Darren in it,' I admitted.

'Oh,' he laughed, looking across to the other tent. 'Oh. That's where he is.'

But he stepped back and opened the flap further so I could crawl inside. I stumbled and tripped my way in, feeling awkward, and all but fell down into the back corner of the tent where the mess was thinnest. As Dougie closed us in, his bare back to me, again I drank in the sleekness of his muscles, shifting under his skin as he moved, but I made myself pull my stare away as he turned back to me. Out of the corner of my eye I saw him tugging a t-shirt over his head and felt both uncomfortable and chagrined.

'Okay.' He settled down into a deep red sleeping bag and smiled at me. I felt a little better. 'Blue or green?' He pointed to the other two bags. I looked at them, just to avoid looking at him. The space was too small, the paper-thin walls of the tent claustrophobic.

'Which one is Darren's?' I asked, striving, unsuccessfully, for nonchalance.

'Blue.'

'Then I'll take green.'

I pulled the sea-green bag over, started to fold myself inside. I planned to escape this awkward torture by falling asleep as quickly as possible. I knew Emma would be disappointed in me, that she'd call me a chicken in the morning, tell me I'd wasted an opportunity. I just hoped to God we wouldn't hear any noises floating over from the direction of the other tent. Surely she'd spare me that much.

'It gets pretty cold in here,' Dougie warned as I rolled over to lie down on the far edge of the huge air mattress. It was much bigger than the one in our tent, a kingsize, maybe. 'It's the height of the ceiling. The space is too big to collect warmth.'

'Okay,' I said, directing my stare in front of me, where Darren's rumpled blue bag marked his absence. I was already cold. Martin's sleeping bag wasn't as thick as mine, the shiny, shell-suit feel of the fabric cooler than my fluffy cotton lining. I buried down deeper so that my nose wasn't sticking out in the frigid air, only my eyes peeking at Dougie. It still felt too much. I closed them, then wondered if he'd continued to watch me. I tried to quietly rotate, planning on turning my back on him, hoping I'd feel a little less self-conscious that way, but he spoke and I froze.

'I'm cold,' he sighed.

My eyes flew open, staring into the roof of the tent.

'Mmm,' I mumbled in agreement.

'We should huddle up,' he said matter-of-factly. He smiled as I turned to eye him warily. 'You know, like penguins.'

Penguins? More like two very uncomfortable people. Or at least one very uncomfortable person. One hopeful-but-pathetically-chicken very uncomfortable person. But he was looking at me, waiting, that half-smile still lingering on his lips. Not sure what else to do – I both wanted and really *didn't* want to do as he suggested – I started to wriggle like an over-sized worm across the tent. The air mattress sloped down towards Dougie's weight and I tumbled the final foot, my arms pinned at my side in the bag, helpless to stop me. Dougie had to catch me to stop my momentum throwing us both against the side of the tent. I still face-planted into his chest, getting a whiff of whatever body-spray he used, trapped in the fabric of his shirt. It smelled amazing. Not that I was able to concentrate on that.

'I'm sorry!' I gasped.

Oh my God. Oh my holy God! How embarrassing. But he was laughing. At me or with me I couldn't tell; I was too mortified to look at his face.

'Don't apologise,' he said through shakes of laughter. 'What guy doesn't want a woman to throw herself into his arms? That's twice in one day!'

'Right,' I choked out. My face was on fire. I wasn't cold now, that was for sure.

Neither was Dougie. Both his arms around me and the length of his torso that I was pressed against radiated heat. He wasn't freezing. I raised one eyebrow, confused and curious, but the thought only lasted a second. Don't be ridiculous, I told myself.

Not quite sure how he wanted us to 'penguin', I shifted round until my back was to his chest. It felt a little less uncomfortable that way. We didn't seem to be as close when I had the length of the tent to look at. One of Dougie's arms draped over my side, the other he tucked under his head as a pillow.

'That's warmer,' he breathed.

I nodded, not sure I could speak without embarrassing myself further. His breath against my neck was giving me shivers. I tried to block it out, listening to the rhythmic ebb and flow of the sea, hoping it would lull me to sleep. Eventually.

When I opened my eyes, it was morning. Dougie's arm was no longer wrapped around me and I had lost the comforting pressure of his chest against my back. I listened to see if I could hear his quiet breathing, but my ears could only pick up the slow, constant whooshing of the waves. I twisted round to double-check that I was alone and saw the dark red sleeping bag lying empty beside me.

I sat up and stretched, wincing slightly. The boys' air mattress might be bigger than mine, but it wasn't any more comfortable.

My shoulders ached and my spine cracked as I twisted. I was in the process of trying to pull the knots out of my hair – matted and brittle from the dip in the sea – when the tent flap was pulled back and I was blinded by light.

'You're awake,' Dougie commented.

He was fully dressed bar his shoes. I wondered how he'd managed that without waking me; I was usually a light sleeper.

'Yeah.' I gave him a half-smile that warped into a huge yawn without my permission. I clapped my hand over my mouth just a second too slow. 'Are you the only one up?' I asked. I couldn't hear the dulcet tones of Darren or Emma.

'Yup. I couldn't sleep.'

'Sorry,' I said, instantly taking the blame. I hoped to God I hadn't snored last night. Surely Emma would have complained if I was a loud sleeper?

Much to my relief, Dougie shook his head.

'It wasn't you,' he told me. 'You were like my hot water bottle. I give you permission to sleep in here any time.' He sighed. 'I couldn't stop thinking.'

'About Martin,' I guessed.

Dougie nodded and I bit my lip, abashed. The thrill and embarrassment of sleeping in the same tent as Dougie had driven our friend out of my mind. Once again I felt the sting of shame.

'I mean, maybe Darren's right. I'd just feel better if I knew for sure.' He sighed, pushed his hands through his hair in a nervous gesture.

'I know,' I said. 'I keep thinking that he wouldn't have just gone, not without saying.'

'As soon as Darren's up I want to take the car up to the main road, hunt for a signal.'

'Before breakfast?' I could easily imagine how Darren would react to that one.

'I'd go now if I could.'

'Well –' I thought about it. 'Why can't we?'

Dougie looked at me quizzically.

'How?'

I shrugged. 'Can't you drive? We could just take the Volvo up ourselves. We'll probably be back before either of them appears.'

I watched Dougie consider my suggestion. He made a face, but it was obvious the idea was appealing to him.

'I know how to drive,' he said slowly. 'And it's not as if there are likely to be any police cars out here in the middle of nowhere. Not this early. We'll be lucky if we even see another car.'

I smiled, pleased Dougie was coming around.

'Where did Darren put the keys?' I asked.

'Behind you.' Dougie pointed to the back of the tent. 'In the black holdall.' I reached round and started to yank at the zipper. 'No,' he called over my shoulder. 'The side pocket.'

But my hands had frozen. There, untidily stuffed around Darren's things, was a very familiar red jumper. I pulled it out. Underneath that were a glasses case and a pair of corduroy shorts that Darren would never be seen dead in.

'Dougie . . .'

I'd found Martin's stuff.

CHAPTER TWELVE

Now

'It seems to me that with Martin out of the way you had what you wanted, Heather. Time with Dougie.'

I glower at Petersen, not dignifying his comment with a response.

'Tell me, how did you feel when Darren found Martin's things?'

'How do you think I felt?' I snarl, goaded into speaking. 'It was –'

Then I catch what he's just said.

'It was Dougie and me who found Martin's things,' I tell him, my voice very deliberately calm and level once more. My fingers curl into my palms, nails digging into soft flesh, as I fight to rein in my emotions. 'Me and Dougie, not Darren.'

'Dougie?' Petersen raises his pitch along with his eyebrows, turning it into a question. 'That isn't what you told me before.'

'Yes, it is,' I snap back.

'No. I have it here, Heather. In your session transcripts.' He grabs up my folder and draws out the stapled bundle of paper, then drops it back into the file before I can focus on the neat lines of type across the page. 'Darren, you said.'

That's a mistake. It must have been Helen. She was probably sucking up to Petersen as she typed, flirting, angling for a pay rise.

'It was Dougie,' I tell him again. 'Dougie and I found Martin's things. In Darren's bag.'

Then

It took Dougie all of five seconds to take in the objects nestled on top of Darren's gear and put two and two together. Swearing loudly, he spun on his heel and stormed away from the tent. I struggled to escape from my sleeping bag then scrambled out after him. By the time I'd got outside he was already hauling open the zipper on the other tent. I heard squeals of protest from Emma. Though the sky was light, the sun was yet to break the horizon. It must still be very early. I hoped that was the only reason.

'What is your problem, Dougie?' Darren's voice, sleepy but aggressive.

'What's my problem?' Dougie was shouting; it was easy to hear him as I trotted across the cool sand, straightening my pyjamas as I went. 'We found Martin's stuff, Darren!'

Silence. I reached Dougie's side in time to see Darren's expression curdle. He looked both belligerent and shamefaced, although there was far too much defiance and not enough contrition to satisfy me.

Emma peeked out from where she'd had her face hidden in the pillow, trying to escape the light.

'What's going on?' she complained.

'Darren hid Martin's things,' Dougie explained, his voice hard. 'He didn't pack up his stuff and leave. Christ only knows where Martin is, but we should have spent the night looking for him, not barbecuing burgers and shacking up!'

'All right, so he left his things behind. But he still might have hitchhiked out of here,' Darren replied, his jaw set. 'We don't know where he is.'

'That's right, we don't know,' Dougie spat. 'But you had no bloody right to lie to us! He might be lying somewhere in a ditch right now. It was freezing last night! He could be bloody dead, Darren!'

Dougie was screaming. I put a hand on his arm and he broke off, breathing hard. Emma looked between the pair, her eyes wide as saucers. They widened even further, though, as she watched Darren slither out of the tent, climb slowly to his feet. He wore nothing but a pair of boxers and his physique was impressive. Even more so because he was quivering with rage. His hands curled into fists. I resisted the urge to take a step back. His anger wasn't directed at me. Maybe it wasn't aimed at Dougie, either.

'Specky was nothing but a pain,' he spat. 'All he did was moan, and let's face it, he made it a crowd, not a party. If he was stupid enough to get himself into trouble, that's his lookout. If something's happened to him, it wouldn't be much of a loss.'

I stared at him, agape. Even Emma looked shocked.

'So if he's hurt himself, if he's dead, that's just no big deal then?' Dougie's voice shook with barely controlled fury.

Darren shrugged. 'I won't lose any sleep over it.'

Emma's quiet 'Darren!' was lost under the roar of anger that emitted from Dougie's chest. He launched himself forward, hands clenched in fists of his own, aiming for Darren's face.

CHAPTER THIRTEEN

'Are you sure you're all right?'

It was the fourth time I'd asked and once again my question was met with a curt 'I'm fine.'

We were hiking up the road towards civilisation, the Volvo waiting idly in the car park at our backs. Darren had refused to let us take it. Dougie, blood still streaming from his nose where Darren had smacked him hard in the face, had been uncontainable. It was all I could do to convince him to wait the three minutes it took me to claw on my clothes before he took off, storming away from the campsite.

'Would you like a tissue?' I asked, trotting to keep up.

'No.' Dougie wiped his lower face on his sleeve, coating his white top in vivid red blood.

I fell silent then, concentrating on keeping up, avoiding the deep pot-holes that rutted the surface of the road. My calves were burning and hunger sapped my energy. I didn't want to ask Dougie to slow down, though. Not when he was in this mood. To be honest, I was a little frightened of him right now.

He seemed out of control and though I couldn't hear what he was saying, I saw his lips trembling as he muttered under his breath.

Then suddenly he stopped short and whirled to face me. I made to back away but then steadied myself.

'I mean,' he exploded, continuing a thought I hadn't heard, 'I know he doesn't like Martin, but for God's sake! He spent the whole night last night *knowing* Martin was missing, properly missing, and he didn't bat an eyelid. All he could think about was getting Emma into the damned tent. What is wrong with him?'

I looked at him anxiously, uncomfortable with the idea of having to reply, nervous of saying the wrong thing.

'And I can't believe he wouldn't let me have the car,' he went on when I didn't respond. 'We could be up there right now, phoning him. Instead we're hiking halfway across the frickin' countryside. And if he doesn't answer . . .'

Dougie trailed off, looked away out over the sea, a darker blue today now that the sky had clouded over. I understood. If Martin didn't answer, how the hell would we know what had happened to him? How would we find him? We'd already retraced his steps, what else could we do?

'Come on,' I said gently. 'Let's just get up there, find a signal.'

Dougie took a deep breath, blew it out and then looked at me and nodded, a ghost of a smile about his mouth. His shoulders dropped and the expression on his face became more like the boy I knew. Apart from the blood.

'Are you sure you don't want a tissue?' I asked as we started walking again, at a much more sedate pace this time.

Dougie reached up to tentatively assess his nose. He winced and dropped his hand quickly.

'Do I look terrible?'

'Red's not really your colour.'

It was a poor attempt at being funny, but Dougie laughed nonetheless, though the sound was sour.

'Here.' I dug a pack of Kleenex from my pocket and held one out to him. 'People with hay fever always carry tissues,' I explained, catching his quizzical look.

'Right.' He took a tissue and tilted his head, using it to try to stem the trickle of scarlet that was still dribbling from his nose. 'I'm not going to forgive Darren for this,' he mumbled through a face full of paper.

I understood that he meant the whole situation with Martin, not the bloody nose. Still, that was something to add to the list. Darren was the world's biggest git. I had no idea what Emma saw in him, besides his muscles. She had been upset with him after the fight, mostly because Dougie was bleeding rather than the fact that he'd lied about Martin, but now she was down there at the beach with him, not up here with us. That spoke volumes.

Dougie was right, we didn't see a single car all the way to the main road. When we reached the top, the only noise came from an electricity generator buzzing quietly. Dougie checked his phone: no signal. Mine was the same. After several minutes, a white van zoomed by. Five minutes after that, an old couple in an aged but spotlessly clean Mercedes came ambling along. They actually stopped, the man rolling his window down to check that we were all right, but his cheerful demeanour cooled rapidly when he caught the sight of Dougie's bloodied face and they didn't linger long.

'Maybe Martin did catch a ride,' Dougie murmured as the car disappeared around the corner.

Perhaps.

We climbed a fence and walked halfway through an empty field. It was the highest point for miles around and we reckoned if we were going to get a signal, it would be there.

'Well?' I asked as he held up the little rectangle. My own phone still showed zero bars.

'Hang on, it's searching,' he replied. He held it a little higher, eyes on the screen. 'Ah-ha!' He grinned at me triumphantly. It looked a little manic on his blood-spattered face. I smiled, making a mental note to hand him another tissue as soon as we'd spoken to Martin.

And I told myself we would. It was the only way I could stop from feeling sick with worry.

Dougie held the phone to his ear, gaze fixed on me.

'It's ringing,' he mouthed.

I waited, my pulse throbbing painfully, heart thudding in my chest. I couldn't hear the rings but I counted them in my head, matching each one to the surge of adrenaline-filled blood pumping around my system. One. Two. Three. Four. Any second now Dougie's face would stretch into a broad grin. Five, six, seven. Any moment, any moment now. Eight, nine, ten. Why wasn't he answering?

My stomach twisted uneasily as I watched Dougie's face cloud. Slowly he dropped the phone.

'It went to the answer machine,' he whispered.

'Try again,' I urged.

He obeyed me silently and I began my count all over again. I tried to hope but already I knew what the result would be. It was still a blow when Dougie shook his head, his expression grim.

'Nothing,' he said, confirming my fears.

'What do we do?' I asked. I felt lost, like a child. 'Should we phone his parents?'

Dougie made a face. I knew exactly what he was thinking. If we rang anyone's parents, or the police, it made it real. Terrifying. I wasn't sure that I was ready to admit that Martin was really missing.

'I don't know.' Dougie echoed my hesitation. 'What would we tell them?'

I twisted my mouth to the side. Was there any way to check if Martin was home without revealing that we'd lost him, that there was any danger? If he wasn't there I didn't want to frighten his parents, not when there was still a chance he might be hunkered down somewhere, ankle twisted or broken, waiting impatiently for us and annoyed that we hadn't found him yet.

'Don't tell them it's you,' I suggested. 'Pretend to be someone else. Ask if he's home.'

Dougie looked doubtful. 'You don't think they'll realise it's me?'

'I'll call then,' I said, though my insides squirmed at the thought. 'I've never even met them.'

To my surprise Dougie let out a laugh. A real one this time.

'Trust me, if you phone up they'll be suspicious. Martin doesn't get calls from girls.'

'Oh.' I smiled uneasily. 'Right.'

'Okay,' he sighed. 'Okay, I'm calling.'

He held the phone to his ear, but quickly he was frowning. I watched him pull the handset away, glare at the screen. 'Oh come on! You were there a minute ago!'

'What?' I asked.

'Signal's disappeared.'

Dougie tapped several different locations on the screen, but the expression on his face didn't change.

'Want to try mine?' I offered. I fumbled around in my pocket and drew out my own phone. 'What network are you on?' I asked.

'EE.'

'I'm on Vodafone. Let me double-check . . . Nope,' I sighed. 'Not a thing.'

'That's so weird,' Dougie said. 'It was fine a moment ago. I had four bars. Maybe I need to get higher.'

'Higher?' I said dubiously. We were as high up as it got.

'I could climb a tree,' Dougie suggested, eyeing up the tall birches that lined the back of the field.

I stared at him, fighting the urge to say what I thought, that he was clutching at straws. But I didn't have any better ideas. How far would we have to walk to find a house? If it came to that we'd have to go back and make Darren hand over the keys. And that wasn't a conversation I was keen to have.

'I'll give you a leg-up,' I said.

With me giving him a punt up to the lowest branches, Dougie was able to scale the sturdiest-looking tree in quick, lithe movements. He paused in the centre, testing out the higher branches with his hands. They swayed easily under the pressure.

'Don't go too high,' I warned. 'The last thing we need is for you to break your neck!'

He chuckled, but stopped trying to climb higher.

'Any luck?'

'No. Yes! We have lift-off! Hang on, it's ringing now.' I waited, both anxious and eager. Then . . . 'What the hell?'

'What?' No answer. 'Dougie, what is it?'

'My battery just died.'

I huffed a laugh, though it really wasn't funny.

'You're joking?'

'No.'

'Hang on.' I dug into my pockets again. 'Catch! See if I have signal.'

I threw my phone up into the tree, wincing apprehensively, but Dougie's deft hands caught it easily. I watched him jab at the screen.

'How do you turn it on?' he called down.

'It is on,' I replied. 'Is the screen locked?'

'No. Heather, it's definitely not on.'

I looked up at him, mystified. It had been on a minute ago. Maybe my fingers accidentally hit the switch when I threw it, although you had to hold it down for at least five seconds. I described the way to start it up, then waited. And waited.

'Nope, it's not turning on. Could it be out of power?'

'No. I still had half a battery. That should do me till at least tomorrow.'

'Well, it's not working.'

'Chuck it down,' I sighed, exasperated.

Dougie obediently dropped it into my waiting hand and I plunged my thumb down onto the power key, waiting for the little red Vodafone symbol to dance across the screen. It didn't.

'That's not right,' I murmured quietly. Was it broken?

'I told you,' Dougie called down.

'I don't understand,' I said, raising my voice so he could hear. 'It was fine a second ago.' I looked about me. 'Could it be the generator thing? Can it drain batteries?'

'Dunno.' Dougie's voice was closer now. I looked up to see him slipping down through the branches. 'Just our luck this weekend.'

He scuttled lightly onto the final branch and hovered there for a moment, judging the distance to the ground. As he bent his knees, preparing to jump, I heard a deep crack resound from the trunk. Dougie's face dropped in time with the branch and both of them tumbled to the ground.

'Dougie!' I cried out, already reaching for him. He was sprawled on the ground, tangled up in the whippy, leaf-covered shoots spiking off from the broken branch. Even as his hands tore at the foliage I knew something was wrong. Peeking out from the confusion of glossy green was his ankle, turned awkwardly under him. His mouth twisted in a grimace of pain and he gripped his leg just above his foot. He groaned, still trying to extricate himself from the chunk of tree.

'Are you all right?' I gasped.

Dougie huffed. 'Yeah, I think so.' I took hold of his hand and hauled him to his feet. He hissed in pain as soon as he tried to put any weight on the damaged ankle. 'Maybe,' he amended.

'Is it broken?' I asked.

Please let it not be. How the hell was I meant to get him back down to the campsite and the car if he couldn't walk? There was no way I could carry him that far.

'No, doesn't feel like it. Hurts, though.' He blew out a breath, tried gingerly to step on his right foot. I watched him grit his teeth. 'I think it's just sprained.' He laughed, though the sound was slightly hysterical.

'What's funny?' I asked, my eyebrows rising in puzzlement and disbelief. Laughing was the last thing I felt like doing.

'It's just . . . could it get any worse?'

I smiled, though the muscles in my jaw had to work harder than usual to achieve the effect.

'Don't say that,' I warned. Then I sighed. 'You're not having much of a birthday trip. What are we going to do, Dougie?'

We still had no idea what had happened to Martin and now Dougie probably needed a visit to A&E.

'I don't know,' he murmured. 'Let's just get back to the campsite. Then we'll work it out. Darren'll have to drive us somewhere.'

I wasn't so sure. The look on Darren's face when we left had been unambiguous: he was furious. And in my experience a furious Darren was not a helpful one. Still, maybe if he saw the state Dougie was in he'd warm up a little. That's if I could get him there.

'Think you can walk?' I asked, eyeing him dubiously. He was trying to stand normally but it was obvious that it was agony to put any weight on his foot.

'I'll try,' he offered.

It was very slow progress. Dougie attempted to walk by himself at first but he couldn't manage anything more than a snail's pace, limping a few inches at a time. His face was drawn and his top teeth were gnawing down on his lip hard enough to draw blood. After only a few hundred metres, he had to surrender.

'Look, I'll wait here,' he said, preparing to lower himself down onto the grass verge. 'You can walk back down and get Darren to come up with the car.'

I paled. I did not want to have to face Darren without Dougie.

'Maybe I could carry you?' I suggested.

Dougie snorted.

'Are you Wonder Woman at the weekend?' he asked.

'No,' I admitted. 'But look, put your arm round my shoulder. I'll be your human crutch.'

That worked a lot better. Dougie had to walk in a slightly awkward crouch because I was so much shorter than him, but it meant he was able to take a step without dropping his full weight onto the rapidly swelling joint. It was hard work and my arm, wrapped around his waist and gripping him so hard my fingers went white, quickly started to ache. But I knew we only had a couple of miles, maybe a little less, to go.

The sun was at its peak by the time we limped back to the car park, although it was hidden behind a thick bank of clouds. Hungry, knackered and aching, I dropped Dougie against the bonnet of the Volvo. He slumped down by the dirty grey metal, his mouth pressed into a thin line. A sheen of sweat glistened on his forehead.

'How does it feel?' I asked stupidly.

128

'Sore.' He flashed me a half-smile. 'I can't wait to get my trainer off. It feels like it's about to explode out of the fabric.'

'Maybe we shouldn't,' I suggested. 'We might not be able to get it back on.'

'Doesn't matter. I'm not going anywhere except in the car. Come on, let's go talk to the delightful Darren.'

I stared at Dougie for a moment, trying to decide if he was delirious or joking. He looked wary under the wink he gave me, so I went with the latter.

Although it looked nothing the same – it was broad daylight and this time our things were strewn around the campsite – I had a strange sense of déjà vu when I hit the sinking softness of the sandy beach. For some reason I had the same tense, uncomfortable feeling I'd had last night when we'd come back to the darkened site to find Martin not where we'd hoped he'd be. It was the silence. It was the emptiness. It was the fact that, once again, no one was there.

'Emma?' I called.

No answer. I looked towards our tent. I really didn't want to have to go in there looking for them. Dougie was already struggling with the uneven, constantly shifting surface, though. I couldn't ask him to wade about all over the beach. Making an embarrassed noise under my breath, I plodded over.

'Emma?' I called again, still hoping her head would peek out and I wouldn't have to interrupt. No such luck.

I drummed my fingers against the fabric of the tent, just in case they hadn't heard me yelling, just to give them a few more seconds, then I gingerly eased the zip down. I squinted into the interior cautiously, ready to shut my eyes. Then I opened them wide in confusion. The tent was as empty as the beach.

'Dougie?' I spun on the spot. Dougie was over by the other tent; the flap was wide open and it too was clearly unoccupied. 'They're not here.'

'What do you mean they're not here?'

I moved to the side and gestured to the vacant tent.

'They're not here,' I repeated.

'For God's sake!' Dougie hobbled over to peer inside for himself. As if I could have missed them amongst the melee of clothes, sleeping bags and toiletries. I hadn't. They were gone.

CHAPTER FOURTEEN

'You don't think they went looking for Martin as well, do you?'

'No.' Dougie's voice was certain. But where else could they be? The car was still there so they hadn't gone far.

'Do you think they just went for a walk?'

'Maybe.' His doubt was easy to hear.

I drummed my fingernails against the plastic armrest of my chair. The sharp, staccato noises jarred my nerves, but it was better than sitting still, doing nothing. I was finding it a challenge just to stay in the chair.

It was incredibly frustrating. I wanted to drive somewhere, raise the alarm for Martin. I wanted to get Dougie to a hospital and have his ankle X-rayed in case there was a fracture under all that swelling. He'd propped his foot up on one of the other chairs, and scrabbled around at the bottom of the cooler and put the last dregs of ice into a towel that was now wrapped around the joint, but had taken my advice and left his shoe on. He wasn't complaining but I could see that it was hurting him.

Most of all I wanted to find Emma and wring her neck! How could she be so inconsiderate? I expected nothing better of Darren, but not Emma. They hadn't even waited around to find out if we'd managed to get in touch with Martin!

'I'm getting a jumper,' I announced, lurching to my feet. I wasn't cold; I just wanted an excuse to move about, to do something. Inside the tent I scrabbled in my bag, hunting for my zip-up top. A crumpled sheaf of paper floated to the ground as I did so. It had been caught under the flap, the reason I hadn't noticed it before. Curious, I grabbed it. Opening it up, I recognised Emma's sloppy writing.

> *Going to find more wood for fire. Think there's a cove just round the headland. Back in an hour. Em x*

I pursed my lips as I glared down at it. The note did not make up for the fact that they'd disappeared. Nor did it excuse their lack of concern about Martin. And I still hadn't forgiven Emma for siding with Darren. At least we knew where they were, though.

'Found a note,' I called out, emerging from the tent, jumper in one hand, scrap of paper in the other. 'They've gone for more firewood at the cove.'

Dougie's eyes narrowed and I knew that he was still annoyed as well.

'It says they'll be back in an hour,' I said, handing him the note. 'Don't know how long ago that was. They shouldn't be long, though –' I broke off in the face of Dougie's dissatisfied grimace.

'This is ridiculous! We can't just wait around – we need to

132

do something about Martin.' He looked at me. 'Can you check your phone again?'

There wasn't much point. Even if it turned on, there was no signal down here. I did as he asked, however, digging out my mobile and banging down on the power button. Nothing.

'Still dead.'

He made a frustrated growl under his breath.

I stared at him thoughtfully. Did we have to wait for Darren?

'Can you drive?' I asked. It was a different question than before: I wasn't sure his ankle would hold up enough to push the pedals.

He made a face. 'I don't know. Maybe.' He pulled his leg off the chair and pressed his foot onto the sand. Grimaced in pain. 'Maybe not,' he admitted. 'Can you?'

No. I'd never had a lesson. Never even reversed my parents' car out of the driveway. The Volvo was like a boat and the thought of trying to navigate the steep, narrow pot-holed road up to civilisation was terrifying. Even more frightening was the thought of Darren's reaction if he found out I'd driven his car. I wasn't entirely convinced that he'd be above punching *me* in the face! But Dougie was looking at me hopefully. I shifted from foot to foot on the sand, uncomfortable.

'I don't know . . .'

'I'll help you,' he offered. He grabbed my hand, his fist warm around my icy fingers. 'Come on, Heather. We still don't know where Martin is.'

I couldn't say no. 'I'll try,' I mumbled.

Dougie directed me to where Darren kept his keys – thankfully he hadn't taken them with him in a fit of pique – and

I helped him limp back to the car. Dougie lowered himself gingerly into the passenger seat while I yanked open the door to the driver's side. I couldn't even reach the pedals and had to yank the seat forward with an ear-splitting screech.

'Right,' I said. 'What do I do?'

'Putting the keys in the ignition is a good start,' Dougie offered, grinning at me. I didn't grin back, I was too nervous. My hands shook a little as I fired the key into the slot.

I twisted the key. Nothing happened. It wouldn't turn, not even a little bit. I twisted harder, but I was worried about snapping it.

'What's wrong?' Dougie asked.

'It won't turn,' I complained.

'Twist hard.'

'I am!'

Dougie sighed and reached over me. I sat back, a petulant expression on my face, and watched him try. My scowl became smug when he had no more success.

'Hang on, the wheel lock's on.' He jiggled the steering wheel, then went back to twisting the key. This time it rotated, but the engine didn't spark. It didn't even cough. It was a replay of the scene by the motorway: nothing but a series of dissatisfying clicks.

'Heap of junk!' Dougie exploded. He banged down on the middle of the steering wheel, making the horn blare out. 'The battery's gone again.'

I said nothing; I'd worked that out for myself.

Dougie sat hunched across me, still gripping the wheel like he could make the car start with the power of his mind.

'Now what?' I asked, after a full minute of silence.

He sighed, aggravated.

'Now we wait for Darren and Emma,' he said after a moment. 'We'll have to hike back up to the road and you won't be able to help me all the way up there. Unless you want to go by yourself?' He looked at me and I quickly shook my head.

Once more, we slowly made our way back to the still-deserted beach. Just for something to do, we made lunch. Neither of us had eaten breakfast and it was hard to decide if I felt sick because I was worried about Martin or just because I was hungry. I made myself eat, forcing in one mouthful at a time.

They still hadn't arrived by the time we'd finished eating. With nothing better to do, we sat and watched the constant movement of the water. We didn't speak. There was nothing to be gained by berating Darren and Emma, or guessing where Martin was. That just made the anger and fear spike by degrees. After a while I dug the brooch back out of my pocket and started to stroke it, running my fingers around the curved edge, tracing the carvings with my fingertips. Like before, the metal remained cold, despite having spent the morning snug against my body.

Eventually I became aware of Dougie staring at me, staring at it.

'I want to take this back,' I said softly. 'I feel like we shouldn't have taken it. It's not ours, and it means something to someone. They put it there for a reason; that's where it belongs.'

When Dougie didn't respond, I turned to stare at him. His expression was unreadable.

'Well?' I asked.

'If you want to,' he said tonelessly.

I tried not to make a face, but I didn't like his reaction. I pursed my lips, feeling the need to explain myself further.

'I just . . . I just feel like it's unlucky or something. Look at everything that's happened since we picked the damn thing up.' Dougie was frowning so I went on hurriedly. 'I mean, we had that big fight and Martin stormed off, then he went missing. Then all that trouble with the phones, your ankle –' I pointed at his swollen leg. 'Now the car won't start, and Emma and Darren aren't here. They should have been back by now.'

Dougie huffed a laugh.

'Darren and Emma'll be fine,' he said, crossing the last item off my list. 'As for the rest of it . . . Martin was uncomfortable with Darren coming along from the start –' (This didn't surprise me, though I was a little put out that he hadn't said anything to me himself.) ' – and the bloody Volvo is an unreliable piece of crap, no matter what Darren says.'

'I know, but I still want to take it back. It feels . . . it feels weird, having it. I don't like it.'

'Well, I'm not in any fit shape to go hiking,' Dougie said. 'And finding Martin is kind of a priority –' He broke off, looking closely at my face. 'But if you want rid of it –'

Before I realised what he was going to do, he'd taken the brooch out of my hand. He shifted upright in his chair and, curving his arm back, launched the little circlet into the air. It arced across the cloud-covered sky then landed with a splash into the choppy waves, several metres into the sea. I gaped at the water, then at him. I hadn't meant that, I hadn't meant that at all.

'Gone,' he said, looking at me solemnly.

'Dougie!'

The uncomfortable feeling I'd had about the brooch went into overdrive. There was absolutely no way to get it back now. I knew roughly where it had landed, but the constant motion of the waves would already have shifted it and the sea was dark and murky and uninviting.

Now I felt worse than a thief. I was a vandal. A desecrator. A . . . a . . . I wasn't even sure what the word was. My stomach churned.

But I didn't want to fight with Dougie – not with everything else that was going on – so I bit back the angry words that were forming, bitter on my tongue.

'I want to go and look for Emma and Darren,' I said, standing abruptly.

He started shaking his head before I'd even finished.

'My ankle –'

'I know,' I cut him off. 'You stay here. I'll go. That way we definitely won't miss them.' And I could get away for a little while and cool my ire. It was just a brooch, after all; there was no reason for the whispering in my head, telling me that discarding the thing so flagrantly was a very, very bad move.

'You want to go on your own?' Dougie said dubiously. 'Heather, you don't even know where the cove is.'

'Well –' That was a point. Needlessly, I dusted my sand-free hands against my jeans whilst I thought of a counter-argument. 'It's another beach, right?' It wasn't really a question but Dougie nodded anyway. 'Surely I can just follow the coast round?'

'Probably.' He looked at me, unconvinced. 'But what if you get lost?'

'I'll be fine. I just . . . I just don't want to sit here any longer.'

I didn't give him another chance to argue. Twisting away, I headed to my tent to change into better walking shoes, drag another layer of clothes on. It had clouded over and was getting chilly on the beach; it'd be even colder up on the headland – the tide was in too far to follow the rocks round the shoreline.

Dougie watched me leave, his expression unhappy. I guessed he was worried about what would happen if I, too, failed to return and he was stuck there on the beach, unable to hike his way out. I wasn't going far, though. And anyway, his parents knew exactly where we were. They'd come looking for us eventually.

That thought cheered me. We were due back in three days and we easily had enough food to last that long. If we couldn't get Darren's car going, and if Dougie wasn't fit to walk back to civilisation, his dad would come and get us.

The only problem was Martin. I couldn't bear three more days of worrying about what had happened to him. I hoped to hell he was back home, vilifying us to his parents and the rest of our friends. I hoped I'd get the chance to kill him for buggering off.

It was a short trudge up the steep hillside to the low cliff that curved round the edge of the land. The path was compacted dirt coated with loose gravel that skittered out from under the treads of my shoes, and in places I had to use the long grass to steady myself. Up top, the view was glorious. The sea stretched in front of me, undulating to the horizon, and far out I could see a boat. To my back were the heather-covered hills but I didn't turn to look at them. I knew the cairn would be there, a beacon in the middle of the landscape; I imagined it silently condemning me.

I started off again, following a thin path that was little more than downtrodden grass. The cove couldn't be far. I hoped not, anyway, because the sky was darkening. I knew night wouldn't fall for at least another couple of hours, but the murky half-light was unnerving. It made the world a little blurry, a little less defined. I didn't like it. Strange shapes kept leaping out of the corner of my eye, making me start until I recognised them for the whipping branch of a tree or a bird launching itself into the sky.

'Emma, I am going to kill you,' I muttered as I stalked along. It made me feel a bit less isolated and alone to hear someone speak, even if it was only me.

I wondered how long our little friendship group was going to survive after this trip was over. Martin was not going to want to be anywhere near Darren after this, which was no real loss, but where Darren went, Emma went. To be honest, I was rapidly losing the desire to be in Emma's company myself. Darren seemed to bring out a whole host of new, unattractive qualities: vanity, selfishness, feigned weakness so that boys would fawn over her. I could hear her coquettish giggle in my head, setting my teeth on edge. Feeling vicious, I parodied it then giggled again as I listened to the simpering peals vibrating back at me. Then I heard another sound. A colder sound.

I heard Emma scream.

CHAPTER FIFTEEN

Now

'Emma was screaming, you said. These are your words. Do you remember telling the police that, Heather? That you heard her, from the path?'

I ignore him. My eyes are on the clock, watching the minute hand tick round. Three minutes. I smile to myself smugly. Another hour gone and once again Dr Petersen has yielded little more from me than a word or two. I see him glance at the wall, too, register the time. He'll be annoyed, and that makes me even happier. All the qualifications and certificates in the world can't mask the fact that he's failing to make any progress whatsoever.

No matter what he says, what he thinks, I am winning.

I shift in my seat, preparing to rise. To begin the long walk back through the plush hallways until we get to the polished linoleum and bare white walls that family members and visiting dignitaries never get to see, deep within the bowels of the institution; Petersen's personal little empire. My escort coughs lightly behind me and I know he's warning me: he's there. If I should make any sudden movements – explode forward, launch myself at Dr Petersen as I have done in the past, and quite successfully, I might add – he will stop me. At least, he thinks he will. I am not so sure. He's big, though. And young.

It doesn't matter; I have no plans to attack Dr Petersen today. I'm just getting ready to leave. To go back to my non-life and stare at the walls. The television. The other 'patients' who actually are total whack-jobs. I stare a lot. I'm doing it to Dr Petersen right now, waiting for him to give up the ghost and dismiss me.

He turns away from the clock, back to me. I see a twitch as he registers the change in the way I'm looking at him – expectant relief rather than complete disdain and loathing – but he smothers the expression before I can read the emotion underneath.

'Is something wrong, Heather?' he asks me calmly.

Too calmly. My brain registers the odd tone – too nice, too smug – but I'm so desperate to get out of the room I'm not paying proper attention. Instead I speak. Might as well, there's nothing he can do now with his perfect schedule and all that.

'Our hour's up,' I say. A monotone. Another thing I do a lot.

'Oh, I see.' He's still calm. Still self-satisfied. What am I missing? 'Well, Heather, I cleared you a double slot today. I thought you and I needed to reconnect, and what with this being the anniversary of the event . . .'

His words melt away. There's ringing in my ears and shock rebounds around my head. Two hours, not one. This sends me reeling.

Because it's hard. I sit here and pretend that I don't care, but it's hard. Of course I care. Not about Dr Petersen, but Martin . . . Emma . . . Dougie. Even Darren. Not talking about it, swallowing it back and forcing it down – deep, deep down – isn't helping. On the outside I'm a hard shell: detached, emotionless, cold. But on the inside I'm burning, suffering my own personal purgatory. And he knows. That bastard Petersen knows, and he will not rest until he pulls it out of me piece by piece.

Hate courses through me and I grab onto it, use to it brace myself until I can feel the ground under my feet again. Until I can feel some semblance of control come back to me. It's fragile, though. Rage comes in waves, unlike contempt, and when it ebbs back out again, that's when I'm vulnerable.

I take a deep breath. Make myself look at Dr Petersen.

God, how I hate you. But you will not break me.

'Fine,' I spit through tight lips.

He smiles at me; that's another point chalked up to him. The rage burns hotter. I am not performing well today. Probably because it *is* the anniversary and yes, I *was* aware of that fact before he so kindly reminded me.

'You didn't like Darren, did you, Heather?'

There wasn't much to like. I don't nod or speak, just stare at him, waiting for whatever's coming next. He sees that and drags the moment out, taking a sip from an expensive bottle of fizzy water. The hiss as he twists the cap is oddly appropriate: it's snakelike, just like him.

'You were jealous of him. Of the way he was stealing your friend from you. Weren't you?'

I raise one eyebrow in superb disparagement. Dr Petersen sits back a little and I'm even able to crack the barest hint of a smile.

No, I was not jealous of Darren. I might be a little bit now, though – at least he doesn't have to sit here and listen to this.

'Do you want to know what I think, Heather?' No, but Petersen isn't really asking. 'I think you needed to get Darren out of the way. I think he was suspicious, a thorn in your side. Was it easier with him than with Martin?' I look away. Not at the floor, that would send entirely the wrong message. I go back to the wall, those fancy glass-framed certificates. Foolish Dr Petersen, they're potential weapons too. I try to use the wry humour of my thoughts to damp down my anger, but I can't drown out his voice. 'After all, with Darren gone, Emma might have come back to you afterwards. Was that it, Heather?'

I swallow back a wave of sadness, because Emma is not coming back. Not ever.

But I don't want to think about that. I will not think about that. I grit my teeth, engineer synthetic anger and use it as armour. It can't protect inside my head, though, and that's the bit Dr Petersen is most interested in. I feel a wave of panic that nearly propels me out of my chair. I am not controlled, I am not composed, and I want the hell out of here before I do something stupid like let him in.

'I need to go to the bathroom,' I say.

It's a child's tactic, but I'm clutching at straws. I look at him pleadingly, hating myself more than him at this moment. Please, please, after all you've put me through, give me this.

He shakes his head.

'We are not finished here, Heather.'

'I have to go,' I insist. 'I have my period.'

That's a lie. He looks down at my file as he considers it and I wonder if the truth is written in there. They keep such meticulous records: the drugs I take, the drugs I don't take; my weight, my height, the length of my fingernails; my mood; what I'm eating and how much of it. I would not be surprised to know they have my menstrual cycle charted too.

They must have taught strategic mercy at whatever nut-job university Dr Petersen obtained his PhD from, because he acquiesces with a subtle nod. I rise, thinking I'm leaving, but it's a discreet door to the left that my escort guides me over to. He opens it and I see a tiny room, less than a metre square and fitted with a minuscule circular sink. Beyond that is a second door, half ajar, revealing a gleam of white porcelain. Not an escape then, but a reprieve at least. Dr Petersen acknowledges my lie by neglecting to offer me a tampon or any other such accoutrement.

I glance uneasily at the escort as he keeps close to my heels – surely he doesn't think he's coming in with me? – but he pauses in the sink room and lets me proceed, alone, to the cubicle.

There's a mirror here, in the toilet rather than by the sink outside. I don't know why – does Dr Petersen send his patients in here for self-reflection? I catch my face staring back at me and for a millisecond, just the smallest fraction of time, I see something else. Something black and evil and terrifying, hovering over me like a malignant aura. I start and can't stop myself from crying out, but I muffle the sound before it can reach beyond this claustrophobic square of space. Another blink and the thing is gone. But my racing heartbeat remains.

I sink down onto the closed pan and drop my head into my hands. I concentrate on breathing normally. I know Dr Petersen's patience will not let me draw out the rest of our 'session' in here; I have only five minutes at best before I'll have to face him again. It's important to be calm, collected, when that happens.

In. Out. In. Out. I count the breaths. Slow them gradually. Taming my pulse is harder. It speeds through my veins, screaming.

A gentle tap on the door. A summons. I stand, sniff, then swallow. Just to keep up the pretence, I flush the toilet. Then I smooth my clothes and open the door. It's almost too small for me to squeeze in beside my escort to use the sink but I make a show of washing my hands, using the fancy soap dispenser, which daintily releases a splodge of pearly liquid that smells like oranges. Pretending I'm not unnerved by the man-mountain standing just inches behind me, I take my time coating and then rinsing the fingers on my good hand. All too soon the door is open and Petersen is smiling pleasantly at me from behind his desk.

The leather is still faintly warm as I sink back down into my chair. It should be comforting, but it isn't.

'Where were we?' Petersen asks.

Trying to look as if I'm just idly glancing around the room, I let my eyes flicker to the clock. Forty minutes. I can last forty minutes.

'Emma.' He says her name triumphantly, as if his question was real, as if he hasn't sat and planned this line of attack while I hid in the bathroom. 'You disapproved of her relationship with Darren, didn't you? In fact –' he ruffles several note-covered sheets in front of him – 'you were quite disparaging about it. You said since they'd met she'd become silly. Shallow. Pathetic, you called her more than once. Do you remember calling her those things, Heather?' Pause. 'Did you think that you were better than her?'

Yes.

No. Maybe.

No.

I hadn't believed her, though.

As angry as I was at my parents, the police, Dr Petersen – all the people who refused to listen to me – I hadn't believed her.

CHAPTER SIXTEEN

Then

The sound rent the air. It froze the breath in my lungs, freezing me. Like a statue I stood there, listening to it bounce off the water, the hills, before finally falling silent. There was an instant of sweet relief, then Emma screamed again.

This time I rocketed towards the noise, stumbling over tufts of grass and large pebbles, my feet fighting to find purchase on the uneven ground. I didn't know where I was going, only that I had to follow the sounds ringing in my ears.

Then, just as suddenly as it had started again, it stopped. I ground to a halt, staring about me, wide-eyed. I was still on the narrow cliff-top path, the sea pounding the rocks down to my right. It was darker than it had been just five minutes before, though I knew it wasn't time for nightfall yet. I looked up at the clouds and they were tumultuous, black and bulging. A cold mist descended in a feather-light curtain, dropping like a fog. Water droplets caught in my eyelashes and the world around me receded to no more than a few metres in every direction. Cautiously, I started moving forward again.

'Emma?' I shouted.

My voice bounced back at me, but nothing from Emma. I tried once more.

'Emma? Where are you?'

Still nothing. I continued on and just a minute or so later came to a fork in the trail. One path carried on before me, skirting the curve of the coast. The other branched off to the right and I could just see it begin to dip down towards the water before the misting rain obscured the view. I guessed it must lead to the cove.

Clenching my hands into fists to stop them from shaking, I started down the second path. The way was bumpy, already slippery. My shoes couldn't find any grip and I slipped and slid my way down. The sound of the sea scratching at the shore grew steadily louder until abruptly the hard-packed trail gave way to mounds of small stones that clattered noisily under my weight. I'd reached the cove.

I looked around me. The rain seemed to be worse down here, as if it was lifting from the sea as well as dropping from the sky. The cliff walls were dark, streaked with white where lime had leached through. The beach itself wasn't sandy but pebbly and strewn with seaweed and driftwood. Dougie's dad had been right: this was a good place to find firewood. The one thing I didn't see was either of my friends.

'Emma?' I called again, then, slightly more quietly, 'Darren?'

They didn't reply but a bird squawked angrily from somewhere above me. I shifted from foot to foot, uncomfortable. Even with my jumper on I was cold and there was an eerie feel about the place, as if dozens of pairs of eyes were watching me from the tiny dark crevices in the rock walls. I took a half-step back, my feet responding to my body's urge to get the hell out of there, but I managed to stop before I could give in to the urge to turn and run.

Where were Darren and Emma?

I forced myself forward. Stones scattered in front of me, the noise making me catch my breath. I made a second, more thorough assessment of my surroundings. Though it was a small cove, hemmed in by the high cliff walls, there were plenty of places two people could conceal themselves.

'Emma, this isn't funny!' I said loudly. If they were playing a joke on me . . .

I knew they weren't, though. The new, unimproved Emma screamed a lot: when she didn't get her own way, when she wanted boys – or anyone – to notice her, when there was a spider. But I'd never heard her scream like that before. It had been real, terror-filled.

I was halfway towards the water when I heard something. I paused, cocked my head, trying to pinpoint the direction, trying to work out what it was. It wasn't continuous, but started and stopped in an uneven pattern, and it was oddly muffled. After several long seconds I realised what I was listening to.

'Emma?' I hurried towards the sound, my eyes on a large rock erupting out of the pebbles, near the far cliff.

The closer I got, the louder the sobbing was until I was positive I would find her there. Still, when I rounded the boulder I skidded to a stop, shocked.

Emma was huddled on the ground, her back wedged into a corner of the rock. Her arms were folded up to protect her chest, hands covering her mouth, and her feet were in constant motion, scrabbling, trying to propel her further backwards, although there was nowhere to go.

'Emma!' She didn't react. Her eyes were sightless, gazing in my direction yet looking straight through me. 'Emma!' I closed the distance between us, crashing to my knees beside her. I grabbed her shoulder but she still took no notice of me. I shook her, hard, and finally got her attention. Her eyes bored into me, petrified.

'Heather!' Her fingers were claws, digging painfully into my collarbone.

'Emma, where's Darren?'

She shook her head, mouth opening and closing uselessly.

'Emma,' I pulled her forward and banged her back onto the wall, trying to jolt her back to reality. 'Where's Darren?'

'Gone,' she whispered. Her eyes were crazed.

'Gone?' I frowned. 'What do you mean, gone?' Then a thought occurred to me. 'Emma, did he go in the water?' Nothing. 'Is he in the water, Emma?' I was shouting right in her face. Instead of answering, she started crying.

Convinced now that Darren – idiotic Darren – had tried to show off by wading into the swell pounding the rocks, I whirled round and started scanning the jagged formations jutting out of the water. My eyes hunted for a glimpse of the orange t-shirt he'd been wearing earlier. Jesus, he could be anywhere! If he'd bashed his head off one of those rocks . . . If he'd gone out too far . . . It was cold enough that he might have just lost consciousness, be floating somewhere, facedown.

I took a half-step, still not sure what I was going to do. Something icy cold wrapped itself around my wrist and tightened like a manacle.

'Don't leave me!' Emma gasped.

She'd come forward to grab me, but as soon as I turned she scuttled backwards, pulling me with her.

'Emma –'

'Don't leave me,' she repeated.

I shook my head at her, frustrated.

'We need to help Darren,' I said. 'Where did he go in? Think, Emma!' I snapped, because she was rocking again, eyes sightless.

'Don't go in there,' she mumbled into her fingers, hands back up at her face.

'What?' My voice was sharp.

'Don't go in the water, Heather. Don't, don't go in –' She broke off, coughing out more sobs.

I gritted my teeth. My initial terror was rapidly dwindling. There was nothing wrong with Emma. But Darren . . . I was getting pretty worried about him.

'Emma!' I grabbed at her t-shirt again, made her look at me. 'Where's Darren?'

She gazed wildly about, eyes searching the sky, then she fixed her sights on me.

'Gone.'

'What the hell's going on?' Dougie came hobbling across the beach as soon as he saw our silhouette against the skyline. We must have appeared as a single confused smudge, huddled together the way we were. I was fully supporting Emma's

151

weight, her arm gripping my neck so tightly she was choking me. Tiny as she was, she felt twice as heavy as Dougie had earlier. She wasn't injured; she just refused to move on her own. It had been carry her or leave her. I'd deliberated for at least a minute before hauling her to her feet.

'Help,' I gasped, stumbling into him and momentarily forgetting about his ankle.

'What's wrong with her?' he asked. I couldn't speak but bent over and gripped my knees. 'Emma? Emma, are you all right?'

Emma didn't reply either but she launched herself into his arms. I eyed her suspiciously – this was much more like typical Emma behaviour – but she was shaking from head to toe and those little gasping cries were still juddering out of her lips. Dougie stared at me over her shoulder, completely bewildered.

'Where's Darren?' he asked me.

I lifted a shoulder, an apologetic grimace on my face.

'I don't know, she wouldn't say. She just kept telling me "he's gone".' My breathing was returning to normal, although the muscles in my legs were burning, my back aching.

'What do you mean, gone?' Dougie demanded.

'Gone,' I heard Emma mumble against the fabric of his jumper.

'I'm sorry, Dougie. That's all I can get out of her.' I ran my hand through my hair, agitated. 'She's totally freaked out.'

Dougie nodded awkwardly, because Emma was tucked under his jaw, and tried to smile at me, but the worry was plain in his eyes. First his best friend, now Darren. What the hell was going on?

'Help me get her to camp?' he said.

Together, we half-dragged, half-carried Emma down to the fire pit, which was flickering welcomingly. The flames drew me in and I was grateful to Dougie for lighting it with the last of the driftwood. More than the glow that chased away the gathering dark, I was desperate for the heat. I was shaking almost as much as Emma, chilled down to my very bones.

Even with his badly swollen ankle, Dougie took most of Emma's weight, supporting her entirely as he tried to manoeuvre her into one of the folding chairs. He dropped her gently, but she wouldn't even hold herself up, slipping down and folding like a rag doll onto the sand. Dougie sighed and reached for her, but I stopped him.

'Leave her there,' I said. 'She's freezing.'

'Yeah, but –'

'Just leave her,' I repeated.

Emma didn't look up, didn't acknowledge us, just gazed into the flames, rocking gently.

'What the hell happened?' Dougie asked again.

I had no answer for him. Only Emma knew, and she wasn't talking. I stared down at her, watched her rub her arms, the skin already turning pink from being too close to the blazing heat.

'I'll get her a jumper,' I muttered.

I disappeared into the shadowy darkness of our tent and dropped to my knees. The air mattress had almost completely deflated and my knees dug painfully into the ground. I ignored the discomfort, rooting around in Emma's backpack, chewing down hard on my tongue. Tears were blinding me and I didn't want Dougie to see.

Emma wasn't acting. She was terrified and it had something to do with Darren's disappearance. I hadn't even been able to get her to confirm that he'd gone into the water. When I tried

153

to go and look for him, scanning the waves, she'd erupted, hauling me back, away from the shore. I'd done the best I could, fighting Emma off every second, but in the end, I'd had to abandon the search and get her out of there.

I was scared. Darren was gone. Martin was still missing and we had no way to get away from the beach. The Volvo was dead, Dougie was in no fit shape to be hiking God knows how many miles to the main road, and neither was Emma. Panic bubbled in my throat but I swallowed it back, took a deep breath. My fingers closed around the fuzzy warmth of Emma's pink cardigan and I dragged it out, pulled it to my chest. Her perfume rose out of the wool and the familiar smell cleared my head a little.

Scrubbing my cheeks to make sure there was no evidence of my little meltdown, I scrambled to my feet and lurched back towards the safety of the fire.

'She any better?' I asked as I approached.

Emma was still hunkered down on the ground; Dougie sat staring at her, anxiety etched across his face. He shook his head at me, blinking ferociously. I looked away.

'Emma?' I dropped down so I was on her level, held out the cardigan to her. She had stopped rocking and though her face was still deathly pale at least she wasn't wailing any more. 'Put this on,' I ordered.

She did as I asked, obediently folding her arms into the garment, then buttoning it right up to her throat, but her eyes continued to stare into the brightness at the heart of the fire.

'What do we do?' Dougie asked, his voice tight. I ignored him, concentrating on Emma.

'Emma.' I reached out and took one of her hands in mine, forced it to lie still. 'Emma, look at me.'

She did, though I wasn't sure that she was actually focusing on me.

'Emma, where's Darren?'

Her face folded, tears brimming over straight away. She started shaking her head, the movement quickly escalating, threatening to get out of control. I reached out my other hand and grabbed her chin. Maybe I should start with something easier.

'You guys went to get firewood?'

A nod.

'Down at the cove?'

Another nod.

'Did you have a fight?'

A shake of her head. No.

'Did Darren go off somewhere, then? By himself?'

No again.

I looked at her, a crease of confusion between my eyebrows as I tried to work out what could possibly have happened. Had I missed him?

'Emma, is Darren still at the cove?'

She paused before answering and my stomach dropped – had I left him there? I didn't want to go back out into the dark. To my relief she shook her head slowly from side to side. Another no.

I was out of suggestions.

'Emma, where is Darren?'

'Gone,' she repeated, the word twisted through tears.

'Gone where, Em?' I said it as gently as I could manage, but frustration threatened to destroy my outward calm. We were going round in circles.

'Was there someone else there, Emma?'

I jumped. I had almost forgotten Dougie was there, silently watching. I went back to Emma just in time to see her finish nodding her head. What?

'Who?' I asked, too sharply, too eagerly. She shrank back but I didn't register the gesture, pounding her with questions. 'Did you see him? Was it just one man? What did he look like?'

'Not who,' Emma whispered.

'Not who? What you mean, not who? Emma, talk sense! Were they old or young? Did you recognise them? Did you see which way they went?'

'Not who,' she said again, even quieter this time. 'Not who, *what*.'

CHAPTER SEVENTEEN

'She's totally off her nut.' I sighed and buried my face in my hands.

'Maybe,' Dougie said quietly beside me.

'Maybe?' I tuned to glare at him. 'She thinks a creature from the deep came and swallowed him!'

That was how Emma had explained it. In between gasps and sobs and tears she'd described how the air at the cove had gone still, the water smooth. She'd stopped trying to kick stringy wet seaweed off a broken log and turned just in time to see a black mass burst from the water. Handless, it had nonetheless managed to grab hold of Darren, pluck him from the shore like he was weightless, then vanished with him, disappearing into the sea.

'Totally off her nut,' I repeated under my breath.

Dougie heard me but he didn't react.

Emma was asleep in the boys' tent, knocked out by two antihistamine pills Dougie had unearthed from Martin's bag. I was too wired to even think about going to bed. Tension

157

gathered in a knot between my shoulder blades and my knee jiggled constantly as my left foot worked itself into the sand. Besides, the fire was nowhere near burned out and I didn't want to leave it unsupervised. Nor did I want to prematurely extinguish it with spadefuls of wet sand, as Dougie had suggested. For the first time in my life, I was afraid of the dark.

I looked over at Dougie, suddenly noticing that his hair was damp, gleaming slightly in the firelight. He was wearing different clothes, too. I frowned, confused.

'Did you go in the sea?' I asked.

'Eh, yeah.'

'Swimming?' Alone and injured?

'Not intentionally.' He twisted his mouth into a sheepish grimace. 'I thought the cold water might help my ankle, reduce the swelling. But I lost my balance, got totally soaked. Clothes and everything.'

'Are you all right?' I asked, leaning forwards and scrutinising him more carefully. 'Is your ankle . . . is it worse?'

'I hurt it a bit when I fell, but I'm fine. Just got a bit wet.'

We lapsed back into silence, but I couldn't bear to let it last very long.

'What time is it?' I asked.

Dougie tilted his watch so that it caught in the light from the fire.

'Just after midnight.'

I snorted. 'Happy Birthday.'

It took a moment, but Dougie laughed too. The noise didn't last long and it didn't lift the oppressive atmosphere. I sighed.

'Dougie, what are we going to do?'

158

Again, there were several seconds of silence.

'I don't know.'

'What . . . what do you think happened to Darren?'

I watched him carefully. He was handling Darren's disappearance fairly well so far, better than Martin's. And Darren's sudden vanishing act couldn't be explained away the way Martin's could. He'd had no reason to go, no spur. Unless he'd had an argument with Emma and stormed off. But that didn't explain the state Emma was in.

'I don't know.' Toneless, emotionless. Dougie gazed out into the dark rather than at the fire.

'You . . . you don't believe what Emma said, do you?'

'I don't know . . .'

'Dougie –'

'No.' He cut off my words. 'I don't believe her. But . . .'

'He wouldn't have just disappeared,' I finished for him.

'Right.' He pressed his knuckles into his eyes. 'Darren's a thoughtless tosser at times, but he wouldn't just go. Besides, his car's here. I just . . . I just wish we could do something. Now.'

'I know,' I said soothingly, because he was looking more agitated by the second. 'But we'll go as soon as it's light, Dougie. We'll get to the road and use Emma's phone as soon as we get any reception and if we can't get a signal, well then we'll just keep walking till we find someone. I mean, we're not in the middle of nowhere, not really. That girl said there were plenty of people round here, they're just dotted about.'

I stared at Dougie. He still had his face hidden in his hands, grinding his fists into the sockets like he wanted to rub out the memory of the last couple of days, start afresh. I didn't see any trace of tears but his skin was a blotchy red, his jaw clenched. I didn't know what to say.

Suddenly he lifted his head, gazed at me. The fire was slowly dimming, throwing his face into shadow. It made him almost frightening, especially with the dark gleam of his eyes boring into mine.

'Let's try and sleep,' he said. 'I want this day over with.'

There was no discussion over sleeping arrangements. Without a word we both gravitated towards the biggest tent, where Emma was already quietly sleeping. With everything that had happened, no one wanted to go to bed alone.

We crawled into our individual bags and then, without seeming to think about it, Dougie shifted over towards me and draped his arm around my waist, sliding into the same position we'd occupied the night before. I didn't complain. I needed the comfort.

I didn't think I'd sleep, but when I opened my eyes it was lighter in the tent. Before sunrise, I was sure, but not by much. The daylight was grey, silhouettes and shadows taking on their proper shapes but still colourless, muted. The air was cold, the tip of my nose freezing. Despite this, I was absolutely sweltering. For a moment I couldn't work it out, it seemed wrong somehow, but then I gradually became aware of the rigid band around my middle. Dougie was holding me so tight it was hard to breathe.

Not wanting to wake him, I tried to shimmy my arms up so that I could reach the zipper and let some air in to cool my skin. I had to knock his hand out of the way to do so, and behind me I heard a murmured groan.

'Sorry,' I muttered quietly. Emma was still sleeping too.

Dougie didn't reply, although I was sure I must have woken him. Curious, I twisted round so that I could look at him.

He had his eyes shut, but scrunched tightly, and his mouth was puckered. His hair lay flat against his head and strands were plastered across his forehead. Worried, I reached out tentatively and pressed my fingers to his face. It was burning hot and his skin was tacky with sweat. His moaned again, pulling away from my touch. His arm slid off my waist, freeing me. I sat up, trying to move carefully, aware that every shift of my weight sent the air mattress rippling under both Emma and Dougie. Slowly, I slid my hand under the edge of his sleeping bag, felt around his shoulder. He was feverishly hot and his t-shirt was sticking to him like a second skin.

Scared, I yanked my hand back, gripped it with my other. It felt warm, like it had conducted some of the heat vibrating off Dougie's skin. Was he sick? Last night he'd seemed, well, not fine, but okay. Not unwell.

He wasn't okay now, though. Quickly, I did an assessment of my own state. I felt normal. Not hot or woozy. Stomach felt fine. Whatever he had, I didn't seem to have caught it.

I remembered the gleam of his wet hair in the fire. The dunking he'd taken in the sea. Was that it? It had been cold last night, the water even colder.

'Dougie,' I whispered. His eyebrows twitched, but he didn't stir. 'Dougie.'

I reached forward and shook his shoulder, gently at first, then harder. I wasn't sure why I wanted to wake him. I only knew that I didn't like being alone. I told myself that I wanted to talk to him, to see how he felt, what other symptoms he had, but I wasn't entirely sure that was true.

'Dougie!'

Emma mewled quietly, rolling over in her sleep, but I wasn't interested in her. I stared down at Dougie, as if I could wake him with the power of my mind. It seemed to work. His eyelids fluttered then opened completely. At first his gaze was unfocused, confused. Then he looked up at me and I watched awareness dawn.

'Is it morning?' he croaked. I was alarmed to hear a deep rasp as he churned the words out.

'Sort of,' I said quietly.

He looked around him, took in the drab light, Emma's still, sleeping form.

'What's wrong?' he asked.

I chewed the inside of my cheek as I considered him.

'How do you feel?' I asked.

'What?'

'How do you feel?'

'I feel . . .' He thought about it. 'Freezing.' As soon as he spoke the words he started burrowing down deeper into his sleeping bag. 'Why is it so cold in here?'

It wasn't. Not really. The air in the tent was rapidly warming in tandem with the morning sun outside.

'It's not,' I replied, my heart sinking. I did not want Dougie to get sick right now.

'It is,' he disagreed. 'Where's my jumper?'

Wordlessly I handed it to him, watched as he sat up and started wriggling his way inside it, his whole body shivering as it was momentarily exposed to the air.

'Urgh.' He clutched his head then flopped back down to the air mattress.

'What is it?'

'Dizzy,' he said, one hand still stretched across his forehead.

'You're sick,' I said. For some reason I had to say it out loud.

'I'm not,' Dougie told me. 'I'm fine.' But even as he spoke he was trying to retreat further into the heat of his sleeping bag.

'How's your ankle?'

Dougie made a speculative face and I heard a quiet rustling beside me as he experimented with his foot. After half a second he stopped abruptly and his expression twisted.

'Sore,' he admitted.

'Let me see it,' I pressed.

'In a bit,' Dougie said, pulling his covers up higher, looking at me defensively. He shivered again.

I studied him closely. As the light slowly brightened, his skin was looking worse and worse. He was pale, slightly jaundiced. After another convulsive shudder he swallowed and wrinkled his nose.

'You all right?'

He didn't answer but a moment later he was in motion. Despite having baulked before at the idea of emerging from his cocoon, now he was fighting his way free, thrashing and pulling at the sleeping bag, rocketing upright, heedless of his damaged ankle. I watched, confused, as he tore out of the tent, then just seconds later I heard the sounds of retching and coughing. He was throwing up.

I swallowed back my own nausea – nothing to do with Dougie's illness – and followed him outside. I grabbed a bottle of water from the now ice-less cooler before I rounded the tent to where he was hunkered over in the grass.

'Thanks,' he gasped as I twisted the top off and handed him the bottle. He took a deep swig then spat a mouthful of water down on top of the contents of his stomach. 'I'm fine,' he promised. 'You don't have to watch me.'

The smell of his vomit was bitter and acidic, but I didn't leave him. If he was running a fever he might pass out. Instead I waited while he took slow, measured sips of water, breathing shallowly and evenly, trying not to chuck it back up. Eventually he felt well enough to move and I helped him to his feet, shoving my shoulder under his arm as a crutch as he limped back towards the blackened circle that was our fire pit. Emma still hadn't emerged. Through the hanging tent flap I could just make out her huddled form. I wasn't sure whether to wake her or not, unsure what kind of state she would be in. She'd been hysterical the night before, right up until the drowsy meds had kicked in.

'Do you feel like eating anything?' I asked Dougie as he flopped into one of the chairs. He shook his head, looking green. Tugging the collar of his jumper up around his neck, he slumped down and continued to take tentative mouthfuls from the bottle of water.

Just for something to do, I pulled out a rice cracker and started to nibble on the end. I wasn't really hungry, though, and before I'd eaten half of it I threw it down into the hole, thinking it'd be burned up by the fire or eaten by a scavenging bird if we'd lit our last flame on the beach.

'Do you think we should take Emma with us?' Dougie asked, pulling me out of my reverie.

I blinked, stared at him as I considered his words.

'We can't leave her here on her own,' I said. Then I took a deep breath. 'Are *you* going to be able to make it out of here?'

'Yes.' Dougie responded at once; his tone decisive, his face set. I kept my scepticism firmly off my face. 'As soon as Emma's up. That's when we'll go.' He was looking at the waves as he said this and I couldn't help the feeling that he was trying to convince himself, not me.

Emma didn't show any sign of rising and after watching Dougie spend twenty minutes almost getting a crick in his neck turning round every three seconds to stare at her, I took pity on him, curled myself out of my chair and headed for the tent.

'Emma,' I called. 'Emma, are you awake?'

She didn't respond but I didn't believe she was still sleeping. She was too motionless, her position in the sleeping bag too tense. Just peeking out above the deep blue of the bag her shoulders were hunched up, hiding her neck from view. I knelt down on the air mattress beside her. The transfer of air shifted her body, but she still didn't move a muscle.

'Emma,' I said again. I laid a hand on her shoulder. She twitched under my touch, lifted her shoulders up even higher. 'I know you're awake.'

She sighed, twisted round in slow motion. Her eyes gazed at me, huge glassy orbs. I knew she was thinking about yesterday, about Darren, but I didn't know what to say. I didn't know whether to bring it up, to ask her about it. Would she just repeat her crazy story about the monster that lived under the waves?

I tried to smile.

'Come on, we're going to get out of here. We'll hike up to the main road, find a house or flag down a car. You need to get changed, grab something to eat. Then we'll go.'

Emma had gone to sleep in last night's clothes but I hoped something as routine as getting dressed would help snap her back to reality. She probably wouldn't eat, but I thought I should suggest it. For some reason I felt like the adult, even though I was the youngest. But with Dougie ill and Emma gone la-la, I was somehow in charge. I didn't like it, but there wasn't much choice.

Emma changed her clothes in slow motion, obediently putting on whatever I held out to her. She was like a zombie, her face completely unanimated. We didn't speak. When she was fully dressed I gestured that she should move outside and she did so, shuffling her feet like an old age pensioner.

Dougie wasn't on the beach.

For a moment my heart froze and I was gripped by a sudden panic, but then I heard coughing, spluttering. He was back in the long grass, hunched over, throwing up the water he'd drunk. Between him and the chair he'd been sitting in was a series of mismatched footprints, the tracks on the left dragging where he'd limped along. He was lopsided even as he vomited, holding his injured ankle gingerly just above the ground.

I didn't ask if he was okay when he came back. He clearly wasn't. I wouldn't have thought it possible, but his colour was even worse than before. His skin was sallow, his lips white where he had them pressed together. Wincing at every step, he slowly closed the distance between us.

'Are you ready to go?' he asked in a dull voice.

Surely he didn't think he could manage to hike up to the road? It was at least two miles. It would have been an ordeal just taking into account his sprained ankle. Retching and burning up under a fever, it would be torturous.

'Dougie, I don't think –'

'I'm going,' he snapped, obviously anticipating what I was going to say.

I didn't want to argue with him. Instead I watched silently as he stuffed several water bottles and a giant bag of crisps into a backpack. Then he slung the straps over his shoulders. He already had his shoes back on, although the left was unlaced. It was obviously too painful to tighten.

'Have you got your phone?' he said, addressing Emma for the first time.

She hadn't seemed bothered by being ignored. She'd just stood motionless, face blank, waiting.

She blinked at the question. Then she frowned ever so slightly, like she didn't understand.

'Your phone,' Dougie repeated impatiently. 'Have you got it?'

Emma made a small movement that might have been a shrug. Then she looked away, towards the cove.

'I'll check in the tent,' I offered, because I could see Dougie was getting ready to explode at Emma and I wasn't sure there would be any point. She seemed completely empty, like nobody was home behind those vacant blue eyes. It was hard to be worried for her, though, when I was so concerned about Dougie. And Martin. And Darren.

Part of me was clinging desperately to the idea that Martin had just gone home. Darren I wasn't so sure about. The suspicion that he was floating in the water refused to go away. I should have checked the cove more thoroughly, I knew that, but Emma had been so out of control that it'd been hard to even get close to the churning sea. And her vehement pleas that I not go in the water had scared me enough that I'd only dared search from the shore, the rocks.

I should have gone in, I really should have. That guilt was hard to deal with on top of everything else. I tried to push it down, out of sight. It nagged at me, though, making my stomach churn.

I found Emma's phone easily. It sat on top of a pile of her clothes, pink metallic cover bright in the dull grey of the tent. I pressed the buttons, hoping to see the screen light up. It didn't. I repressed a sigh. I supposed it wasn't surprising. We'd been at the beach several days and Emma liked to keep her phone on, using it as an MP3 player and a camera. All the apps she ran ate up battery life, and the handset was dead.

'Emma's phone's no good,' I said as I returned to Dougie and Emma. They didn't seem to have moved an inch, although Dougie looked like it was costing him a lot of effort to stay standing. 'Dead.'

Dougie made an agitated noise under his breath.

'Guess we just walk until we find someone then,' he said. He shifted on the sand, adjusting his weight. 'Come on, I want to get started.'

He started the slow, slow trudge towards the car park.

'Emma.' I tugged gently on her elbow. 'Emma, we're going.'

It was as if she hadn't heard me, though I was standing right next to her. I pulled harder on her arm and she let me drag her along. We shambled forward in tandem for several steps then she stopped dead and refused to move, no matter how hard I hauled at her. I turned, stared at her.

'What?'

'I'm not leaving.'

'Sorry?' I hadn't misheard her; I just couldn't believe what she was saying.

'I'm not leaving. Not without Darren.'

I expected her to burst into tears but her pale face was calm and composed. Her jaw was set in determination.

'Emma, that's why we're going. So we can get help for him. We need to get help.'

But she shook her head at me, absolutely resolute.

CHAPTER EIGHTEEN

It was going to be impossible for me to drag Emma and support Dougie on the climb up the hill. I stood between the two of them, helpless.

'Emma, please –' I said, tightening my grip on her arm.

But her face darkened. Taking a step back she wrenched her arm free with surprising strength.

'No,' she said, the loudest I'd heard her raise her voice since she stopped screaming.

'Emma, Darren isn't here!' I hissed.

'I don't care.' She glared at me, eyes finally full of life. 'I'm not leaving without Darren.'

'But –'

'NO!'

And before I could stop her, she turned and ran back down the beach. I saw her disappear into the tent. Angry, worried and feeling completely helpless, I made to follow her.

'Leave her,' Dougie said over my shoulder.

Leave her? Here, by herself? I turned to stare at Dougie,

only to see he'd dropped down to rest on the low stone wall. My immediate fears over Emma vanished as I took in the nauseated expression on his face, the way he was swaying slightly, mirroring the slow, undulating movement of the waves.

'Dougie, are you sure about trying this?' I asked.

He ignored my question, hoisted himself onto his one good foot.

'Look, we need to get help. That's it.'

There wasn't much to say to that.

I held my hand out in case Dougie wanted me to support him, but he seemed to want to travel under his own steam. He hobbled awkwardly across the uneven packed dirt of the car park. I followed a half-step behind, walking slower than a funeral march, watching his every movement, waiting for the inevitable.

It didn't take very long. One moment Dougie was scuffling determinedly along, shoulders rolling with each uneven step; the next he was leaning ominously. I caught him before he toppled, but only just.

'Are you all right?' I gasped, hanging onto his jumper and trying to lower him gently to the ground – he was too heavy for me to hold up. 'Did you trip?'

'No,' Dougie mumbled. 'Dizzy.' He groaned. I released him, sure he was going to throw up again. He didn't, but rolled over and lay with his face inches from the mud, each breath sending up a little puff of dust that coated his sweat-covered skin. I hovered over him as he moaned and convulsed periodically. Nothing came out of his mouth, though. He must have already emptied his stomach. 'Christ,' I heard him hiss.

We stayed like that for a full minute, then another. Dougie stopped heaving but he didn't try to get up, either. Eventually I crouched down, tentatively rubbed his back.

'Dougie, this is stupid. You can't possibly go anywhere like this.' I said it as gently as possible, acutely aware of how he would react. He didn't disappoint me.

'No!' he growled. 'We've got to get help. We've got to let someone know. Help me up!'

I did as he asked but as soon as he was upright he staggered, as if he was blind drunk, and I had to move quickly to support him, stuffing my shoulder under his arm, bracing him with a hand on his chest.

'Dammit!' he hissed.

'Let's go back to camp,' I suggested. 'Just for now,' I had to add quickly, because Dougie immediately opened his mouth to argue.

But after a moment he nodded and I started to slowly guide him back down the hill. I wanted to lead him to the tent but he resisted, pulling me towards the chairs.

'I like the fresh air,' he said, even though he was shivering again.

I dropped him down into a seat, got one of the water bottles out of the bag and prepared to do battle. He was in no shape to go anywhere. I knew it and he knew it. I also knew that probably wouldn't stop him. There was only one way to keep him here.

'Look,' I said, swallowing hard. 'You stay and watch Emma and I'll hike up and find someone.'

I didn't want to. I *really* didn't want to, but it was obvious Dougie couldn't and Emma wasn't going to leave. He was right, too. We needed help. Now.

I just . . . The thought of wandering about on my own, flagging down a stranger . . . Maybe getting lost, stuck in the dark . . .

I took a deep breath to quell the panic. Thought about Martin and Darren; Emma, lost in her own head; Dougie, burning up in front of my eyes.

Something gripped my fingers and I looked up from the hole I'd been burning in the sand with my gaze to see Dougie staring at me. Slowly he shook his head.

'No,' he said. 'Nobody goes on their own.'

I didn't point out that he'd been willing to let Emma stay alone. I was too overwhelmed by a sudden rush of warmth that he wouldn't let *me* go off by myself, that he wanted to protect me, keep me safe.

But it was hard, sitting there. Dougie sank down so he was half-lying in the chair, his head resting on the back. He closed his eyes and although I didn't think he was sleeping – every so often he would sigh or groan, then his eyelids would flutter open – it was clear he didn't want to talk. Emma had closed the tent flap, shutting herself in her own little world. That left me. Not on my own yet very much alone. Well, I had my thoughts for company and they were not pleasant.

First I tried to work out how many hours Martin had been missing for. Thirty-six? Maybe longer? If he really had cadged a lift home, would he have forgiven us by now, be thinking about sending a reconciliatory text? One I might get tomorrow if Dougie was better and we hiked back up, if I could get my phone to switch on?

And if he hadn't left, if he was stuck somewhere, injured or trapped, was thirty-six hours enough time for the cold to do damage? It was warm enough during the day but night was a different matter, and then there was the rain that had fallen . . . How long did it take to get pneumonia?

I didn't know the answer to that. Same as I didn't know how long a fever could rage before I should start to get worried. Or more worried. A day, maybe? A day was all I was going to give Dougie before I walked up by myself, no matter what he said. He wouldn't be able to stop me; he could barely stand.

And Emma. Lost-her-marbles Emma. I didn't know what to do there, either. I couldn't imagine what had made her snap so completely. Had she and Darren had a massive falling out? Or had she really watched him sink under the waves?

He was in the water. I was sure of it. There were so many simple things that could have gone wrong. He might have waded out too far, started swimming and been caught in a current. He might have been prancing around on the rocks, showing off. One slip and it would be easy to smack his head, knock himself out. Then the gentle current would just let him drift away. There were a lot of ways to get into trouble in the dark, frigid waters of the sea.

But the waves, they pushed one way. If something had happened to Darren there was a chance he would wash up on the beach, like all the flotsam and seaweed collected in the cove. After all, hadn't that been why they'd gone there; because it was such a great place to collect driftwood?

I was standing before I realised I'd made a decision.

'I'm going to the cove,' I announced.

Dougie opened one eye and gazed at me blearily.

'What? Why?'

'I just want to . . . check. Maybe I missed Darren. Maybe he fell and he's lying on the rocks, or maybe he was in the sea but he made it onto the beach and was too exhausted or hurt to get back here. Maybe . . .' I didn't finish. Maybe he'd *been* washed back up, not off his own steam, but as a 'gift' from the sea. 'What harm could it do?' I asked, because Dougie was looking at me uncertainly.

'On your own?' he said.

'Just to the cove,' I replied. 'It's not far. I won't go up the road. You're right, I don't really want to hike up there by myself.'

In all honesty I didn't really want to go to the cove by myself either, but I just . . . I had to check. I had this funny, eerie feeling that wouldn't go away. And it was killing me just sitting here. Waiting for nothing.

'It'll be fine,' I said, because he still didn't look convinced. 'It's practically within hearing distance. If anything happens, I'll yell. I'm loud,' I added.

For the first time that day he cracked a smile.

'I know,' he assured me. 'I remember the jellyfish.'

Despite the sunshine that had dominated the weather for weeks, it was another overcast day. Not quite as cold as yesterday, though, so I left my jumper on my chair. I tried to ignore the fluttering in my stomach as I walked quickly up the short hill to the path that wound round the coast. I hadn't enjoyed my first visit to the cove and I wasn't looking forward to going back. But if there was any chance Darren was there . . .

Really, I was assuaging my own guilt. I couldn't stop wondering if maybe I'd been so busy trying to calm Emma, to get her out of there, that I'd missed him.

175

The walk wasn't familiar to me yet and I hesitated when I came to the fork, not entirely sure which way to go. The day before, Emma's screams had been my guide. Today there was nothing but the cawing of gulls and the rush of the breeze in my ears. I wondered if the wind ever stopped blowing up here. Somewhat uncomfortably, I set off down the trail and eventually emerged on the pebbly beach.

There were several large rocks and boulders in the cove that could conceal a slumped human figure – one of which I'd found Emma huddled behind. I checked each one, walking all the way round to be sure, then concentrated on scanning the flotsam that had collected along the shoreline and the shallows.

I didn't see anything at a glance that resembled Darren's wide silhouette but I made myself look properly, determined to be thorough. My trainers crunched against the shifting stones with every step and the sound seemed to reverberate off the rock walls.

I was halfway to the shoreline when it caught my eye. A smidge of orange. Darker than it should be, but definitely orange. Nothing on this beach should be that colour. I sucked in a deep breath through suddenly tight lungs and tried to find it again, that tiny fragment of man-made colour.

There, bobbing up and down, in and out of sight. In the water.

I started forward, unaware of my feet pounding, arms pumping. My eyes were fixed on the flash of dark umber, convinced I'd lose it if I so much as blinked. I broke the surface of the water without noticing the shocking cold of the Irish Sea. Splashing my way forward, I reached out long before he was within my grasp.

'Darren!' I gasped.

The shape of his body was clearer now, the outline just visible through the murky water. His back and shoulders were lifted a little above the surface, nestled against a jagged rock that, now the tide was out, just broke the waves; his orange t-shirt shouting his presence to the world . . . to me. His head was twisted to the side, face half-in, half-out of the water. Part of his mouth was clear. Enough for him to still be breathing?

I had to hope as I snatched at his shoulders, hauled him onto his back. His skin was pale, waxy. His eyes were open but the pupils were hidden, rolled back into his head. My hopes plummeted as his head dropped back, hanging lifelessly over my arm. Was I too late?

'Darren!' I shook him roughly and his head flopped from side to side. 'Darren! Look at me!'

No response. Just the heavy weight of his massive frame, limp in my arms. I dropped my face down to press my cheek against his mouth, praying I would feel the soft flutter of warm breath against my skin. Nothing, just the chill of his lips bumping against the side of my face, unwelcome kisses as the sea lifted him rhythmically with the waves.

Trying to remember it was Darren, trying not be repulsed by the knowledge that I was probably clinging on to a dead body, I ran my hand across his clavicle until I came to his neck. I pressed two fingers firmly against the base of his throat, hunting for a pulse. I couldn't find one. The skin was stone cold, hard beneath my touch. My face scrunched up as tears burned my eyeballs. Too late, far too late.

Had he been right here yesterday, still breathing as I left?

I cried a little harder, crumpling under the weight of guilt.

Something encircled my arm. Not the gentle, tickling touch of seaweed or jellyfish. This grip was tight, firm. I screamed, jumped, yanking my body backwards, ripping both my arms free. Then I saw Darren's face. His eyes were black, focused. Staring right at me. But only for a second, before he slipped beneath the water, disappearing.

He was alive. Darren was alive.

'Shit!' I exploded forward, desperately searching the water. It wasn't deep here, where was he? I was soaked and frozen but I didn't care. I dropped down onto my knees, wincing as jagged stones smashed into my shins. I didn't stop hunting, though, crashing about, hands scraping over sand, seaweed, rocks. Where was he? He was here, just a second ago. Where was he?

'Darren!' I screamed. My throat was tight; his name came out broken and scratched.

But nobody answered. There was utter silence. Emma was right; it was deathly quiet in this cove. I wasn't thinking clearly enough to realise that the beach was sheltered on all sides by rock walls, keeping out the wind. The sea was calm, whispering gently. The only sound came from my frantic splashing as I beat at the water.

Abruptly I stopped and stood there, panting. Now that I wasn't disturbing the surface, I realised it was clear enough for me to just make out the bottom. I could see dark swirls of seaweed, twigs, snapped off grasses and fronds, pebbles. But not Darren. No body, clawing for the surface or lying still. He wasn't there.

Confused and frightened, I twisted round, gazed about me. He wasn't on the shore, or floating off into the depths. He wasn't anywhere.

'Darren!' I screamed for him anyway.

Somebody called back, wordless, guttural. It wasn't Darren. I knew that voice, though.

'Martin?' I was ran out of the water, turning left and right on the beach, dripping water everywhere, not remotely aware of the cold. 'Martin?'

He shrieked again, sounding in pain. Hesitantly, I took a step in the direction I thought his voice was coming from, but the sound seemed to surround me, echoing off the walls.

'Martin? Martin, where are you?' The tears were back and they stole the volume from my voice.

'Heather!' My name came at me from everywhere and nowhere. I was turning so fast I was getting dizzy. 'Heather, help!'

Two voices, Martin and Darren. Calling together. Scared, angry, in pain.

Accusing.

Why hadn't I helped them? Why *wasn't* I helping them?

I cried harder, running this way and that.

'Where are you?' I yelled.

This time I got nothing back but bawling, screeching, tortured cries.

Where were they? The cove was small. Standing dead in the centre, I was able to see everywhere, everything. Panicked, scared as I was, it took a long time for the truth to sink in: I was alone.

So what the hell was making that noise? I clapped my hands over my head, trying to shut it out. Was this what had happened to Emma, was this what drove her over the edge?

Desperate now to escape, I started to run, palms firmly cupped against the sides of my head. It made me clumsy, unstable. The constant shifting of the stones on the beach beneath my feet was too much for my precarious balance and I tumbled.

I hit the ground hard, skidding. Instinctively I clawed at the undulating carpet of stones and rough sand, trying to stop myself. My hand folded over something smoother and colder than the rest of the pebbles. I turned my hand over, staring at the thing nestled in my palm.

The brooch. How could it possibly be here? Dougie had hurled into the water, back at the camp. The odds against it swirling in the water and being spat out in the cove for me to find were astronomical. But more than that, I was beyond the tideline. I shook my head, disbelieving.

Then another scream rent the air and all thought vanished. I lurched to my feet and hit the narrow path at full sprint, my eyes fixed on the trail, the tiny copper brooch held fast in my palm like it was glued there.

CHAPTER NINETEEN

Now

I'm thirsty. It's warm in the room; I blame that for my dry mouth. My discomfort peaks as I watch Dr Petersen take another sip of his expensive fizzy water, but I don't ask him for a drink. I swallow; try to eke some saliva back into my parched mouth. Not that I have any intention of talking.

We are taking a break. Not my idea, but I am not about to complain. From the look on Dr Petersen's face, he's not happy about it either. I can only guess that this is some sort of requirement – that after so long I have to be given a chance to recuperate, or reflect. I am not allowed out of the room, however, and there has been no mention of refreshment.

Dr Petersen glances at a fancy Rolex watch strapped around his wrist, hairs on his arm silvery grey with age, and I realise my respite is almost up. He goes back to perusing my notes, but he's no longer reading. Perhaps he's just counting down the seconds in his head. His eyes stare down at the paper, but they aren't moving.

At last – and yet, still much too soon – he sighs, pushes away my file and fixes me with a pleasant smile. I can't help but wonder if he hates me as much as I hate him, if that smile is a struggle for him and if what he really wants to do is scowl. No – I am sure he enjoys our little meetings. I'm like a Rubik's cube to him, a puzzle he already knows the answer to but he keeps working away at. Because the challenge is in the solving, in making the little coloured blobs bend to his will.

I never managed to solve a Rubik's cube. I'd get so far, maybe a row of yellows, or four little reds grouped nicely in a square, then I'd get stuck and no matter how much I twisted, I wouldn't make any progress. I'd get bored, give up. Unfortunately Dr Petersen appears to have more tenacity than me, in this respect at least.

He opens his mouth to speak, and I wonder where we're going now.

'Are you a religious person, Heather?'

What does that have to do with anything? I blink but keep my face expressionless, waiting for the rest. Dr Petersen doesn't speak, but continues to watch me, obviously waiting for an answer. If I don't say anything, how long will this go on?

Possibly quite a long time, I realise a minute later. It's awkward, sitting here in silence. The escort's breathing in the background is loud. Irritating, really. Is it on purpose, so I don't forget he's there? Now that I'm tuned into it, it's even harder to ignore. I want something to cover it. Anything, even if it means I have to speak. Besides, it seems an innocuous question. I am not giving much away by telling him this.

'No,' I say quietly.

'Do you believe in God?'

I fail to see how this is different from his first question, but I answer anyway.

'No.'

'What about life after death?'

I squint a little, still trying to puzzle him out. Just when I think I have my ducks all in a row . . .

'Everyone wants to believe in an afterlife,' I tell him. 'They want to think that death is not the end.'

'Do you?'

'I don't know.' I make my voice deliberately short, curt. Because I think I might be starting to see where he's heading, and I want to cut it off here and now.

'Ah,' he says, as if he hasn't heard me say this before. Then, 'And that's the problem, isn't it? The not knowing.'

I pin on my smile. I am right. The smile doesn't last long, however. This theory that Petersen has tried to convince me of again and again isn't something I want to talk about. Not that there is much I *do* want to talk to Dr Petersen about, except maybe my release, and I'm pretty sure that isn't a conversation we'll be having any time soon.

But the escort is still breathing; slowly, loudly. Constantly.

'Nobody knows,' I say, striving for disdain, as if this should be obvious.

Petersen smiles.

'Is that what so fascinates you about it? About death?'

'I'm not fascinated by death,' I answer. It's the truth.

'No, you're right,' he agrees. I blink in surprise at Petersen's admission but he isn't done. 'It's not death, is it? It's dying.

183

Those precious moments when you can watch life drain away. Wonder where it goes.'

There is something very wrong with this man.

I clamp my lips shut and attempt to do the same with my ears. Just to cover the sound, wheezing in and out and in and out, I start drumming loudly on my knee with my good hand. Dr Petersen will think it's a sign that he's getting to me, but I will just have to live with that.

'Heather?'

Death, dying. It's not fascinating: it's terrifying. Unexplained, uncharted. Unexplored. Nobody knows what the final journey will be like, not until you're so far down the path you'll never be able to turn back and tell anyone what you saw.

Deep, deep down, it's why we're all really afraid of the dark. Because there's nothing worse than not knowing what's out there.

But I'm not going to try to explain that to Dr Petersen. I don't care how long he waits, how loud that damned guard breathes. I clamp down on my tongue with my teeth, squeezing so hard it hurts.

Perhaps Petersen sees the determination in my face, because he quickly moves along to the next question on his little list.

'Do you believe in spirits, Heather? Demons, creatures from another world?'

I chew down harder. I must have drawn blood because my mouth is suddenly filled with a metallic taste that's both alien and familiar.

This is what Dr Petersen brings up when he really wants to elicit a response from me. If I was thinking straight I would be surprised he's waited so long in this session to spring this one on me. But I'm not. I'm not thinking at all. I'm concentrating all of my efforts on staying right here. Right in this room, right now. It should be funny, because that's something I've never wanted before, but I'm not laughing.

Because I do believe. I believe in spirits, demons, whatever you want to call them. Creatures that shouldn't exist in this world but do, beings that don't have to live by the same rules as the rest of us. Things that you can't fight, can't kill. I do believe in those.

The druids, who made their horrific sacrifices to appease the beasts, they knew what they were doing. They knew what would happen if the demon's hunger went unfulfilled.

So do I.

CHAPTER TWENTY

Then

'Dougie!' I hit the beach at full tilt, my breath coming in ragged gasps. Forgetting that he was ill, forgetting his injured ankle, I threw myself at him, collapsing, still half-sobbing, into his arms.

'What? What is it? Heather, what's wrong?'

'It's . . . it's . . .' But I didn't know how to describe what had happened at the cove. Instead I just gripped him harder, locking my hands around his neck, burying my face in his shoulder. Though the beach was quiet, I could still hear their screams echoing in my head. The terror I'd felt refused to lessen and I was shaking violently. My pulse thumped round my system, and even with my soaking wet clothes I was overheating.

Warm as I was, Dougie was hotter. His skin seemed to radiate heat, reminding me that he was sick. He was in no shape to be holding me up. Though it was the last thing I wanted to do, I pulled back, put the space of a footstep between us.

Now, though, he could see my face. I worked hard to mould it back into its ordinary shape, but my chin was trembling and my eyes were screwed into slits as I tried to hold back the tears. I sniffed deeply, trying to get a grip on myself.

'You should sit down,' I quavered.

Dougie ignored my advice. Closing the distance I'd put between us, he gripped my arm.

'Heather, what happened? Did you go to the cove?'

Not really capable of talking, I made do with a couple of jerky nods.

'Did . . . did you find anything?'

'I don't know.' My voice came out oddly distorted, choked with emotion. 'It was . . .' I broke off again, breathing hard. Just thinking about it was bringing the fear back, tight around my chest like a steel band. 'There was something there.'

Dougie caught the strange emphasis in my words.

'What do you mean, *something*?' he asked, his face intense.

'I . . . I'm not sure.' I shrugged in apology. I was beginning to calm down, to regain my senses. What had happened seemed . . . impossible. I was no longer sure about what I'd seen, heard. Had I imagined it?

But then . . .

'Dougie, I found –' I presented him with my left hand.

Dougie's eyes narrowed, then widened as he saw what I had. Slowly he prised my fingers loose and pulled the brooch from my grasp.

'Where the hell did you get this?' he asked.

'It was on the beach. At the cove.'

'Washed up?' He looked dubious. 'I guess it could happen.'

But I was shaking my head.

'No, it was up above the tideline. It was buried beneath some pebbles.'

'That's not possible,' he murmured.

I took a deep, steadying breath. 'I know.'

Two dark green eyes stared deep into mine.

'Heather, what happened?'

I told him. Told him about the body that disappeared, the screams that came from nowhere. How I'd accidentally come across the brooch, fallen right on top of it. I didn't look at him as I spoke, afraid I'd see the same thing in his face that Emma must have seen in mine: disbelief.

When I finished, there was a long moment of silence. I managed to wait all of ten seconds before I had to look.

Doubt was written across his face.

'You don't believe me,' I accused.

'I don't think you'd lie,' he hedged.

I scowled. That wasn't the same thing.

'You think I imagined it.'

He made a face that was easy to interpret: yes, but that's not what you want to hear.

No, it wasn't.

'How are you feeling?' he asked. His hand reached out to press against my forehead; a pointless gesture as his skin was so much hotter than mine. 'Do you feel chilled? Overheated? Sick to your stomach?'

I pulled away from his touch.

'No,' I replied, somewhat frostily.

He chewed on his lip as he considered me.

'I'm sorry, Heather, it just sounds a bit –'

'Crazy,' I finished for him.

He grimaced at me, his eyes apologetic.

'But this . . .' He turned the brooch over in his hands. 'This is weird. How did it get there?'

'I don't know,' I said, watching the way the light reflected on the coppery surface. 'Don't you think it's a bit of a funny coincidence?'

'What do you mean?'

'It being there, right there, at the cove. Maybe . . . maybe it's linked.'

'Linked?'

I paused, not sure I was ready to admit my theory. Even to me it sounded nuts.

'Think about where we got this,' I said, hoping he'd guess what I was thinking so I wouldn't have to say it.

'The cairn?'

'The *burial* cairn,' I reminded him.

'But it was just left there,' he argued. 'It can't have been there long, it's not even old.'

'It looked old when you pulled it out,' I argued.

'Yeah, but, that must have just been dirt. Look at it now. Metal doesn't stay all shiny like this, not for that length of time. Not left outside.'

I knew he was right, but I still couldn't let it go.

'But everything that's happened, it's all been since we found it.'

'You think –' His lips twitched and I knew, even with everything that was going on, I knew he was laughing at me – 'you think the brooch is causing all of this?'

'Don't you think it's a bit strange that we steal this, then just after it – and I mean, like, just hours after it – everything starts going wrong?'

'It's just a coincidence, Heather,' he said quietly. 'Nothing more.'

'I don't think so,' I said obstinately. I felt stupid, my cheeks flooding with red, but I ploughed resolutely on. 'Right after we find it, Martin goes AWOL, the Volvo dies and you sprain your ankle. Then you chuck it away and Darren goes missing at the beach it washes up on, Emma goes crazy and I –' I broke off, ground my teeth together.

I was getting angry; annoyed that Dougie wouldn't even consider my words. He hadn't been this derisive when Emma had told her insane story. Why wouldn't he even consider mine?

'Heather –'

I didn't let him finish, sure he was going to try to persuade me I was talking nonsense.

'Dougie, what if we've . . . woken something?'

'Heather, there's nothing here.' Dougie leaned forward in his chair, forcing me to meet his gaze. 'It's just us. Maybe –'

'I didn't imagine it,' I hissed. 'It could be . . . what you were saying. About the druids.'

'That was a story, Heather!' Dougie exclaimed. Then he took a deep breath, obviously reining in his emotions. 'Look. I believe you think you saw what you say you did,' he said, and I glowered at his careful wording. 'But maybe you're

190

not able to separate what's real and what's not right now. I mean, when I was dizzy before I didn't even know where I was for a minute.'

'I'm not getting sick,' I repeated stubbornly.

'You might be and you just don't know it yet,' he insisted. 'I was fine right up until I wasn't. Heather –' He reached one hand up to rub his forehead, which was shiny with sweat – 'Heather, you're talking about the supernatural here. Spirits and entities and stuff. I mean, just last night you said Emma was losing it. Now you, what, agree with her?'

'I don't know,' I muttered. I wasn't quite ready to align myself with Emma. I certainly hadn't seen anything like she'd described. But I was maybe willing to think about it with a more open mind. But she just . . . she just seemed so unstable right now. It was difficult to believe anything she said.

'I'm not crazy.'

I hadn't heard Emma coming out of the tent, but when I whipped my head around at the sound of her voice she was standing just a few feet behind us.

'Emma, you're awake,' Dougie commented, his voice falsely cheerful, and I knew he was wondering the same thing I was: how long had Emma been standing there listening?

'I'm not crazy,' she repeated, moving forward, footsteps silent in the sand. 'That thing I saw, it was real, and it was there.'

We watched in silence as she rounded the fire pit and lowered herself slowly into the one of the remaining chairs. She was wearing the clothes I'd helped her dress in earlier, but now they were creased, her jumper hanging messily from one shoulder. Her hair was tousled, not in the casual,

I-just-got-out-of-bed style that I knew she spent hours creating, but as if she didn't know what she looked like and didn't care. The make-up she'd put on at least a day before was now halfway down her face.

She looked older than I'd ever seen her. It was in her eyes: as if she'd witnessed true horror. They were frightened and sad and resigned all in one, and I didn't like looking at them. I couldn't seem to tear my gaze away, though.

'Tell me again what you saw,' I demanded.

Now that she was calmer, I hoped I'd get something a little more concrete than the hysterical fragments Dougie and I had had to piece together the night before.

But Emma didn't answer. She was looking at me oddly, head cocked to the side, eyes slightly tightened.

'What happened?' she asked me.

'What?'

'Something happened to you. What was it? Was it the cove, did you go back there? Did you see something?'

'I'm . . . not sure.'

'Tell me,' she ordered.

I recounted my story again. Emma's eyes widened in surprise and fear, then settled into a mixture of satisfaction and resignation.

'I told you,' she said when I finished. Then, with more feeling, 'I *told* you!'

'I didn't see a . . . *thing*,' I insisted, uncomfortable corroborating her story when it still seemed so unbelievable.

'But you think there's something going on. I heard what you said before,' she added as I opened my mouth to argue.

192

'I don't know,' I mumbled pathetically, aware of Dougie's eyes watching me closely. I took a breath. 'I think we should just get the hell out of here.'

Nobody argued with that.

Though it was tempting to hide out our final hours on the beach in our tent, none of us wanted to leave the fire. It wasn't just for the heat, though I was so cold it had settled right into my bones and Dougie was shaking uncontrollably, fever tricking his body into thinking everything was cold, even my arms around his shoulder, desperately trying to warm him.

We huddled by the fire. The world around us was cloaked in ominous shades of grey. Slowly that darkened into unfriendly, threatening black.

We didn't talk much. After appearing almost normal earlier, Emma had retreated back inside her head and was quietly humming to herself as she gazed into the flames. Dougie looked like it was all he could do to stay awake, although he'd resisted my attempts to get him to go and lie down. I didn't push the matter. His presence, even weak and dizzy and barely conscious, was a comfort. As for me, I spent my time scrutinising every inch of the brooch. Tilting it an angle, I used the flickering glare from the flames to throw the engravings into sharp relief. Twisting it this way and that, I tried to make sense of the squiggles and shapes. I wasn't sure why, but I remained convinced that the little circlet, small but big enough to almost fill my palm, was somehow, if not responsible, then at least connected to everything that was going on.

They were so strange, though, those markings. Unrecognisable, but not random. Undaunted, I continued to try to decipher them, spinning the brooch round, peering at it from different perspectives, attempting to force the loops and irregular angles to become something that made sense.

'You know,' I said slowly, squinting down at it, 'if you look at this the right way, that bit kind of looks like a man.'

'What?' Dougie turned to me, his eyes half-shut, jaw juddering. He sniffed, pulled his second jumper tighter around his shoulders, but looked down at where I was pointing.

'The brooch,' I said, ignoring when he sighed. 'This bit here.'

I held it out for his inspection. Rather than straining to see across the short space between us, he pulled it from my grasp. I watched him rotate it this way and that.

'Maybe,' he said. 'You mean this bit, in the middle of the flames?'

'Flames?' I blinked. 'What flames?'

'Yeah, these bits.' He pointed to jagged scratches that I hadn't been able to decipher. 'They're flames, right?'

I wasn't sure – they didn't look very flame-like to me – but I remembered how easily Dougie had interpreted the cairn when I had seen nothing more than a jumble of stones.

'Sure,' I mumbled.

'And these look like gifts.'

Gifts? I snatched it back from him. I hadn't seen any 'gifts'.

'Where?'

'Here.' He stretched over, ran his finger around the lower half of the brooch, opposite the man apparently surrounded by fire. 'See? That's a pot or something, and that's maybe a spear or an axe . . . it's hard to tell. Definitely votive offerings, though.'

'Votive offerings?' I echoed, trying not to sound like I'd never heard the phrase before in my life.

'Yeah, you know, sacrificial offerings to a god or whatever.'

'Right.' How the hell did he know all this stuff? 'So then . . . this might be a god?' I pointed to the man I thought I'd found.

Dougie made a face. 'Doubt it, not with all the flames. Not unless it's the Devil. Or a demon, perhaps.'

'Something evil . . .' My thoughts were racing. I looked back down at the scratched figure of a man, the jagged shapes Dougie said were flames. 'Or could they be –' I squinted, connected lines in my head – 'wings?'

'Yeah.' Dougie lifted one shoulder in a shrug. 'Flames, wings.' He paused, thought about it. 'Might even be waves.'

CHAPTER TWENTY-ONE

Silence. Uncomfortable silence.

I didn't know what Dougie was thinking, but only one thought was spinning round and round my head.

What if the brooch was old? Really, truly old.

What if there was some spirit tethered to it, to the isolated cairn, one that had lain dormant until Dougie rooted around where he shouldn't have? It sounded ridiculous, so ridiculous that I couldn't even bring myself to say it out loud for a second time.

But it wouldn't go away.

And now that thought had cemented itself in the depths of my mind, the darkness – already unwelcoming, frightening – became terrifying. What lurked out there, hiding in the night? It was hard to stop my imagination inserting the muddled description Emma had provided into the villain's role. Now every gust of wind that rolled around us carried with it ethereal noises. Low moans, high-pitched wails, a chorus of whispers. The rush of air tickling my hair was like brushing fingertips, making goosebumps erupt on my arms under the thick sweatshirt I wore.

The fire, a comfort before, became an absolute necessity. Neatly stacked off to the side was our pile of wood for burning. Collecting wood had been the furthest thing from my mind during both trips to the cove and now the stack was pitifully small. I was loath to shrink it, but the flames were retreating into the pile of smoking ashes. Heat still rolled off the embers, but the light was receding, darkness encroaching upon our circle so that it was a strain to make out Emma's outline, just a few feet away. I opened my mouth to suggest delving into our dwindling reserve when Dougie reached forward and yanked up a couple of good-sized branches.

'These won't catch if we leave it any longer,' he said, thrusting them into the heart of the fire pit. Taking a thinner stick, he poked at the smouldering heap until virgin flames leapt up, gnawing hungrily on the fresh fuel. Job done, he chucked the spindly twig into the fire and sat back, satisfied. His face was troubled, though. I knew why.

'How long do you think that'll last?' I asked, pointing towards our reserves. There were only four or five logs there and a few handfuls of dried seaweed and grasses.

Dougie shrugged, made a face. That wasn't reassuring.

'Will it last us till morning?' I pressed.

'Are we going to sit here all night?'

Yes. Or at least that was my plan. There was no way I was going to huddle in the tent in the darkness. The flimsy material could barely offer protection from the weather, what chance would it have against a vengeful spirit?

Dougie seemed to read my mind.

'We could lock ourselves in the Volvo,' he offered.

Steel and glass were a lot better protection than canvas, but . . .

'I like the light,' I said.

There was a long pause, then Dougie said quietly, 'Me too.'

'Are we going to need more wood?' I asked.

Dougie thought for a moment, then nodded. I sighed. I'd suspected as much. Dougie was in no fit state to go wandering around and Emma was still half-in, half-out. Which left . . .

'Well.' I stood up decisively. 'Might as well get it over with.'

'What?' Dougie looked up at me, eyebrows raised. 'On your own? No, Heather.'

'Yes,' I said. 'I won't go far. I won't even leave the beach. I think I saw some driftwood over the far side. Leftovers from other campers, maybe.'

'Heather –'

'Five minutes,' I said firmly. 'Give me the torch. It'll last that long.'

I wasn't feeling as brave as I was trying to sound, and there was no way I was going out there into the darkness empty-handed. The measly glow from the dying flashlight would at least keep me from being completely engulfed by the suffocating black.

Dougie wasn't happy, I could see that, but he handed me the torch without further complaint. As I swept the beam in front of me, sending a narrow strip of light outside the circle of the fire, I caught Emma's silhouette. She was standing, too.

'I'm coming,' she said.

I was surprised but I didn't question it. I was too relieved not to have to hunt for burnable material by myself.

We didn't speak as we took our first tentative steps away from the safety of the campfire. My hand was shaking, making the torchlight tremble. I tried to tell myself it was just the cold – it was chilly away from the heat of the flames – but truly I was scared. Whether I believed my theory about the brooch's wraith I wasn't sure. But being in the dark, far from anyone, two of our friends mysteriously gone, was enough to terrify me anyway.

The moon was hidden behind a thick bank of clouds and we didn't have to go far before the brightness of the fire seemed no more than a memory. The weak light from the torch was cold by comparison, turning the world into layers of shadows. Colourless; nightmarish. My teeth started chattering. To cover the sound, I marched forward with more purpose, heading for the jumbled pile of wood I thought I'd seen along the far side of the beach.

'We're not leaving here, you know,' Emma said quietly as we walked.

I glanced at her, taken aback by the sombreness with which she said the words.

'What? Of course we are, Emma. We're leaving tomorrow, as soon as it's light.'

'No, we're not,' she disagreed, but so low I could almost ignore it. I chose to. Emma's ominous comments were not helping me steady the vibrating torch beam.

'Look,' I said, grinning with relief. 'Firewood.' Right where I thought it would be.

I had to stick the torch under my arm so that both hands were free to grab bundles of logs. Emma didn't help, but stood staring towards the rocks at the edge of the cliff, water lapping over the path Martin had taken the last time we saw him. I turned my back on it resolutely, concentrating on the task at hand. I kept my eyes fixed on Dougie's fire, where I was going to be in about four minutes. It looked tiny from here; I could barely make out his silhouette, hunched in a chair.

'Emma, can you help me?' I asked, a little impatiently. I wanted to be back inside that halo of warmth as soon as possible. No answer. I turned, annoyed. Why had she come if she wasn't going to help? 'Emma?' I asked again sharply.

She was still gazing away from me, standing utterly motionless, her hands by her side.

'Heather,' she whispered. 'Heather, can you feel that?'

Feel what? I shuddered.

'What? Emma, I don't feel anything. Come on, help me with the firewood.'

She turned to me. I trained the torch on her face and saw she was smiling wistfully.

'The wind,' she said. 'It's gone.'

I knew she wasn't commenting on the weather. I held her stare for a brief moment, then started snatching up wood with haste.

'Let's get back to Dougie,' I said as I stuffed a final log under my chin. This would have to do.

'It's too late,' she murmured. Now that the air was completely still I heard her easily. 'Can you hear the waves?'

'They're still there, Emma,' I snapped, to cover the fact that no, I could no longer hear the quiet lapping of the water on the sand. 'Come on!'

She still wasn't moving.

'Emma!'

I started to make for the fire and Dougie, but without turning I knew, I just knew, she wasn't following. I managed to go six steps before I had to stop.

She was right where I'd left her, facing the rocks.

'Emma!'

She didn't even flinch when I called her name. I stood my ground, waiting, hoping, just for a few more seconds, before I gave in to the fact that she wasn't going to come and I couldn't leave her.

'Dammit!' I hissed under my breath. I dropped the wood to the ground and half-walked, half-ran back across the sand.

'Emma!' I repeated as I reached her side. I grabbed for her arm, folding my fingers tightly around the fabric of her cardigan. 'Come on, I want to get back to Dougie.' Nothing. 'Emma!'

Impatient and still trying to swallow the panic I felt that the situation was getting quickly out of my control, I took another three steps until I was in front of her, right in her line of vision. She continued to stare straight ahead, as if she was seeing right through me. My stomach dropped. I'd hoped she'd been getting better, slowly coming back, but she'd never been as far away as she was that second.

She opened her mouth to speak. 'I told you we weren't leaving here.'

My lips popped open in a silent 'O', but I gathered myself quickly.

'Yes, we are! Emma, come on!' Putting both hands on her shoulders, I started to force her backwards. She didn't resist, but she still refused to move of her own accord. Slowly, I shoved her back until we were level with the logs again. Now I had to let go; this whole excursion had been about getting the wood for the fire, after all. 'Don't move,' I warned as I released her.

She blinked, looked at me, right *at* me this time. The expression on her face stopped me from reaching down for my bundle of logs.

'It's here,' she said.

Any doubts I had over whether I believed her story, whether I believed in the 'wraith', were dispelled as my body went into total and utter shutdown at her words. My brain froze; my lungs were too tight to breathe. I'd stopped shaking simply because my muscles refused to move. Panic and fear immobilised me. I couldn't even feel confused that Emma didn't look scared. She seemed . . . peaceful. Relieved.

But then that changed.

Emma looked up, staring at the sky directly above my head. In the space of an instant, her eyes widened, her mouth stretched open into a horrifying parody of a scream mask.

I whirled, searching the inky heavens to find out what had frightened her so entirely. I saw nothing, but then Emma started to scream.

The noise went on and on and on. Longer than Emma had the breath for, and I realised it wasn't Emma screaming I was hearing, not any more. It was the creature. Wailing at us.

And then I saw it.

Black on black, that's what it was. No face, no form, just a deeper, darker, more sinister shade than the murky clouds behind. Raven on charcoal. My eyes could hardly make out an outline, it just seemed to bleed into the inky sky. What I *could* tell, though, was that it was moving. Fast. Plummeting towards us, silent yet shrieking. It had no eyes, but it was staring right at me, dark pits in the centre drinking me in.

I backpedalled. Tripping and falling, I didn't dare take my eyes off it. I bashed past Emma, our shoulders connecting. My searching fingers brushed the soft wool of her cardigan. Feeling frantically down her arm, I grabbed a firm hold of her wrist. Squeezed tight. Then I turned and together we began to sprint back towards the fire.

'Dougie!' I shouted. 'Dougie!'

But the wind was back. Swirling around us in a turbulent gale, it ripped my voice away and I knew he hadn't heard me. I couldn't even hear my own ragged breathing, or the gasps of Emma running beside me. At least she was fleeing with me. I tightened my grasp on her arm, determined not to lose her.

My eyes were fixed ahead, drawn by the dying flames of our campfire. There was no point looking at my feet; the ground was covered in darkness and the torch was back with the pile of firewood. Besides, there was nothing underfoot but smooth sand. Nothing to trip us, nothing to make us fall.

So why was I sinking? Why was I tumbling to the ground, gravity claiming me with terrifying speed? Instinctively I flung my arms out to cushion the impact, letting go of Emma as I hit the cold silk of the beach.

'Emma?' Had she fallen with me? I looked to my left, where she should be, but I could see almost nothing. The night seemed thicker, like a black fog. The wind was roaring in my ears and the two combined robbed my senses. 'Emma!' I felt out in front of myself, hunting for her.

Two hands grabbed me, fingers interlocking with mine. Emma's touch was cold, but it flooded me with warmth. I pulled myself over towards her, so close we were almost cheek to cheek, her frightened face emerging from the darkness. It was ghostly pale.

'Where is it?' I shouted. I should have deafened her, but my words only just reached her.

She shook her head. Her eyes were darting over my shoulder, though I doubted she could see much. I know I couldn't.

My breath was slowly coming back to me, lungs expanding gratefully. I sucked the air in, practically hyperventilating.

'We need to get back to Dougie,' I yelled.

What was happening where he was, less than a hundred metres away? For some reason it felt as though Emma and I were trapped in a bubble, caught in a vicious storm that existed only where we were.

Emma nodded at me, stood up. Still with her fingers hooked into mine, she pulled me to my feet.

'I can't see it,' she shrieked in my ear. 'I can't see anything.'

The wind picked up even more. It was tugging and pushing at us, pinning us in place. My hair was in wild disarray around my face and I had to snatch each breath before it was plucked away. I turned in the direction I thought our campsite lay, looking for the firelight, totally disoriented.

'That way?' I asked, pointing with a finger. It was hard just to hold my arm away from my body.

I saw Emma lift her shoulders up in a shrug. Then she let go of me. Reached up. Grabbed her shoulders. Opened her mouth, lips moving to form a question, eyebrows furrowed in confusion.

Then she was moving. Up. Away from me. Up.

I realised what was happening at the exact moment she did. I reached for her as she reached for me. I screamed as she screamed. Our fingers fumbled against each other, scrabbling for a grip. I felt my skin tear as Emma's nails hooked into my knuckles, dug in. They wrenched deep, bloody gouges as they were torn away.

'No!' I threw myself forward, grabbed handfuls of her cardigan, her jeans. Still she continued to slide away from me. In a last desperate bid to hold on, I jammed her foot under my arm, clung to her leg. She was lifted higher and higher until my own feet were struggling to feel the sand beneath them. I held tighter as I was hoisted into the air, but Emma was writhing frantically and it was almost impossible to cling on.

Then something warm and wet sprayed my face. Startled, I jerked my head back, loosened my grasp just for a heartbeat. Emma's kicking foot slipped through my grip and I was falling again. Crashing back to earth as she soared unnaturally into the sky.

CHAPTER TWENTY-TWO

I don't know how far I fell, but I hit the ground with a dull thump. The impact drove the air from my lungs for the second time in just five minutes and for several moments I could do nothing but lie there, stunned. My face was pressed into the sand and tiny grains clung to my eyelashes, my lips. I didn't notice.

Emma. Still breathless, I forced myself to my feet. Then I spun on the spot, hunting for her. I knew, though: she was gone.

The wind was back to a gentle breeze; the darkness had receded. Dougie's fire was easily visible just half the beach away; the clouds churned above me, steely grey. Emma was nowhere to be seen.

'Emma!' I called her name over and over again, but I was talking to empty air.

'Heather? Heather, what's going on?'

Dougie. I saw his silhouette framed by the fire. I watched as he took one, two, three steps. Away from the flames, into the dark.

No! I took off, running. I didn't want him to leave the safety of the campfire. He paused, catching the movement of me hurtling towards him.

'Dougie!' I didn't even try to stop myself, but crashed into him. He staggered then steadied both of us, his hands automatically coming up to grip my arms. 'Dougie, it's real!'

'What?' He gazed down at me, forehead furrowed in confusion. 'What's real? Heather, where's Emma?'

'Didn't you see it? Didn't you feel the wind?'

He ignored my questions but shook me gently. Dropping his face lower to mine, he looked deep into my eyes.

'Heather, where is Emma?'

I choked out a sob. 'She's gone!'

'Gone? What do you mean, gone? Heather, you're not making any sense!'

He shook me again, getting agitated. Rather than calming me, his actions just accelerated the tears forming in my eyes. I started to cry, gasping and mumbling. My hands were clawing at his chest, pathetically seeking comfort. I wanted him to hug me, but instead he pulled away. I knew what he wanted: an explanation. But I couldn't speak.

I tried anyway, blubbering incoherently, my words a mush.

'Emma's gone, she's gone. The thing . . . the thing she talked about, it's real. I saw it. It came down and it . . . it . . . grabbed her. I tried to stop it, but it was too strong.'

Dougie just stared at me, open-mouthed.

I looked across the beach, now quiet and still. I could just make out the pinprick beam of light from the abandoned torch, where our collection of logs lay discarded. The menacing atmosphere was gone. The panic, the urgency, the horror. It was just a beach. An ordinary beach.

I turned back to Dougie.

'Didn't you see it?' I asked again, a little more composed now. Having the light from the fire, having Dougie beside me, the whole thing almost seemed impossible again. But I'd seen it. I'd *felt* it. And Emma was gone.

'I didn't see anything,' Dougie said, his face troubled. 'I watched you guys walk over, then I saw you coming back really fast. Then it all went dark and I figured the torch had run out of battery. I waited and waited, but you didn't come. Then I heard you screaming.'

'What about the wind?' I pressed.

'What wind?'

The air was now still but for little breezes that barely lifted the tresses from my shoulders.

'The *gale* that was blowing about three minutes ago?' I insisted.

The beach was small. How could that have happened just a hundred metres away and Dougie not have felt it?

'Heather, there wasn't a gale,' Dougie assured me. 'Where's Emma?'

I'd already told him. Twice I'd told him.

'She's gone. It took her,' I said. 'Dougie, this thing appeared out of thin air and snatched her. Just like she said happened to Darren. It's the truth!' I shouted the last words, seeing the disbelief written all over his face.

'Okay,' he said, putting his hands up in surrender. 'Okay.'

But he still wasn't convinced. He was probably just worried that I'd start screaming and crying again. Aggravated, I spun away from him and started pacing round the fire. I ran my hands through my hair, feeling the wild tangles conjured up by the swirling winds. Though I thought I would be past caring about my appearance, I suddenly felt embarrassed. Flashing Dougie a glance, I pulled a bobble out of my pocket and swept my hair up into a messy knot. Then I resumed pacing.

What were we going to do? The beach wasn't safe. That thing could come back at any time. How much protection would a dying fire offer against a creature that was able to conjure winds, pluck up a person, then vanish into thin air?

But leaving . . . leaving meant going out into the dark.

Every inch of me screamed against that option. Out there, out there was unknown, hidden. We'd be totally blind, even more so now that I'd lost the torch. I tried to imagine it: feeling our way to the car park, fumbling up the hill, wandering aimlessly in the dark. Waiting for rescue. Waiting for dawn. Waiting for attack. I shuddered.

We were going to have to stick it out.

I turned back to Dougie. He was standing, arms folded, watching me. The expression on his face was hard to read. It took a moment for me to realise that that was because the light was fading. The fire was dwindling fast. I looked to the left where we'd stacked our reserves. Nothing.

'I'm sorry about the wood,' I said, my voice husky. 'I had it. I had it in my hands, but then –'

'Forget about the wood,' Dougie said quickly.

'But the fire . . .' I gestured to the pathetic remains of our blaze.

Dougie looked towards the spot of light where the torch lay. 'Where did you drop it?' he asked. 'Is that it?'

'You can't go out and get it,' I said, skipping a step and answering the question I knew was coming next. 'You can't. We've got to stay here, by the campfire.'

While the flames remained . . .

Dougie fidgeted on the spot, his gaze still drawn by the pinprick of light rather than our smouldering embers, a murky mixture of red and black.

'It's not safe out there,' I said. 'Dougie!' I waited till he looked at me. 'It's not safe.'

Now that there were just two of us there was no way we were splitting up. And I wasn't going back out there.

He still looked unconvinced, shoulders half-turned away from me, one foot forward like he was considering making a run for it.

'Do you think I'm making it up?' I asked quietly. That got his attention.

'No,' he said at once. 'No, but . . . Heather, if there is something out there, how do you know it's afraid of the fire?'

I didn't. Yet somehow I sensed it. It felt safer here, anyway. At least we'd be able to see it coming.

'Please don't leave me,' I whispered. 'Please.'

I sat down in one of the chairs, making it clear I wasn't going anywhere, and looked at him pleadingly. He made an agonised face, gazed once more out to the torch, winking now, as if it was calling him. Then he looked back at me. I kept my face calm, biting down on my lower lip to stop it trembling, blinking to stop any more tears cascading down my cheeks. Begging with my eyes.

'Heather . . .'

'We'll burn our clothes,' I said. 'Our sleeping bags, whatever. Even the tents –' I certainly wasn't going camping ever again. 'Just . . . just stay here.'

Dougie took a step towards me, his face torn. He glanced over his shoulder and the torchlight sputtered a few times, flashing like an SOS. Then it died. The beach was inky blackness, the pile of logs hidden. It was no longer a sixty-second mission. Not in the cloaking dark. Would that turn the odds in my favour?

Dougie sighed and I held my breath. I watched him limp over to the campfire, hold his hands over the last of the flames. The light was so low his face was almost obscured by the night, hands glowing red.

'We can't burn the sleeping bags,' he said quietly. 'They're made of fire-retardant stuff.'

He smiled ruefully when I grinned at him, momentarily victorious.

'Clothes,' he said. 'We'll start with clothes.'

It felt wrong to throw the others' stuff onto the dimly glowing, charred remains of wood, but we did it anyway, promising to replace it all. I even joked that we'd have to check Emma's labels before we burned them, make sure she didn't bill us for anything designer. Pretending they were fine, pretending they were coming back, made it easier.

The fire was so low we had to use lighter fluid to get enough life back in the flames for the clothing to catch. Once lit it burned quickly. Dougie had to keep hitting it with spurts of clear liquid just to keep the flames going. I didn't know how much was left in the can, but it sloshed ominously every time he tilted it to the fire.

'You want to know something funny?' he asked, briefly illuminated as the lighter fluid sparked another flare.

'What?' I asked, smiling slightly in response to the tight, embarrassed smirk etched across his jaw. I couldn't imagine anything that could be funny right now.

'I was hoping this birthday trip –' I coughed out a laugh and he stopped. 'What?'

'I'd almost forgotten it was your birthday,' I said. 'I got you a present.'

He smiled. 'Was it a good one?'

'It was a book,' I said. 'One of the course books, about fossils.' I chuckled blackly. 'I guess we could burn it, it's in my bag.'

'Don't burn it,' he said softly. There was a moment of quiet. I looked at the smoky flames, then up at Dougie. He was gazing at me oddly.

'What were you hoping?' I asked to cover the awkwardness I felt.

To my surprise he blushed.

'I was hoping, maybe, under the influence of the stars or the fire –' he huffed a laugh – 'or the booze or whatever, I was hoping maybe you and me . . .' He tailed off.

I stared at him, astonished.

'Or maybe not,' he muttered, embarrassed.

I tried to rearrange my features but they were frozen into whatever ugly mask had caused Dougie to take completely the wrong reading of my reaction.

'Pity about the supernatural creature from hell then,' I made my vocal cords work, though I didn't quite manage the light, jokey tone that I was after. 'That would have been nice.'

More than nice. Much more.

He flicked his eyes back to mine, smiled at me. I smiled back, wondering if I would go to hell for the glimmer of happiness that was trying to thaw the ice gripping my chest.

'Give me your hand.' Dougie held out his right hand, palm up, and when I placed mine in it he hauled us both out of our seats. We wobbled a little on the uneven sand and I wasn't sure if it was Dougie's balance that was off, or mine. It didn't matter, his hands were lightly gripping my waist and suddenly that was all I could focus on.

'I shouldn't have waited so long to do this,' Dougie told me, and then, before I could form any sort of reply, he was kissing me. Mouth hot on mine, hands on my waist, sliding up my arms, cupping my jaw.

Kissing me.

His lips were soft, his tongue probing. Everywhere there was heat. The air around me seemed to shimmer with it.

My brain was screaming at me that this was wrong. Our friends were missing. Something was lurking in the dark, something evil. But I needed to kiss Dougie like I needed to breathe.

It was the stress. It was the tension. I *needed* something to release the pressure. We both did.

Several long moments later, Dougie pulled back, his hands still soft on either side of my face, and said something. I saw his mouth move, but couldn't hear the words.

'What?' I asked. Then realised he wouldn't have heard me either. Not over the wind.

The wind.

'Dougie! It's coming!' I glanced down at the fire. It was low again, the flames not even climbing their way out of the shallow pit we'd built to hold them. 'Quick, we've got to build the fire up!'

Dougie was slow to react. He blinked, his expression cloudy, and I noticed his features were waxy, his eyes sunken. I hadn't noticed, but it seemed the fever was beginning to grip him once more. Lack of sleep, lack of food, stress; it was taking over his body again.

He let go of me, though, and weaving only slightly, bent to the pile of burnable objects we'd grabbed from the tent. There wasn't much left, just a couple of pairs of rolled-up socks.

'That's it,' he said, dropping them down into the fire. They didn't catch at once. Mindful of the ever-growing breeze, I squeezed some of the lighter fluid in the heart of the fire. That worked a little. Looking up at Dougie, I could clearly see his face. The mouth I'd been kissing just a minute ago.

I didn't have time to linger on it, though, because behind Dougie something was descending through the sky faster than a swooping crow. A black mass, half-hidden by the camouflaging clouds. The creature. The stinging wind whipped at my eyes as they widened in terror. How fast was it moving? A hundred miles an hour? Two hundred? Faster than I could follow it.

Much, much faster than we could move.

Dougie's mouth pursed as he read my face, but he didn't have time to form the question on his lips. Before my eyes, large talons dug into his shoulders and hooked tight. I saw it in his face: pain, shock and fear.

'No, no, no!' I would not lose Dougie. I wrapped my arms around his neck, clinging fiercely. His hands clutched my waist, fingers digging painfully into my hips. Something was scratching and pulling at my face and hair but I twisted my head away, hiding in Dougie's shoulder. I tightened my grip, grabbing handfuls of his t-shirt. I would not let go.

I would not lose him like I had Emma.

I felt the upward pressure as we were lifted. My feet kicked for the ground but found nothing. The only thing supporting me was air. That, and my grip on Dougie. My arms were so tight around his neck I knew I must be choking him.

'Heather!' he shouted, right in my ear.

I couldn't answer him. All of my concentration was focused on hanging on. I was so heavy; gravity seemed to be magnified by a million, calling me back to the ground. Every foot we lifted higher, it was harder and harder to keep my grip.

But I would not let go.

That thought flashed in my brain the exact second the wraith took a firm hold of my hair and hauled backwards with enough strength to snap my neck. I couldn't help it. My brain, seeking to save my life, took control of my muscles and loosened my fingers one by one.

I fell to the ground even as I fought the urge, reaching again for Dougie. Too late, my hands closed on empty air.

I landed on my feet. The impact forced me to drop into a crouch, hands sinking into the sand. I looked up, poised like a cat, and saw Dougie's flailing legs disappearing up. Up and away as the creature hauled him out towards the sea.

No. No, no, no!

What should I do? I searched around frantically. Every second, Dougie was being pulled further away. Leaving me here alone. My chest constricted with fear.

'What do you want?' I screamed at the sky.

What could it want? What could it possibly want? Sacrifice? Our lives taken to slake its thirst? Offerings to an evil spirit?

Offerings. That's what I had. An offering. Cursing my own stupidity, I dug into my pockets. My hand was shaking so badly I struggled to grasp what I was after, but finally I pulled it out.

'Here!' I screamed, brandishing the brooch. 'Here! Is this what you want? Come and get it! Come and get it!'

It worked. The creature howled and Dougie's body dropped. There was a sickening crunch as he crumpled onto the rocks nearby, missing the relative softness of the sand by my feet. He lay unmoving, half in, half out of the water.

There wasn't time to go to him, to check if he was okay. My heroic action had done what I hoped: it had saved Dougie. It had also put the spotlight firmly on me.

I tripped backwards, unable to tear my eyes away from the creature as it swooped towards me. The brooch was still clutched in my hand, half raised, clearly visible. I snatched it away, hiding it behind my back. I wasn't sure what to do. I didn't know how to destroy the brooch, or if that would help. The only thing I could think of was to get rid of it.

Taking one panicked breath, I turned and began to run. I bolted past the glowing embers of the fire, expecting every second to feel claws hook into my back, wrench me skywards. Air rushed around me as the winds that announced the coming of the creature whipped up in warning. My eyes hunted through the darkness, looking for a weapon, an escape route. I found neither.

The wind was picking up. The back of my neck prickled, as though it sensed the presence of danger. Too terrified to think clearly, I did the only thing left to me: I hurled the brooch away with all the strength I could muster. Though it was pitch black, the dark even more suffocating than usual, the brooch seemed to glow, emitting its own light. I watched it arc away from me, then drop back towards the ground. My throw was pitiful; I hadn't even cleared the sand. Instead, the spinning disc flew neatly in through the semi-circular doorway to Dougie's tent. I lost sight of it as it nestled down amongst the sleeping bags.

Now what? The brooch was still here, still far too close. But so far away that I couldn't retrieve it. If I went into that tent, I wouldn't come back out. Not with the creature so close behind. I stared helplessly ahead of myself, hoping desperately that the brooch would magically reappear, fly far away and take the creature with it.

Though my eyes were fixed, my feet kept running. I didn't see the hole, the hole I'd dug with my own foot, sitting waiting by the fire. My ankle twisted awkwardly beneath me and my leg buckled under my weight. I fell, landing on the sand with a thud.

My heart stopped. I took one quick breath, hunched my shoulders, closed my eyes. Waited for it.

The whispering screeches of the wraith grew nearer, so close it seemed they were hissing in my left ear. But they passed me by. A shadow blocked out the light of the world for a heartbeat and then continued on. Towards the tent. Towards the brooch.

I didn't pause to wonder. I threw myself to my feet, using the chair to scramble my way up. The soft wool of Dougie's jumper still covered the arm of the chair, and it came away in my hand. I stared at it, stared at the fire. At the lighter fluid sitting neatly beside. Click, click, click. A plan formed in my brain.

Swinging my arm, I slapped the garment into the fire, clinging on to it by the sleeve. There wasn't much heat left, but I snatched up the lighter fluid and squirted it wildly. It landed on the beach, my clothes, my hand, but enough sputtered onto the smouldering ashes and the jumper quickly caught fire.

'Yes!'

I turned and bolted for the tent. The wind was even stronger, sending blizzards of sand up into my face, blinding me. I ran on, trailing the burning bundle of cloth behind me. In one smooth movement I zipped up the tent flap, sloshing the rest of the lighter fluid over the flysheet.

I'd no idea if the creature was inside. Couldn't see it; couldn't hear it. But the brooch was, and I had to hope that meant the monster would be somewhere nearby. I swung the jumper round, slapped the flaming end against the side of the tent.

As soon as the burning embers touched the shining fabric, flames erupted out of nowhere. The blaze was blinding, engulfing the tent, reaching up into the sky like a dozen writhing snakes. An agonised hissing rose above the roar of the fire. The sound escalated to a snarl, then a scream. It peaked in waves, deafening me. It sounded like dying.

The creature.

Good. Die. That was what I wanted.

I stepped back, away from the sound, away from the intense heat prickling at my skin. The noise diminished as I put one metre, then another, between me and the fire. But not the warmth. If anything it grew worse. My face was hot, but the source of the heat was lower, spreading across my abdomen. Burning, blistering. Excruciating.

I was on fire. My jumper, where I'd spilled just a few drops of the lighter fluid, was wreathed in flames. The brilliant light of the tent had dimmed the smaller fire, but I was aware of it now. Shrieking and dancing on the spot, I beat at it with my hand. The flames fought back, forcing me to slap at my scorched clothes again and again. Each second that passed, I could feel the heat cooking my flesh. A nauseating smell wafted up, burning plastic from the nylon in my clothes mixed with something almost like food. Me. I gagged, pounding my stomach harder with my bare hand.

Finally I won. The ragged material hung smoking, gaping holes revealing my t-shirt underneath. It was blackened too, but I ignored that. My every attention was focused on my hand. Or what was supposed to be my hand. I lifted it up, illuminating it in the glare of the raging fire still surrounding the tent. In silhouette, it was skeletal. Skin and muscle had been scorched away, revealing raw sinew and bloody bones. My arm shook as I tried to flex my fingers. I could feel nothing. Nothing but agony. Scalding, burning agony. It ran up my arm, straight to the centre of my brain where it pulsed, like a siren. My vision shimmered, blurred to black at the edges. Then my whole body went into shutdown.

CHAPTER TWENTY-THREE

Now

I'm crying now. There's no way to hide it and I don't even try. Let Dr Petersen see. Let Dr Petersen see and let him think he's won. I don't care.

I thought I'd forgotten the fear, the panic, the sense of helplessness. I thought I'd buried it deep down where it could no longer hurt me. I haven't. The flood of icy blood in my veins, the pounding of my pulse, the adrenaline spiking my system, my hairs standing on end. I feel it. Feel it just as strongly as I did back then.

I let out a choked gasp and realise I've been holding my breath. My hands are clutching each other, and my ravaged right is screaming in protest. I can't seem to unglue them, though.

I look up, those tears Petersen's been working so hard for sparkling in my eyes. What now?

He's gazing at me strangely, and I wonder if I'm seeing a glimpse of the real him. He looks . . . confused. As if for the first time he might be considering that I'm telling the truth. I feel the first flicker of hope in more than a year.

But the moment passes. We're back to who we always are: him, sceptical and superior; me, crazy.

'You did it, Heather,' he says softly, his eyes focused very intently on me.

I don't respond, but the question is clear in the furrow of my brow.

'You did it,' he repeats. 'You killed your friends.'

Don't react. Don't. I close my face down just in time to stop the pain and outrage from showing.

I knew he thought it, of course I knew. I could see it in his eyes, in the curl of his lip. But it hurts to hear him say it. Every time.

But Dr Petersen isn't finished. He continues in the same quiet, monotonous voice, as if he's trying to lull me into a trance; like he's a hypnotist, trying to burn this fact, this deceitful 'fact', into my brain.

'You killed them. Martin and Darren and Emma. You murdered them. Strangled Martin and Emma, drowned Darren.' He raises a hand to stop me before I get halfway through shaking my head. 'They found the bodies, Heather. They found them, half buried in the cairn. Not broken like they'd been dropped from a great height, or clawed at by giant talons. The autopsy report found bruising round the necks of all three, identified asphyxiation as the cause of death.' Petersen pauses, making sure he has my complete and utter attention. 'If you hadn't passed out from your burns, would you have succeeded in killing Dougie, too?'

221

Burns.

I flinch at the word. Burning. Sizzling, blistering, melting. Sometimes I wake up in the middle of the night and believe for a few terrifying moments that I'm still on fire. I scream, then. Scream until pounding feet thunder up the corridor and my door swings open with a series of clicks and the orderlies pile in.

But I am saved from the heat of my memories by the mention of Dougie. Anger takes the sting out of my scalding thoughts. I would never hurt Dougie. Never. I gaze at Dr Petersen steadily. He looks back, letting the silence go on and on . . .

And on.

And on.

Finally he sighs, leans forward. One hand reaches out as if he's going to touch me, but he thinks better of it and rests his palm flat against the satiny wood of the desk. Good. If he lays a finger on me I will do my best to rip it off before my escort manages to restrain me.

'You killed them, Heather. Your friends. Somewhere, deep down, you know the truth. Admitting and accepting it is part of the healing process.'

He takes a slow breath. I resist the urge to spit at him.

'I want you to tell me what you did. I want you to tell me that you took the lives of three of your friends, attempted to take four. That you did it on purpose. And that you tried to hide the bodies. Admit it, Heather, and we can start to move on.'

No.

The first time I heard this version of events, I was in a hospital. A normal one. I was strapped to a bed – to keep me still and stop me aggravating my injuries, I thought – and there were tubes under my nose, sticking into my arm. My right hand was coated in bandages up to my elbow and I was so tired it was like trying to see through a fog. I did notice a policeman standing just outside my room. I noticed, but I didn't wonder why he was there. Not then.

It was days before I could stay awake long enough to talk to anyone. Then a man in a suit visited me. He asked me what had happened and I told him. He went away and another man came. I didn't know his face then, though I've been looking at it at least once a week ever since. Dr Petersen asked me what happened and I told him, too. He didn't frown like the other man had, he smiled. All the way through, right to the end. I remember thinking how odd that was.

Then he told me a story of his own, one where I had a starring role.

In Petersen's version of events I lured Martin away from the campsite, up towards the cairn, where it was quiet. Private. Then I plied him with alcohol until he passed out, and once he was unconscious, I put my hands around his throat and squeezed. Hard.

And stuffed the body inside the cairn.

Back at the beach, I explained Martin's disappearance away, hid his stuff. And congratulated myself on a job well done. But Darren and Emma had seen me leave with Martin, and they became suspicious. And so I had to silence them.

One murder turned into three.

Afterwards, I panicked. I doused the tent in petrol and set fire to it. I spilled some on my hand, too, and it caught fire along with the tent. That was the only part I recognised; I could feel the burning pain even if I couldn't see the damage under the pristine white bandages. Dougie – who'd been ill and passed out in the other tent while I'd apparently done away with three of his friends – tried to stop me, and I hit him with a rock. Hit him so hard I fractured his skull and put him into a coma. Then I passed out from the pain in my hand before I could finish the job.

A story. A story that was told to my parents, repeated in court.

A story that became the truth. To everyone except me.

'Why would I do that?' I ask, accidentally speaking my thoughts aloud. 'Why would I kill my friends?'

Dr Petersen starts. I've never even entertained this story before. He scribbles a quick note to hide his glee then considers me.

'You know why, Heather. Curiosity.' I stare at him, appalled. 'Death. You're obsessed with it. You wanted to watch, to witness life drain away. You wanted to feel the power of playing God.'

I don't know what to say; how to respond. Dr Petersen has shocked me to my very core.

I say nothing.

Tick tock. Tick tock.

This conversation is over. I stare at the clock until Petersen has no choice but to acknowledge what I'm looking at. His face crumples. Out of time.

'We'll continue this next time, Heather. But I want you to think about what I have said. You know the truth. It's there, right in front of you. Grasp it. Help yourself.'

I do help myself: out of the chair. Then I turn my back on Petersen and his stories. My escort opens the door for me and I am gripped by a sudden desire to run. I won't get anywhere, I know that, but I can't bear to stay in this room another second. Not another millisecond.

I am practised at swallowing back foolish urges. I walk sedately through the door, past Helen who's still tip-tap-typing. She doesn't look up to acknowledge me as I pass.

There's a headache throbbing at my temples. Tension has kept my head gripped in a vice for the last two hours. It's always the same. I know that the ache will take all night to dissipate, longer if I let myself dwell on the session, vindictively snarling snide responses at the imaginary Dr Petersen in my head. Usually I try to forget about it as quickly as possible, but I know that's not going to happen today.

It's what he said about Dougie. It's rankled me. The idea I would have turned on the one person to make it through this nightmare with me . . . For the millionth time I wish I could visit him. I've asked, but of course they will never let me. All I know is that Dougie's in a hospital somewhere, bleeping machines monitoring his breathing, his heartbeat. He must still be there. No one's told me so, but I know. Otherwise they would have switched him off, let him fade away. Then it would be four lives against my name.

Walking slowly back down the corridor, plimsolls squeaking on the highly polished, marble-effect linoleum, I glance around, make sure no one's watching. Then I close my eyes – just for the briefest of seconds – and say a prayer.

I need Dougie to wake up.

I need him to wake up and tell Dr Petersen and my mum and everybody else that I'm not a murderer.

I need him to wake up and get me out of here.

CHAPTER TWENTY-FOUR

Then

I left the hospital in a wheelchair. It wasn't that I was incapable of walking so much as nobody wanted me to. Because if I could walk, I might run. I really *wasn't* capable of that, but no one seemed to want to take the chance.

I was confused. Confused and scared. I'd told them what had happened. Told my story so many times I'd lost count. But that didn't seem to be enough; didn't seem to make anyone happy. I was alone too. My parents had been to visit me several times in the little room I had all to myself in the hospital, but the more I'd seen the smiling man – who I now knew as Dr Petersen – the less I'd seen them.

I was loaded into the back of a vehicle that seemed to be a cross between an ambulance and a prison van. There was a trolley-like bed, an array of equipment hanging above it, but the person pushing my chair – a sombre man in a spotless white uniform – reversed me up the ramp and guided the wheelchair to a purpose-built space against the other wall. I heard a series of clicks as he locked the chair in place. Right across from me, dead centre in the railing of the bed, were a series of loops. Dangling from one was a set of metal handcuffs. That was when the first block of ice dropped down into my stomach. As the doors slammed closed on my right, and the engine started up, I felt the chill of a couple more. What was going on?

I twisted my neck round to stare at the man. It was the only part of me I could move – I was strapped into the chair with a seatbelt-type contraption. He had taken a small, folding-down bucket-seat, like an air hostess without the smile.

'Where are we going?' I asked.

I hadn't questioned anything up to this point as the whole manoeuvre had been sprung on me so suddenly. One minute I was in bed, forcing down the lukewarm hospital breakfast, the next I was in a wheelchair, trundling quickly along the corridor, down in the lift, through the foyer . . .

'You're being transferred to another facility,' he said. He looked at his watch as he spoke, avoiding eye contact. He was tense, his rigid posture adding to my discomfort.

'Oh,' I said. 'Why?'

This time the orderly turned to face me, but his eyes were guarded, his expression unreadable.

'I don't know,' he said.

I didn't believe him.

'Where am I being transferred to?'

He turned away from me again and spoke to the neatly folded sheets on the bed opposite.

'Dr Petersen will be able to answer all of your questions when we get there.'

Why not tell me now? I tried to slow my breathing, but it felt like there wasn't enough oxygen in the cramped space. I plucked at the strap across my front, but that wasn't the thing making my chest tight. I looked to the doors, desperately wanting them to open, but the gentle vibrations shaking the chair told me we were still moving.

'How long will it take to get there?' I asked, my voice croaky, my throat choked.

'Not long,' the orderly replied.

That was the end of our conversation. I wasn't wearing a watch, so it was hard to keep track of the minutes as they crept by. I paced them out by drumming the fingers of my good hand against my knee in double-time. Under the bandage, my other hand itched to join in, but there wasn't room to move a millimetre under the painfully tight dressing. I made do with jiggling my whole arm restlessly.

When the door finally opened, I barely had a second to glance at my surroundings before my view was blocked by two men wearing uniforms identical to the one the orderly wore. They went straight to my chair and unhooked it from the wall of the vehicle.

'Journey all right?' one of them asked.

Before I could answer, the man who'd ridden with me spoke.

'Fine. The court had the paperwork all in order so the discharge was pretty straightforward.'

Court? What were they talking about?

'Where are we?' I asked, trying to turn my head to see out of the door. But they spun the wheelchair around, taking me out of the ambulance backwards, and it was another ten seconds before the vast expanse of driveway came into view. There was a thin strip of lawn, neatly mown, but what caught my eye was the very high, very sturdy-looking metal fencing, topped menacingly with spiked tips. Before I had time to do more than register the intimidating enclosure, I was whirled around once more and at last I could see the building.

It didn't look like a hospital. More like a cross between a school and an office block. There were lots of windows but nothing that looked like an entrance. One of the orderlies began to push me closer and I saw a small door, almost hidden amongst the glass. I realised this wasn't the front. I was going in the back way. For some reason that amplified the anxiety bubbling in my stomach.

'Where are we?' I asked again. I didn't really expect them to answer and they didn't disappoint.

Inside, I found myself in a very short corridor. We paused in front of a door with a small window too high for me to see through. To my left was a larger window and behind that sat yet another orderly, like a teller at a bank.

'Heather Shaw?' he asked. Again, he wasn't talking to me.

'Yeah.' Confirmation came from behind me.

There was a beep and the door clicked open. One of the three men escorting me reached out and opened it and I saw another corridor, lots of closed doors running off it. We traversed the length of it, went through a second door – this time with a pass card that one of my entourage swiped smoothly against a discreet wall panel – and behind that there were more corridors, more locked doors. I didn't bother to try to wrangle any more information from the men around me, but waited with growing alarm. How big was this place, and why did it need so much security?

The silent tour of my new surroundings ended at another door. Somehow I knew this was my destination, even though this door looked much the same as any of the others. I could clearly see the large, complicated lock on the outside, but when one of the orderlies reached out and twisted the handle, to my surprise this door opened silently, already unlocked. The only unlocked door I'd seen so far.

I understood why at once: there was already someone in the room. A familiar figure, dressed impeccably in a three-piece suit, with a genial expression on his face that I didn't like, although I was never quite able to put my finger on why.

'Heather,' he said, standing up.

Only then did I realise that he was sitting on a bed; that this was a bedroom. Panic burgeoned once more. Why would I be brought to a bedroom with a lock on the door except to be put in it? What was going on? Dr Petersen, at least, might give me some answers.

'What's happening?' I asked.

He smiled at me, a reassuring smile. It didn't work.

'What's happening?' I repeated, louder this time. I was almost shouting. Dr Petersen didn't like that. He gestured to the men escorting me to bring me inside, then I heard the sound of their retreating feet and the click of the door closing. I didn't hear the lock engage but still I felt trapped, like an animal in a cage.

'Let's get you up and out of this chair, shall we?' Dr Petersen said, cutting me off before I could scream my question at him a third time.

I closed my mouth, because I wanted out of the restraining straps of the chair very much. Hands at my shoulders started unclipping the straps, startling me. I'd thought Dr Petersen and I were alone in the room. The remaining orderly came around and released my wrists, giving my legs a wide berth as if I might lash out at him. He moved back quickly as my arms came up, but I merely wanted to ease the tension in my shoulder, the cramps in my good hand. The restraints had been too tight.

'I know you've been sitting for a long time, Heather, but if you have a seat on the bed there, I'll explain everything to you.'

Unsteadily, I rose from the wheelchair. On stiff legs I took the three steps required to cross the length of the room, then dropped down onto the bed to face Dr Petersen, who had taken a plastic chair, similar to the ones from school, directly across from me. There wasn't much else in the room. Just a small table, a bedside cabinet and a window, so high up that from my position on the bed I couldn't see the view. Everything was a shade of white or beige. Clean, clinical. Even the air smelled hygienic, burning my nostrils with the faint hint of bleach.

'I suppose you have a lot of questions for me,' Dr Petersen said, pulling me from my inspection of the room.

'Where am I?' I asked. This was the most crucial question on my list.

'You are at my facility,' Dr Petersen replied.

'And what happens at your facility?' I fired back.

Dr Petersen's smile widened. 'I treat patients,' he said simply.

I frowned. That wasn't an answer. He was being deliberately vague and that was only exacerbating the very bad feeling I had.

'Treat patients for what?' I asked. 'I'm not ill.' The only thing I needed help with lay under the swathes of bandages on my right hand.

Another ingratiating smile. 'There's plenty of time to talk about that later.' He stood up and I knew he was about to leave. The orderly shifted from his position against the wall.

'I want to talk about it now!' I snapped. Unconsciously I rose, took half a step forward, but quick as lightning the orderly was in my face, blocking my path. Over his shoulder I saw Dr Petersen hold up two hands in a calming gesture.

'All in good time, Heather. First I want to give you a chance to settle into your new environment. Someone will bring you something to eat shortly, then I suggest you concentrate on getting some rest. We'll talk again tomorrow.'

He turned his back on me, walked out of the door. The orderly put both hands on my shoulders, pushed me gently backwards. A second orderly replaced the departing form of Dr Petersen in the doorway, something with far too many buckles clasped in his hands. I thought I knew what it was, although I didn't want to ask and discover for sure. Surrendering, I let the hulking figure in front of me guide me to the bed, where I obediently sat down. He backed away, one cautious step at a time. The door closed. Locked. For a brief moment there was a face at the tiny square of glass, high up in the door. Then it, too, was gone and I was alone.

I sat there for a long, long time before I finally started to cry.

CHAPTER TWENTY-FIVE

Now

I lie on my back and stare at the ceiling. My stomach is churning and it has nothing to do with the tray of food that was delivered to me this morning, because I haven't eaten any of it. It's lying on the table, as far across the room as possible because the smell of congealing scrambled eggs was making the nausea so bad I actually hovered over the toilet bowl, waiting. Nothing came up, though.

It's not easy to get rid of dread.

Six days and twenty-one hours have passed since my last appointment with Dr Petersen. Usually I'd have a mid-week session too, but I was granted a temporary reprieve that day. Dr Petersen had not been lying about the release form for the surgery on my hand. At the preliminary consultation the surgeon was optimistic, fairly certain he could graft some skin, implant false nails. I'd never have a 'normal-looking' hand, he told me. But it wouldn't be too far off.

That thought had cheered me through the last few days, but when I woke up this morning, dull grey light filtering in through the tiny window, I felt only cold, unmoving trepidation.

I do not want to go back into Dr Petersen's office.

I don't have a clock, but it's easy to measure the hours as they pass. The orderlies have a set routine that they follow every day. Food round. Meds round. The token hour of 'exercise' for those of us with nothing else on our schedule. Checks round. It's just gone half ten. Not three minutes ago a face peeked in at me, making sure I'm not attempting to hang myself with some ingenious rope made out of strips of my bed sheets bound together with desperation and despair. I'm not; I'm not that inventive. Although I might be getting that desperate. I'm beginning to realise that I may never get out of here.

A rattle at the door turns my head. I roll up into a sitting position, my face expectant. The churning in my stomach has gone into overdrive.

I hear a whoosh as the door is pulled back. An orderly who has been tending to me for almost a year, but whose name I still don't know, gives me a perfunctory smile.

'Time to go, Heather.'

I sigh, swallow; take a second to gather myself. But I don't try to resist. I know from previous experience that there is no point. It does more harm than good. The orderly takes a step back as I approach, ever cautious, following protocol to the letter.

We walk past door after door and as usual I hear the strange orchestra of sounds that belong in a place like this: screaming, wailing, shouting. Banging. Voices, talking to themselves. It never ceases to unnerve me; this is the only time that I'm glad there are locks on every door. Crazy people frighten me.

I both relax and grow tenser as we cross the threshold into the plush, visitor-friendly section of the facility and the noise diminishes, replaced by more normal sounds. Business-like conversations, the click of heels, the tap of fingers typing at one hundred words per minute, phones ringing. I pause in the waiting area – Helen's domain – ready to take one of the seats against the wall, but a hand on my shoulder urges me on and as soon as I feel the pressure I realise that Petersen's office door is already open, waiting for me.

I am relieved that I won't have to wait, can just get on with it, but at the same time I was counting on those few precious minutes to compose myself, to prepare for the coming assault.

When I enter the room Dr Petersen is not at his desk. I frown, look around and spot him at a filing cabinet almost behind me. He is rooting through the top drawer and I have never noticed before that he is so short. He has to stand on tiptoes in his shiny black shoes to see all the way into the back. This knowledge raises an illicit smile across my lips. It will probably be the last genuine one for a while.

'Heather,' Dr Petersen acknowledges me slightly breathlessly. My eyebrows rise up my forehead in surprise. It's very unlike him to greet me this way, very unusual. He's usually ensconced behind his desk. I wonder if it is an elaborate trap, some new strange strategy he has devised to deal with me. But no, he definitely seems on edge, uncomfortable. I watch silently as he sifts through files then plucks one free. A relieved look on his face, he slams the drawer closed then dumps the file onto a huge stack of papers untidily piled on his desk. As I move to take my seat, I see that the one on top has my name on it.

'There's been a development, Heather,' he says as he eases himself down into the chair opposite me. He takes a moment to settle himself into a comfortable position, old bones creaking, a twinge of pain on his face.

Development? I keep my face impassive, but curiosity is burning just beneath the surface. What could have happened that would unnerve the unflappable Dr Petersen?

'The judge has sent through a summons. You are to go back for a second hearing.'

If this was a Tom and Jerry cartoon my mouth would pop open, hitting the floor with a comical 'thunk'. This is real life, however, and there is no jaw-dropping. I just stare at him, astonished.

My first hearing was something of a joke. I wasn't even there. I was in the hospital. My parents went, though. They sat in a room with a judge, some lawyers and good old Dr Petersen and, in a conversation that I doubt lasted more than ten minutes, they decided that I was insane. Crazy. Off my nut. Not fit to stand trial. That's how Dr Petersen got away with locking me up without any questions. Perhaps there had been another doctor there to give a second opinion – I certainly saw enough men in white coats while I was lying flat on my back in my isolated room in the hospital, trying to make sense of the world around me – but if there was, he must have agreed with Petersen. My parents didn't even put up a fight. Maybe they thought it was better than jail. Less shameful. Better a lunatic for a daughter than a criminal.

A second hearing. It's not something that Dr Petersen has even hinted at in our sessions together. Judging from the way he's twitching in his chair, the sheen of sweat on his forehead, it's come as a bit of a shock to him too. I like that he's flustered, but I'm too gobsmacked myself to take advantage of it.

'Why?' I ask. What has changed?

Dr Petersen coughs, adjusts his tie, purses his lips.

'The judge wishes to re-evaluate your case.'

Yes, I know *that*, but . . . 'Why?'

He sniffs, takes a deep breath then looks me square in the face.

'A new witness has emerged and the judge feels this person has the potential to shed a fresh perspective on the events at Black Cairn Point.'

Dougie. Who else could it be?

I try to shut the thought down before it can grow into hope. A new witness – it could be a local resident who knows about the cairn; it could be a dog-walker none of us saw. It could be another doctor eager to have a poke about inside my head.

But it isn't. I know it's Dougie. He's awake. Finally, he's awake.

'I want to see him,' I say.

Immediately Dr Petersen shakes his head.

'No.'

'I want to see him.'

Neither of us has even put a name to the new witness. We don't need to. Dr Petersen is refusing to meet my eye and that tells me everything. No wonder he's on edge. If Dougie backs me up, I cannot be called crazy. If Dougie backs me up, I cannot be called a murderer.

If? There is no if . . . he will.

'I want to see him.'

I am going to go on saying this until Dr Petersen realises it is non-negotiable.

Unfortunately I am not in a position to negotiate. Petersen waves away my demand with a dismissive flick of his wrist.

'Your hearing is scheduled for Thursday the seventh of July. I will accompany you there and your parents will also be in attendance –'

'I don't want them there,' I say automatically.

Dr Petersen shrugs. 'You are still under the age of eighteen, Heather. Your parents must be present.'

I make a face but I don't really care. My mind is whirling. Thursday the seventh . . . I try to guess today's date in my head. It's Monday, I know that much. Last week's marathon, nightmarish session was the anniversary – I shudder discreetly – so that makes it . . .

'What day it is today?' I ask. Just to be sure. Just to be absolutely sure.

'Monday,' Dr Petersen responds.

I resist the urge to tut – he knew what I meant.

'What *date* is it today?' I rephrase, trying to repress the acid in my tone. I feel the urge to be nice to him today. I don't want him to be difficult at the hearing just because he is annoyed at me. Of course, I am probably a year too late for that.

Dr Petersen sighs. 'It's the fourth.'

'Of July?'

'Yes.'

I process that. My hearing is in three days. In three days, I might be free.

In three days, I might be heading to jail, a trial date wrapped around my neck like a hangman's noose.

In three days, I might be heading right back here.

Three days is both a lifetime and a heartbeat. I spend it completely alone. The orderlies don't particularly engage with inmates – 'patients' – anyway, but I refuse to leave my room for exercise or for weekly treats like the seventh showing of a bad film. Before I left Dr Petersen's office I repeated my request to see Dougie, but he ignored me as if I hadn't spoken.

That was the last thing I said, and by Thursday morning my throat is tight, my voice croaky from disuse. I eat my breakfast in silence, walk silently to the showers, wait, silently, in Helen's little office-cum-waiting area. As promised, Dr Petersen is escorting me and he emerges exactly on schedule, pin-striped suit hidden beneath an expensive-looking, charcoal grey woollen coat. A huge folder is tucked tightly under one arm – this is the condensed version of my file. All the juiciest bits.

If I am released today, will I get to read it? Somehow I doubt it.

I expect to travel in the 'ambulance' that I arrived in, but instead we walk sedately out of the front door. It's the first time I've seen the official entrance to the place and I can't resist glancing around before I clamber into the back of a sleek saloon car. It looks . . . expensive. Like a country manor house. There is no clue of the madness within. Sticking to my vow of silence, I don't comment. I just hope I will never see this sight again.

For July, there's not much warmth in the air. It's cloudy, misty rain descending from the leaden ceiling of the sky. I tell myself this is not an ominous sign, but anxiety is writhing like snakes in my stomach. The car moves off, purring smoothly. Beside me, Dr Petersen is flicking through his notes. I'm tempted to try to read across him, but adrenaline is starting to fire through my veins and it's making my vision shake. Besides, I don't want to seem like I'm interested in anything Dr Petersen has written, to give credence to his 'professional' opinion. Instead I stare out of the window and wait to see something I recognise.

It takes a while. We weave through buildings that must be commercial, then almost imperceptibly the view melds into a housing estate. A posh one, though. This is an upper-class neighbourhood. I wonder what the residents think about a madhouse on their doorstep. I wonder if they ever wake up in the middle of the night afraid that a crazed lunatic is creeping across their immaculately mown lawns. Probably not.

I don't make sense of where I am until we hit the motorway. There is only one route going north, and the names on the signs are recognisable. I raise my eyebrows in surprise. I am further from home than I'd thought. In fact, I am closer to Black Cairn Point than I am to Glasgow. I crane my neck west, as if I might be able to see the sea. I can't – it's miles and miles away. I get the feeling, though. Anxious, afraid, uncertain. I stop trying to look.

My hearing is in the Glasgow Sheriff Court in a side room. It could be a conference room in a posh hotel. There is a long table, a big window overlooking another building and tasteful art on the wall. At first nobody else is there, just me, Dr Petersen

241

and my minder, but almost as soon as we arrive, others begin to trickle in. A man in a suit with a shiny black briefcase arrives, who I'm sure is a lawyer. He ignores me but shakes Dr Petersen's hand. Then there is a very awkward moment for me as my parents are escorted in. I try not to look at them but I can't help it. My dad smiles tightly, my mum looks pained. I wonder if I should say something, but with Dr Petersen and the lawyer in the room I'm suddenly shy. I fidget in the chair I have been placed in and stare at the door, waiting for someone else to enter and take the pressure off.

Someone does enter. The door swings wide and two wheels glide into view. At first I can't see who's sitting in the wheelchair because whoever is pushing it is making a mess of it, colliding with doors, being overly helpful and getting in the way. I hear a sigh and a very familiar voice mutters, 'I've got it.'

Dougie. My mouth forms an automatic smile that freezes halfway as I see how terrible he looks. He seems to have shrunk, hunched in the chair. His cheeks are hollow and there are dark rings under his eyes. His hair is lank and greasy. He smiles when he sees me, though, and takes a second out from manoeuvring the wheelchair to wave at me.

But we don't speak, because striding in directly behind Dougie is a portly man with greying hair and a serious expression who must be the judge. He goes straight to the seat at the head of the table and everyone else assumes positions around him.

I am the furthest away, at the bottom of the table. I have a sinking feeling that most of the talking is going to be done at the other end of the long mahogany oval, far away from me.

242

'Right then.' The judge's booming voice cuts off any muttering from around the room, calling everyone to order. 'This is the hearing of Heather Shaw, is that correct?' He glances around and the lawyer nods curtly. 'Good. It is –' a quick glance at his watch – 'eleven forty-seven a.m. on the seventh of July. Present are –' As he lists the attendees, beside him a mousy-haired woman is typing away on a small laptop, minuting his every word. She's nothing like cool, collected Helen; her expression is anxious as she struggles to keep up with the judge's brisk speech. 'I am Judge McDowell, presiding over today's hearing. Right, that's the pleasantries done with. Where are we starting with this?'

We start with the lawyer. He reads from a typed sheet in front of him, which I soon realise is a report on my case so far. Judge McDowell nods in several places, so either he's already read the report or he was the judge on my initial hearing; the man who signed me over to the care of Dr Petersen. I hope it is the former. I squirm in my seat as the lawyer reads out the details of my initial testimony to Dr Petersen. Every detail, every word. My cheeks grow hot. If it was not me being discussed, I would say the person who claimed this was insane, no question. Throughout the statement, Dougie listens intently, a slight frown creasing his forehead. There are a few occasions where his eyebrows twitch, like they are about to lift in surprise, but I can't read why. There is no way to ask.

At last, it's over.

'So we are here today to hear the testimony of Douglas Fletcher, is that right?'

'That's correct, Your Honour.'

'And remind me why we haven't heard from Mr Fletcher before now.'

'He suffered a head injury which left him in a coma, Your Honour,' the lawyer says.

'For a year?'

'Yes, Your Honour.'

'That's a bit inconvenient.'

I am tempted to laugh so I bite down on my tongue hard enough to make my eyes water. The judge is smirking at his own wit, but my urge to laugh is encroaching on hysteria. 'A bit inconvenient' is not how I would describe Dougie's injury and its impact on my life for the past twelve months. A living nightmare would be closer to the mark.

'Your Honour, if I might interrupt?' Dr Petersen leans forward and smiles ingratiatingly. My stomach clenches. I now regret every snide, belligerent thing I ever said to him. I even regret trying to stab him. Because he has the power to keep me locked away, and I have handed him the desire. I wait, breath bated, to hear him pour honey into the judge's ear. He doesn't get a chance, however. The judge frowns him into silence.

'I want to hear from Mr Fletcher first, Dr Petersen, then you can have your say.' He turns to Dougie. 'This is a formal hearing, Mr Fletcher, but I'd like to make it as informal as I can for you. May I call you Douglas?'

'It's Dougie.' His voice is quieter than I remember and I wonder if that is because of the year he spent asleep – my throat feels like sandpaper after just a few days – or whether he's as nervous as I am. I smile at him, but he isn't looking at me.

Judge McDowell gives him a look before continuing. 'Douglas, I am going to ask you questions about your trip to Black Cairn Point last year. I want you to answer as fully as you can. I need you to bear in mind that I am a judge and this is a court hearing; you must tell the truth at all times. Do you understand?'

Dougie pales, but nods again.

'Let's start at the beginning, then. Run me through the trip as you remember it.'

Dougie starts with the car journey, talks Judge McDowell through the camping, the drinking, the tension between Martin and Darren. It's weird, hearing his version of events. Like watching the world through coloured glass. He explains Martin's disappearance, Darren vanishing, Emma's strange behaviour. I close my eyes when he gets to the final, dramatic scene on the beach, but that doesn't stop his words from piercing my imagination. I resist the urge to stick my fingers in my ears so I can't hear, don't have to relive it, aware of how that would seem. I must not look like a crazy person today.

Dougie's story finishes a little earlier than mine. He describes how he was jerked backwards, how he felt himself flying through the air. How the world went black for the length of a year. When he finishes there is a brief moment of quiet. Someone coughs. I open my eyes to see it is my dad. Our eyes lock for the briefest second, then I look away.

Dougie's story, bar one or two small details, matches with mine. One or two small details, and one major one. He has not mentioned a wraith, a being. He has not explained how Martin, Darren and Emma disappeared. Just that they did. There is a big gaping hole in the middle of Dougie's story, and I know that Dr Petersen is waiting to jump right in.

'Douglas, my name is Dr Petersen,' he begins. Dougie nods and then his eyes flicker to me. A look passes between us and I realise that Dougie understands: Dr Petersen is my gaoler, but more than that, he is a snake in the grass. I watch Dougie steel himself; he knows what's coming. 'I would like to ask you one or two questions, if I may?'

I want to jump in between them, shield Dougie from Dr Petersen's sly, manipulative ways, but I am glued to the chair by the occasion and I have already given as much of a warning as I can.

'Sure,' Dougie croaks.

'You say that Darren Gibson, and your friend – Martin Robertson? –' Dr Petersen turns his name into a question as he quickly checks it against his notes – 'disappeared. Can you explain to me what happened to them?'

'I told you. Martin walked off alone, and Darren vanished from the cove when he and Emma were collecting firewood. Heather was with me. Both times.' Dougie's expression is set, defensive. I shoot him a grateful look but he doesn't see.

Dr Petersen smiles. 'It is noble of you to defend your friend, Douglas. But you are here to explain to us what happened, not to give Heather an alibi.'

'It's the truth,' Dougie says bullishly.

'Were you with Heather when Emma Collins disappeared, Douglas?'

Horrible silence. It goes on and on. My eyes are on Dougie, but on the edge of my vision I see Judge McDowell frowning.

'Douglas?'

'We were all on the beach.'

'Together?'

Another awkward pause.

'No,' Dougie finally says.

'So you didn't see what happened to Emma Collins?'

No. That's the truthful answer, but I can see that Dougie doesn't want to give it.

'They were only a hundred metres away. I could see the torch. Heather was only gone for a few minutes.'

But a few minutes would be enough. That's the thought I can see on Dr Petersen's face, the lawyer's. I scrutinise Judge McDowell, but his thoughts are unreadable.

'You were ill during the trip, were you not?' the lawyer asks. Dougie twists his head to look at him, confused by the change of direction. 'I'm sorry, Douglas. I am Mr Thompson, I work for the Procurator Fiscal. Can you tell me, were you ill during the trip?'

'I had a bit of a cold,' Dougie hedges.

'Just a cold? It says in your medical records that you were admitted to hospital with a fever. You had a dangerously high temperature as well as your head trauma. The doctor at the time commented that you would likely have been suffering dizziness, nausea, possible vomiting. Do you remember having any of those symptoms, Douglas?'

'So what if I did?' Dougie asks. 'What are you trying to say?'

The lawyer smiles, accepting the yes hidden in his words.

'What I'm suggesting, Douglas, is that you may have been so ill that your memory is lying to you. Taking that into account along with the trauma to your head, you –'

'I'm not lying,' Dougie interjects.

The lawyer smiles wider. 'I'm not suggesting you are,' he assures Dougie – and the judge. 'But you might be remembering things differently to how they actually happened. Because of your illness. I understand, you want to help your friend, but it is important that you don't bend the truth, or fill in gaps, even the tiniest bit, Douglas. Being absolutely honest about what you remember, that is the best way for you to help Heather.'

'I'm telling you what happened,' Dougie spits through his teeth. 'I felt a bit unwell, but I didn't imagine anything. I hurt my ankle as well. Are you going to tell me I imagined things because of that, too? Or that it was Heather who broke the branch, trying to kill me?'

'Douglas.' Judge McDowell steps in, a half-raised hand acknowledging the rising tension. 'Take a breath. We are all here to try to help Heather.'

This time I do snort a laugh, but it's so quiet I don't think anybody hears it. I have only one friend in this room, and I am terrified that he is not going to survive the interrogation tag team of Dr Petersen and the lawyer, Thompson.

'Douglas,' Dr Petersen leans forward again and Dougie shifts position in his wheelchair so he can face him. 'You need to understand that Heather is ill.' I lock my face down so that no one will see how mortified I am to be discussed as if I'm not here. 'She believes an evil spirit is responsible for the deaths of your friends. A dark shadow who swooped down and stole them away.'

I catch my breath, aware that this is a very dicey moment. Petersen has just laid a trap for Dougie, a very clever trap.

248

Agree with me and he's as delusional as I am; maybe we were in it together. Disagree, and I'm a lunatic. Lunatics do crazy things . . . like killing people. Disagree, and Dougie sends me back into Petersen's clutches.

He doesn't do either. He laughs.

I stare at him, not understanding, but Dougie looks confident not wrong-footed.

'That was a story,' he says. 'A ghost story I told us to try and freak everyone out. It wasn't real.'

'It's real for Heather,' Dr Petersen says quietly.

Under the table I grip the arms of my chair with both hands, ignoring the searing pain in my right. This is not at all going the way I want it to. I want to speak, but I know no one will listen. I am the crazy person, after all.

'Is it?' Dougie asks, somehow cool and calm. I suppose it's not his head on the block. He continues before Petersen can confirm his words. 'There was no wraith, no monster.' Dougie pauses, looks at me, takes in my horrified face and smiles grimly. 'But there was a man.'

A man? I blink at Dougie but he doesn't wait to see my expression. He turns and levels a look at the judge.

'I saw a man. Several times. At first I thought he was a dog walker, up high on the hill, but I never saw a dog with him. Not that first time, or the next day, when he came back. He was there, high up, watching us, just an hour before Martin disappeared.'

'A man?' the judge says slowly.

Dougie nods at the same time as Thompson barks out, 'What did he look like?'

Doubt is written across the lawyer's face. Dougie doesn't react to the derision in his eyes but shrugs his shoulders at the question.

'Don't know, I couldn't see. He stayed too far away. All I could see was his outline. He wore dark clothes, I know that.'

'And you saw this man the day Martin disappeared?'

'Yeah.' Dougie jerks his head in a short, sharp nod.

'Did you see him after that? Did you see him the day you say Darren went missing?'

Dougie makes a face.

'I'm not sure. Heather and I hiked up to the road and I thought I saw a van, parked far off, but by the time we'd walked higher it was gone.'

'Can you remember any details about the van, Douglas?' the judge asks.

'It was far away,' Dougie reminds him.

'Colour?' The judge pushes gently. 'Size?'

Dougie opens his mouth but Dr Petersen jumps in before he can answer.

'Heather has never mentioned a man. Not once, in all our sessions together.'

And everyone looks at me.

My parents: expressions carefully blank. The judge: curious. I can't read the lawyer and Petersen is wearing his typical look of disdain. I focus on Dougie, my port in a storm. He is looking at me expectantly. Waiting for something.

I don't know what.

I do the only thing I can think of: I burst into tears.

They're impressive. Loud and wet, my breath hiccupping. It takes no effort: I am so strung out I've been fighting tears anyway.

'I w-was scared,' I babble, swiping at my nose which has already started to run. 'M-Martin and Darren and Emma were gone and then Dougie –' I break off, choke on a sob. 'He was hurt and the fire was out and I couldn't see what had happened to him. I . . . I tried to light it again but I was shaking and the lighter fluid got all over me and when I struck the match –'

My body's shaking so hard that it's tough to lift my hand, but I do. I hold it up and see the judge's eyes take in the deformed claw, the hideously scarred skin. He winces.

'Heather.' Petersen tries to command my attention but it's easy to ignore him, crying louder, huddling into myself. Now that I've started weeping I can't seem to stop. 'Heather, you've never talked about this man. You told me about the wraith, remember? The spirit at the cairn.'

'I – I –' Thoughts whirl around my head. Sudden inspiration hits. 'I thought he'd come after me too!'

I dare to glance up and see that one corner of Dougie's mouth is hitched up in the smallest semblance of a smile.

If the tables had been turned and I'd been the one to fall, the one to slip into a coma, and Dougie had been left to save us, I know for a fact that he would not have been as foolish as me, that he would have been waiting for me to come round, free and living his life. He would have done what I was too slow to understand: made it a story, made it a lie. Left a hole and trusted the police to fill it with a monster they could understand. A serial killer, a local madman. If I had not screamed quite so loudly about things that no one in their right mind would believe in, who would have suspected me?

251

But I am a year too late for my epiphany. All I can hope is that my situation is salvageable. Finally, I tear my gaze away from Dougie's face and look to Judge McDowell.

He's the one who will decide my fate.

CHAPTER TWENTY-SIX

It feels wrong to be standing in the sunshine, but there's not a cloud in the sky. It almost adds cheer to the place, picking out the vibrant green of each blade of grass, the dots of colour from every bouquet of flowers. But there is just too much grey. Row upon row upon row of forbidding slabs of stone. The three in front of me are shinier than most.

Martin. Emma. Darren.

Names on a tombstone. And beneath that, dates which to me feel like yesterday.

Beside me Dougie coughs, trying to clear his throat, looking away so that I won't see his face. Though his friends were buried almost exactly a year ago, like me this is the first time he's ever stood in front of their graves. His parents wanted to take him, to be there for him – to keep him in sight like they have almost every moment since he opened his eyes – but he refused. Refused because I wouldn't have been welcome. No matter what Dougie said in court – or the judge said as he signed my release form – to them I am guilty. To them I am the reason they lost a year of the life of their son. I can't blame them; even my own parents treat me with suspicion.

I sigh heavily, and out of the corner of my eye I see Dougie turn in my direction.

'You okay?' he asks.

I nod my head, knowing he'll see, because I'm not altogether sure I can talk. Standing here, looking at their names etched deep into the flecked granite, it makes their deaths real. I mean, I knew that; I knew they were gone. But there's a difference between knowing it and feeling it. Today I feel it.

Dougie reaches up, rubs my back. I smile briefly at the warmth of his hand through the thin cotton of my t-shirt, still keeping my gaze straight ahead. His touch is mostly friendly, I know, but there's still a thrill attached to the gesture. Half and half. Like us; after everything we've been through together, we're more than friends. But not more than that. That's okay, though. Right now, with Dr Petersen's voice still rattling around my head and open spaces feeling too wide, too free, it's about all I can handle.

I am grateful to have a friend at all.

Besides, there's plenty of time. In just a week we are going to university together, to do the archaeology course we were supposed to start last summer. As if the last twelve months never happened.

'Are you ready to go?' I ask quietly. I am hoping he'll say yes. I don't like being here. It's empty, dead. I can't feel any connection to the three people beneath my feet. Wherever they are, it isn't here.

'Yeah,' he says, and we turn in tandem, begin to wind our way down the rows, heading for the exit.

There's something I've been meaning to say to Dougie but haven't. But I know I really should. I know it needs to be said, and better now than later. Without it, I'll never really be able to put all this behind me.

I walk slightly closer to him so that our shoulders bump.

'Thank you,' I say.

Dougie looks at me quizzically and I make myself meet his gaze. Our footsteps slow.

'For what?' he finally replies.

I take a deep breath.

'For standing up for me. For backing me up. You could have . . .' I tail off, then make myself continue, '. . . you could have left me in that place.'

Dougie's puzzled smile freezes on his face. We have purposely avoided talking about the camping trip and I can see he's in no rush to do so now.

'You didn't have to help me,' I say. Because he didn't. With the dark cloud of suspicion hanging over me, with everyone else already having condemned me to the gallows. He didn't have to do that.

The smile is back, and this time it's untroubled. 'What else was I going to do, abandon you?'

That had been my fear. I should have had faith, but after a year in that hellhole, a hopeless year, faith had been hard to come by.

'We were in it together,' he says. 'You and me.'

'Yeah,' I whisper. 'Together.'

There is a lull in the conversation as we once more begin the morose trip out of the cemetery. Chitchat seems disrespectful in this place. Dougie frowns and stares down at the ground as we walk.

'There is just one thing that troubles me,' he finally says as we meander out through the gates of the cemetery. 'You said that we went swimming together –' I look at him curiously as we walk, nodding slowly. Where is he going with this? 'But you went after Martin. The two of you took the back path up to the road. You watched him flag down that car, cadge a lift off that old couple. That's what we agreed.' He pierces me with his eyes and I stop dead in my tracks.

'I –' I start to speak but words escape me. Dougie reaches out a hand and grips me firmly by the upper arm. I don't try to get away; I couldn't even if I wanted to.

'It didn't exactly go to plan,' I remind him.

The book Dougie dropped in front of me was obviously really old. The spine was cracked and the writing inlaid on the leather front was so faded I could hardly read it.

'Blood and Dust,' I read. 'The Dark Rites of Human Sacrifice.' I looked up from where I was lying sprawled across his double bed. Dougie sat at the desk, spinning the chair round so that he could face me, a feverish light in his eyes. 'Where did you get this?' I asked.

'Bought it off some guy on the internet. He's got a shop down in London, specialises in druid stuff.'

'Wow.' I flipped it open, wrinkling my nose at the dusty smell that wafted up from the pages. 'The writing's funny, looks almost like Macbeth.' We'd been reading the Scottish Play in English, ploughing through the Shakespearian language. 'Can you read it?'

'Most of it,' Dougie replied.

I pulled my gaze away from the scrunched lines of tiny writing.
'Enough?'

'Enough.' He nodded.

The half-smile on my face widened until it was a grin, then I giggled.

'Are we really going to – ?' I cut off the rest of my question, too overcome with the idea.

'We're going to,' Dougie confirmed.

'Can you imagine?' A delicious shiver ran down my spine, excitement making my nerves shiver.

'We won't have to,' Dougie promised. 'It's my birthday soon . . .'

I saw it.

Saw the very moment. The instant. The second the light drained out of his eyes.

Saw it, and savoured it.

I felt power rush through me, adrenaline flood my veins.

With hands ghostly pale, I reached out and closed his eyes. The bruises were already beginning to bloom on Martin's neck.

No, not Martin's neck. He wasn't here anymore. On the body. That's all this thing was now. A lifeless body. It was just like Dougie had said.

We'd hiked with Martin to the cairn – it seemed fitting. A burial mound. A tomb. Ancient, sacrificial.

'Now, remember,' Dougie murmured. 'Remember what we agreed.'

'He hitched a lift,' I replied. 'I saw him go.'

'Darren knows.' His voice was soft and came out of nowhere, slithering from the darkness behind me.

257

I jumped, whirled around to see Dougie's face lit by the light of the torch, his expression grim.

'What?' I asked faintly, though I'd heard him.

'Darren. He knows.'

My heart stopped for an instant, then began to beat again in double time.

'How?' I whispered.

'He found Martin's stuff, the book at the bottom of my bag. He went up to the cairn.'

Fear zinged through me, but it was quickly replaced by outrage.

'What was he doing raking through your bags?'

'I don't know. Acting on suspicions?' Dougie shrugged. 'I've just overheard him telling Emma what he's found. They're going to hike out tomorrow and call the police.'

'What are we going to do?' A much more important question.

'What we have to,' Dougie answered. 'You deal with Emma. I'll take care of Darren.'

There was steel in his eyes. Steel, and excitement.

Dougie lifts a finger to my lips. 'It worked out in the end.' The finger leaves my mouth and he runs a hand through my hair, pinning it back behind my ear. 'You did well.'

Did I?

'But you got hurt,' I blurt out. 'If I'd handled Emma properly –'

'You did well,' he says again, disregarding my words. He flashes me a grin. 'We did. It was just like we'd talked about, wasn't it?'

258

Well, not exactly. I hate to bring up the names, but . . . 'Darren . . . and Emma.' My best friend. Her boyfriend. We haven't talked about that.

'They should have left it alone,' he tells me, no hint of recrimination or regret in his words.

'They should,' I say. 'If they'd stayed wrapped up in each other, like they were supposed to . . .'

I reach up, cup my hands around his jaw and he grins at me. Then suddenly we're kissing and it's all tongues and gasping and clashing teeth. Right there in the cemetery. I go up on my tiptoes, desperate to be closer.

'It doesn't matter anyway,' I whisper, breaking away. 'We did it.'

The light in his eyes is devilish and full of excitement, matching mine. 'We did it,' he agrees.

Claire McFall

Claire McFall is a writer and English teacher who lives and works in the Scottish Borders. Her first book, *Ferryman*, is a love story which retells the ancient Greek myth of Charon, the ferryman of Hades who transported souls to the Underworld. *Ferryman* was shortlisted for the Scottish Children's Book Awards and the Grampian Children's Book Awards, longlisted for the Branford Boase Award and the UKLA (UK Literary Association) Book Awards, as well as being nominated for the Carnegie Medal.

Her second novel, *Bombmaker*, is a YA dystopian thriller in which the main character Lizzie struggles to survive in a London dominated by gangs and plagued by terrorism.

You can find out more about Claire at www.clairemcfall.co.uk and on Twitter: @mcfall_claire

HOT KEY BOOKS

Thank you for choosing a Hot Key book.

If you want to know more about our authors
and what we publish, you can find us online.

You can start at our website

www.hotkeybooks.com

And you can also find us on:

We hope to see you soon!